T0039317

PEGGY GOODY

THE HOBGOBLIN WAR

Peggy Goody

the Hobgoblin War

Book 5

Charles S. Hudson

Order this book online at www.trafford.com
or email orders@trafford.com

Most Trafford titles are also available at major online book retailers.

Print information available on the last page.

ISBN: 978-1-4907-8231-7 (sc)
ISBN: 978-1-4907-8230-0 (e)

Trafford rev. 05/22/2017

www.trafford.com

North America & international
toll-free: 1 888 232 4444 (USA & Canada)
fax: 812 355 4082

TABLE OF CONTENTS

Chapter 1
THE DECISION

Savajic used his pendant and transference spell and left Black Eagle far behind. He and Peggy appeared in the great hall and Cooper was there, ready to greet them.

I have taken the liberty of laying out tea and biscuits in the study, and if you will leave your things here, Miss Peggy, I will see that they are put in your room.

Thank you, Cooper, said Savajic, and guided Peggy towards his study. Sit down, Peggy, I want to bring you up to speed on our progress so far. I have put two wall screens into play; one here in the study and one in my workshop. To activate them you just say 'screen'; to deactivate it, say 'clear.' I will enter your voice pattern so that you can use them in my absence should the need arise.

I will give you a list of the war council members and the names of the intelligence officers who have been hand-picked by Commander Churmill. I want you to memorize it and then destroy the list. Everything that we do and say is strictly on a need-to-know basis; we have to treat everyone not on the list with suspicion. Is that understood? Peggy nodded her head yes.

My first duty is to inform Enzebadier that you have left Black Eagle and intend to join forces with us. He turned to the wall and commanded screen. The wall turned into a screen. Then he said, Enzebadier, and immediately he was there.

Is everything all right? he asked.

There is no need for concern, Savajic said, but I need to tell you right away that Peggy has left Black Eagle and has come to live with me. I want her to link up with us and join our team.

Enzebadier stroked his beard and said, Has there been another attack on her?

No, said Savajic. It's just the opposite. Peggy feels that she is a danger to the students. The Black Watch have obviously made her a target, and as they step up their efforts to kill her, innocent students could get hurt, or even killed. She is also concerned that when she is put in a competitive situation with other students, she could cause them harm. In an incident while playing surf polo she put the opposing captain in hospital; her strength and powers are so great now that even Professor Battell Crie cannot stand against her.

I personally think that she has made the right decision, and her timing could not be better. We need to contact the planners on the bridge and Peggy can haze with me, and give us the opportunity to breach the Black Watch security.

Enzebadier looked directly at Peggy and said. Before you join forces with us, Peggy, I must impress upon you that you understand all the implications of such a step. Nothing that you are about to do will be a training exercise or practice. There will not be any second chances. If you get things wrong and fall into our enemies' hands, it could be fatal for you. I know that this is giving you the worst possible scenario, but it is never a bad place to start. You are already an equal to some of the most powerful wizards, and as I understand, you have powers that we can only dream of. Nevertheless, anyone is vulnerable. Take a lesson from what happened to Baldric Zealotte. He had the power of Kanzil in his sword, but because of his arrogance, he let his guard slip and Goodrick trapped him in a time bubble and sent him spinning off into space.

Have you considered what your mother would think of this? She believes that you are studying at Black Eagle under our protection. If you join with us, you would not be able to discuss it with her, and that means deceiving her each time she asks you about your schooling.

Peggy looked at Enzebadier and protested, This is something that I desperately want to do, and I feel in my heart that I have an important role to play in this impending war. I have changed, and I know that there is no going back for me. I know that my destiny has been set. You are right about my mother; but we have powerful spells that we could use that would stop my mother from asking me the sort of questions where I would have to lie to her.

That is true, said Enzebadier, but should you be killed, all our magic will not bring you back. I have no objection to your proposal, but having said that, I would like you to discuss this in some detail with Savajic before finally making your mind up.

The screen went blank and the wall reappeared. Savajic watched Peggy closely. Her jaw was set and tense, and the knuckles on her hands were white as she gripped the sides of the chair and her face was pale. She was about to make the most important decision of her life.

Her shoulders dropped and her body relaxed. She looked directly at Savajic. Let's do it, she said; and the die was cast. There would be no going back. From today on she would be at war with all that was evil.

Savajic changed the subject. Before I get started on intelligence, I need to discuss the Christmas holidays with you. As you know, I have asked Rose and you to come and stay here over the holiday period. I have not spoken to Owen yet, but I thought it may be a good idea to invite Lilly and Charlie, depending on whether they can come, of course.

Peggy was already missing Charlie's company and her face suddenly brightened up. That's a great idea, she said. But will they be allowed to come? Because it's a time when families like to be together.

Savajic smiled. We are wizards, remember? And wizards worship Gasieus, our creator. We take a Christmas holiday purely to respect the human way of life and their beliefs. So in that respect, we do not insist on family gatherings. It may have slipped your mind with all that is going on around you, but Christmas is only fifteen days away.

One more date on our calendar, Peggy, is the Black Eagle gala. Black Eagle always arrange a Christmas ball before breaking up for the holidays and we have been invited. I myself will be going, and I would be delighted to be your escort, should you wish to go.

Try and stop me, she said. I can't wait.

Excellent! said Savajic. I will arrange it all, and then we must get on with some more serious work.

I have tried to put myself in the shoes of the Black Watch commander and think how he would think. My main objective would be to complete the bridge across the worm fields in preparation for an all-out attack on Greco. The attack would be a total surprise to the Gnomes, and would almost guarantee success. And if this was to happen just before Zealotte returns, the commander, whoever it is, would be held in great esteem by him.

Chapter 2
Savajic's Reasoning

Now, I believe that the chosen one to be commander is Sealin Belbur, but he is held in Lockstay Prison at this moment in time so that would indicate that a prison break is being planned for the not too distant future, possibly just before the completion of the bridge. I believe that although he is in Lockstay, he is still somehow pulling the strings to the whole operation; if we could somehow plant a couple of undercover wardens to befriend him and to aid him with his escape, it could save a lot of bloodshed and make sure that he got to the bridge safely.

We know that the Gnome army has been seriously depleted because of the centuries of peace they have enjoyed, and if we know this, so will the Black Watch. Now suppose that if we contacted King Kelbot and told him of the Hobgoblins' plans to wage war against his nation, I wonder if he would listen to us.

I'm sure he would, said Peggy. He would be very foolish not to, and after all, he is the king, and would want to keep his people safe.

Peggy, my priority in this whole situation is of course the wizard world, and its survival for the future generations; and to this end, a war between the Hobgoblins and the Gnomes could have a very beneficial outcome for the wizard world, because I now believe a wizard war to be inevitable.

Let me explain. The Black Watch are heavily involved in this and have persuaded the Hobgoblins that they can win this war easily; not that they need any persuasion. They have had a deep hatred for the Gnomes for thousands of years and would dearly love to get their hands on their gold reserves. Zealotte, remember, is still trapped in a time bubble and consequently knows nothing of this, so he will not have any expectations, or for that matter, will not know any of the wizards that are alive today, or that the Black Watch is still in existence. Their plan, I believe, is to take Greco and make it a power base for Zealotte on his return. But if we were to turn the tables and defeat the Hobgoblins, then Zealotte would be on the run from the minute he lands.

Since our meeting with Demodus, I have been giving his words to us much thought. He said that he had no intention of waging war with the Fairies or the Wizards or you yourself, Peggy. To my mind that leaves only one plausible target for his army and that is the Gnomes. Remember that he was sentenced to exile in the wastelands of the Arctic at his trial in Greco, and that might be the motive for him to want to get his revenge.

Now suppose it was possible to broker a peaceful solution between Demodus and King Kelbot, the Gnome king. But surely, said Peggy, if he intends to attack Greco, and he has created an army just for that purpose, he will not want to stop now.

I know what you're saying is probably right, said Savajic, but I don't want him to stop his army from fighting. Can you imagine if his army was positioned and waiting to attack the Hobgoblins?

My research into Gnome history shows that Demodus was the most famous Gnome that ever lived. He was their greatest champion and was never defeated. He was also a very rich and successful merchant who shared his wealth with the poor and sick and was loved by the nation. His home still exists and has been turned into a museum, and his statue still stands proudly in its grounds.

He lost his father in a terrible accident while travelling and he never really got over the shock of losing him. It turned his mind, and he finished up on trial for murder.

Ever since then, he has paid dearly for his crime; but through it all, he has an ingrained love for his people and was proud to be their champion. If we could show him another path to redeem himself and save his people and become their champion once again, he might just be for turning.

Now we must focus all attention on the quarry and the bridge. It is crucial that we have accurate information and try to engage with one or more of the planners.

Chapter 3
THE BRIDGE

Savajic had set up the screen in his workshop to show Peggy the discoveries he had made on his trip to spy on the Hobgoblins. The screen came to life and a road came into view; Savajic started his commentary.

"We are now in Hobgoblin territory, and the road that you see leads directly to the bridge that is being built across the worm fields. As you can see there are large slabs of slate being transported along the road, using Levita and Proti spells, obviously involving wizards." The screen panned down to the slate slabs. "I am down level now with the road, behind a façade, and will soon be approaching the start of the bridge."

Peggy spoke up. What are the creatures walking with the slabs?

They're Hobgoblins, replied Savajic, realizing that she had never seen one before. They are nasty creatures that rule over the smaller Goblins and treat them like slaves. Wherever they go, they cause trouble and look for fights. The Goblins and the Hobgoblins have strong magic and must not be underestimated.

As they watched the screen, the entrance to a massive bridge appeared, then just as suddenly disappeared. There is an elaborate façade covering the whole of the bridge so that it can be kept a secret. Fortunately, I had my anti-façade baton with me and was able to see through and capture everything that was going on. Savajic pointed out to Peggy the two planners who were there. These are two of the very best planners we have. One is Brixun Mortah, who is from England, and the other is Showvel Hanpix from France. We believe that they are working under threat, and if they do not do what is asked of them, then their families will be harmed. This is where you come in, Peggy. If we go back to the bridge, we could haze and get onto the bridge and with a bit of luck, talk to one of them and find out what is going on.

Suddenly, a Troll came into view. Wow! What's that? exclaimed Peggy. It's massive.

It's a Troll, said Savajic. They have the strength of twenty men and are fierce fighters. We don't know why they are there but we need to find out.

Do you think the bridge will be completed by the time Baldric Zealotte returns? Peggy asked.

To be truthful, we don't know how long it has taken them to get this far or when they started to build it, but with our best planners working on it, I would guess it would be. And if I am right in my assumption that Sealin Belbur will want the war to be over before Zealotte is back on Earth, then it will be.

Savajic shook his head and said, I still can't believe we had no knowledge of this. If they had not tried to be so clever and set up the false trail at Black Eagle to waste our time, they may just have gotten away with it. But by us gaining the clue of the worm fields and you, Peggy, thinking that they may be building a bridge across, we are now one step ahead of them.

Chapter 4
Reconnaissance

Savajic waved his hand at the screen and said, Bridge. Immediately a side elevation view of the bridge appeared. It showed the start point of the bridge and the edge of the worm field; they were some hundred yards apart. The Hobgoblins were so frightened of the Snack Worms that they were taking no chances, and had created a hundred yards of no man's land. Over to the right it showed how far the bridge had progressed and then the far edge of the worm fields. It looked to be about halfway across, which was quite a feat considering they were twenty miles wide. From the end elevation view you could see that the dimensions of the bridge were quite staggering; twenty-five yards wide with walls six feet high running down on each side, and the bridge itself was suspended twenty feet in the air.

It looks massive, said Peggy. You could move a whole army across in a few hours. Then she asked. How far from the bridge do you have to travel to get to Greco?

Savajic thought for a while then said. It's about one hundred and seventy miles, and in between the bridge and the gates of Greco is a great forest. So, you can see that if the Gnomes knew nothing of the bridge and the Hobgoblins could gain the cover of the forest, they could be at the gates of Greco before the Gnomes even realized that they were under attack.

Peggy, I cannot tell you how important our work will be over the coming months. If Baldric Zealotte should return and somehow get hold of the Sword of Destiny once again, I not only fear for the fourth-dimensional world but also the human world. Kanzil wants his sword and his power back and he wants Zealotte's soul, and I am sure that the more souls Zealotte can corrupt and send to the magma on his way, the more Kanzil will like it. And so, I believe that Kanzil will use all his power to make Zealotte victorious.

This war will not just be between the Hobgoblins and the Gnomes. The wizards are going to have to take sides, wizard against wizard, and if Kanzil sends an army of Fire Imps, then that will involve the Fairy army too. The outcome of this war could change the world forever and send it down a path of evil. We cannot let this happen. So you can see how important it is for us to gather as much information as possible so that we can be in a position to make the first strike.

Now, Peggy, I have to get you kitted out for our trip to the bridge. You will need to carry the same equipment as I do. Do you have any anti-odor potion?

Yes, Peggy replied. I always keep some with me.

Good, said Savajic, pleased that Peggy was thinking ahead. We will take a break for lunch and then after we can come back down and go over the equipment and you can practice and get used to it.

Chapter 5
PREPARATION

Over lunch, Savajic told Peggy of his plans. First, we are going to the quarry where the slate is being cut, because there must be planners working there. I'm sure the Hobgoblins would not be able to keep pace with the tremendous demand put upon them. Plus, the slate is being transported by Levita and Pulshy magic, which would need wizard magic. We need to carefully document both the planners and the wizards that are keeping guard because they will be members of the Black Watch. Then we can move on to the bridge and do exactly the same.

If we get the opportunity to talk to one of the planners, we will, but we have to be one hundred percent sure that it is safe to do so. Two days' provisions should be sufficient for us and give us ample time to complete our mission. Now, Peggy, let's go over the equipment piece by piece so you can get used to it, and then you can relax before dinner.

At dinner, Peggy was pleased to find out how easy she felt in Savajic's company. Apart from lessons, she hadn't really been alone with him for any length of time and she was really enjoying it.

I can't stop thinking about Demodus, Peggy suddenly said. How has he managed to stay alive all these years? It's quite a mystery. And how has he come to have the Sword of Destiny after it being hidden for so long? That's an even bigger mystery.

Savajic rubbed his hands slowly together. He was deep in a train of thought. He looked at Peggy and said, "Have you ever heard the saying 'what goes around comes around'?"

Yes, said Peggy. I heard my mother say it many times. Why?

Well, when I was talking earlier about brokering a peace between Demodus and King Kelbot, I had forgotten about the Sword of Destiny, and with that in his hand he could conquer any army.

Peggy, to answer both of your questions, I believe that Demodus is about to come full circle and fulfil his own destiny, and we seem to be a part of it.

We have so many things to do that I will list as many of them as I can think of and cross them off one by one. Tomorrow we start at the quarry and then the bridge. With a busy day ahead, they both decided to retire for the night and get a good night's sleep.

Chapter 6
THE SLATE QUARRY

Peggy and Savajic had both eaten a hearty breakfast and were going over their planned visit. How long do you think you can hold both of us in haze? Savajic asked.

A good hour, answered Peggy. And if I lie on the ground for ten minutes I can keep repeating it.

That's great, said Savajic. Much better than I thought. We will use a Parto spell whenever possible, to reserve your energy. But if we are to try and speak to one of the planners, we will need to haze to allow us to get close enough to talk.

Before we start out, Peggy, have you any concerns?

No, said Peggy. I'm a bit nervous, but that's all.

Savajic smiled. So am I, he said. It's only natural. Right, let's get dressed for action and double check your kit. We will meet up on the terrace in fifteen minutes.

Savajic had set the coordinates on his pendant and they were ready to go. Hold on tight, he said to Peggy. She linked arms with him. He said the words, and they were gone.

As soon as they were there, Savajic instantly put up a façade and they both relaxed behind it. Then they started to lay out their equipment. Savajic had camouflaged their boards. He wasn't going to risk them reflecting in the sun and giving away their position.

They were ready to go, and Savajic suggested they keep close together and haze; that way they could follow the road back to the quarry and get a good idea of the amount of slate being moved.

They were travelling fifty feet up from the road and had a good view of everything that was moving. It really was on a grand scale. Every twenty-five yards there was a massive sheet of slate suspended in the air being guided down the road towards the bridge by a single Hobgoblin. Peggy couldn't help thinking it resembled a giant blue-and-gray snake winding its way down to the bridge.

Savajic figured they had travelled four miles before they arrived at the quarry, and that gave him a good idea of the rate the slate was being cut at. A massive open quarry loomed in front of them. There was no blasting or splitting going on; the wizard planners didn't work that way. They were using the latest state-of-the-art rock-cutting equipment. They had developed powerful anti-matter lasers with ultra-sonic sound beams running down them in a triple helix with a pitch so high even Peggy, with her animal instinct, couldn't pick it up. It was a masterpiece of engineering.

Four wizards were working on the slate, each one operating separate units. Two were cutting out gigantic cubes and moving them out into open space, where a third wizard was cutting them into sheets and then the fourth wizard was cutting them to size. As each sheet was finished, it rose into the air and lay on its side and began to move away. A line of Hobgoblins was waiting to guide them along the road to the bridge. It took no effort for them because under the Levita spell, the sheets were weightless.

Savajic and Peggy both had their cameras in action and were carefully recording everything they could. Savajic whispered to Peggy, Look up to the top left of the quarry. Can you see the wizard standing there? Peggy nodded, not wanting to speak. Well, it's our first piece of luck, because it's George Buttress. He's a planner, and he was in my class at Black Eagle and we were very good friends. As soon as we have everything we need we will move up to him and attempt to make contact. How are your energy levels holding out, Peggy?

I'm good for at least another thirty minutes, she replied.

Good, said Savajic. As soon as you are ready, make sure your camera is secure and we will go over to him.

Peggy put her camera safely away and they began to move. They hovered behind George, and Savajic spoke to him. Don't look around, George, it's Savajic Menglor. I'm here on a spying mission and need to gain as much information about the bridge and who is forcing you all to do this.

George lifted his hand to his face and pretended to rub his nose to hide his lips as he spoke. Be careful, Savajic, they are watching our every move. My family are being held prisoner and under threat of death if I don't do what they ask of me. This is my team working in the quarry, and their circumstances are the same as mine, and so are the planners on the bridge. The Black Watch have taken over our homes and they will kill our families without a second thought. Can you come back at 8.00 p.m., when it starts to get dark, and follow me back to base camp? The Hobgoblins are terrified of the worm fields and won't go anywhere near them when it's dark.

Understood, replied Savajic. I will be back at 8.00 p.m. He squeezed Peggy's hand and said, let's go, and they kicked off and flew back to their own base camp.

When they landed, Savajic said. Let's eat now, Peggy, and then I want you to get some rest. You will need to get your energy level back up to its maximum because we could have a long night ahead of us.

Peggy lay on her back and closed her eyes. She could feel her body drawing energy from the earth beneath her and she knew Mother Earth was making her strong for what lay ahead.

Wake up, Peggy, Savajic's voice came drifting to her in a whisper. It's almost time to go.

She opened her eyes and yawned. How long have I been asleep? Nearly six hours, replied Savajic. How do you feel?

I'm good, she said, and ready to go.

They checked to make sure they had everything that was needed and mounted their boards. Stay close and in contact at all times, said Savajic. It gets very dark and we cannot afford to get separated. He held Peggy's hand and she hazed.

They rose up into the night sky and headed for the quarry and when they arrived, there were powerful arcing lights blazing out, giving a ghostly look to the place. They dropped down close behind George Buttress. We're here behind you, George, whispered Savajic.

Right, said George. We're just about to leave, and they leave us alone at night because they know we will not try to escape because of the threat to our families. As soon as we leave follow close to me, and as soon as we are back in our hut we can speak. Brixun Mortah and Showvel Hanpix are in the same hut as me so we can give you some very useful information to take back with you.

Brilliant, said Savajic. You won't see us but we will be close behind you.

The hut was quite a large one and had plenty of space inside for a sitting area and three beds. The planners were three of the most powerful wizards in the wizard world, and their magic provided everything else they would need to make themselves comfortable.

George pushed the door open wide, allowing Savajic and Peggy to slip in past him. He followed and closed the door behind him.

Don't expose yourself yet, he said. Just wait a couple of minutes until the other two get here. Almost as soon as he had finished speaking, the door opened and the two planners from the bridge entered.

Good evening, Brixun, Showvel. A smooth day I hope?

As smooth as possible, I suppose, considering we had to put up with those unbearable creatures all day, replied Brixun. Let's get our exclusion spells in place so we can get some peace and quiet. They drew their wands and each placed an exclusion spell around the hut.

Now we can relax, said Showvel.

I have a very pleasant surprise for you both, announced George. Show yourself, Savajic.

Brixun and Showvel looked at each other and echoed, Savajic?

Peggy came out of haze and appeared standing next to Savajic. The look on their faces was of total shock, how could this be? And who was the young girl? And how had Savajic found out about the bridge?

The questions came pouring out. George held up his hands. I suggest we should all sit down and let Savajic tell us the full story over dinner.

Brixun said. An excellent idea, and waved his wand across the table. It was instantly covered with food of all kinds and five place settings appeared, and they all sat down around the table.

Before I start, said Savajic, let me introduce you to Peggy Goody, a very special young wizard and a very close friend. She is a human who has mixed her blood with mine to become a wizard, and she has learned much wizard magic under the guidance of Enzebadier and myself. She has attended Black Eagle. She has fairy magic and a fairy speed no other wizard is capable of, and Mother Earth has given her animal instinct. She can also transfigure into any bird or bear on earth, and she can make herself and anyone holding onto her invisible, as you have just witnessed.

Now, Peggy, let me introduce you to the three top planners of the wizard world; Brixun Mortah, Showvel Hanpix, and George Buttress. One by one they shook Peggy's hand and greeted her.

Savajic put his hand up to his mouth and cleared his throat with a polite cough and then began. I'm not sure how much you know, so please forgive me if I repeat some of the things you are already aware of. We have established that the Sword of Destiny is back in the world, and fortunately for us, we know the location of it and are confident it is in a safe place for the time being.

For centuries, the Black Eagle observatory has been tracking the time bubble that holds Baldric Zealotte prisoner, in the hope it would land on some dead planet and he would end his days there, but alas, it has never happened. Professor Gellit has discovered a new meteor in space and it has caught and is pulling the time bubble holding Baldric Zealotte prisoner in its gravitational pull, and it is heading towards Earth. We believe Earth's gravitational pull will bring it back down. If this happens, then as soon as it lands, Zealotte will be back in the world and because he has been in a time bubble, he will not have aged a single minute. And worst of all, he still has his wand.

The bridge, we believe, is the idea of the Black Watch. They intend to use it to set the Hobgoblins on a path of war with the Gnome world. We are working on many possibilities to prepare ourselves for Zealotte's return, but the Black Watch seems to be under every stone we turn, so we have to show extreme caution with every move we make.

I am hoping you can provide us with the information that will point us to the families that are under threat and also, if you have any plans to sabotage the bridge.

Brixun spoke up. From day one, we worked on a plan to destroy the bridge. Our first part of the plan was to work on the Hobgoblins' fear of the Snack Worms, and we managed to convince them that the worms could jump and the bridge would have to be twenty feet from the ground to guarantee their safety. They agreed right away, and pretended it was their idea. This has given us the opportunity to build the bridge supported by a Levita spell for its foundation.

We set about its construction with a willingness the Hobgoblins couldn't understand and because of our willingness to push the construction hard, they have given us quite a lot of freedom, which we use to our advantage. The bridge is designed in two-mile sections, each section having its own separate Levita foundation; although to look at it, it is seamless. This will enable any one of us three to individually collapse sections of the bridge at will. We could trap a whole army without an arrow being fired in anger or we could simply feed the Hobgoblins to the Snack Worms. We have been counting on wizard intelligence to find out what was going on here and now seeing you here is a massive relief to us.

To be honest, Savajic said, the Black Watch have shown they have a remarkable organization and must have some very high-ranking wizards in positions we have no knowledge of. Fortunately for us, they tried to be too clever and set up an elaborate false trail to keep us occupied. I won't go into detail, but part of their plan was to kill Peggy and get me and the security forces concentrating all our resources at Black Eagle. Not only did they fail twice with attempts on Peggy's life, but she managed to eliminate one member of the Black Watch, and she also came up with the idea that there was the possibility of a bridge being built across the worm fields.

As soon as I was able to locate its position and verify its existence, we were able to set our own plan into action. Peggy has left her schooling at Black Eagle to help us, and with her unique magic we have been able to contact you here without being detected. And now I have the exact coordinates of the hut so we can transport directly here in the future at 8:00 p.m., just before you put up the exclusion spells.

Brixun looked at Peggy and said. We are very fortunate indeed to have you on our side, Peggy, for you are truly a remarkable young wizard. And I am sure I speak for us all when I say we will sleep peacefully tonight. George and Showvel both nodded in agreement.

Thank you, said Peggy. She was beaming, and it made her feel really important.

They had cleared the table and were soon busy working on the information Savajic had requested about all the families under threat, and when they were finished, Savajic had a comprehensive list that was going to prove invaluable. I think we have everything I came for, said Savajic. May I just remind you to trust no one. No matter how close they are to you, everything must be strictly on a need-to-know basis. Peggy and I will be your only contacts. Talk to no one else, no matter what they may say to you. Please remember, the safety of your families depends upon your discretion.

Savajic and Peggy shook hands with the three planners, and then he set the pendant coordinates for their base camp. He linked arms with Peggy and they disappeared.

As soon as they were back, Savajic began to pack everything away. He said there was no point in them staying any longer because they had everything they had come for. Peggy started to pack her things away. She didn't say anything, but she was a little bit disappointed because she would have liked to have seen the bridge. But then again, sleeping in a comfortable bed after a nice, hot bath did seem more appealing than a night in the open air on top of a mound, and there would be plenty of time to see it on another visit.

Is everything packed away? Savajic asked.

Yes, I'm ready, she answered. They linked arms and disappeared, and when they reappeared in the great hall, Cooper was waiting for them with a tray of biscuits and two mugs of hot chocolate. Peggy took two of the biscuits and one of the mugs and said to Savajic, I hope you don't mind but I'm taking mine up to my room. This will taste a lot better when I'm lying in a hot bath.

A good idea, Peggy, I think I might just follow suit, said Savajic. I will see you at breakfast. Sleep sound. He turned to Cooper and said, I'm going to retire now so that will be all for tonight.

Very good, said Cooper.

Chapter 7
PEGGY MEETS ENZEBADIER

Savajic and Peggy tucked into their breakfast with vigor, for they both had good appetites. Savajic finished eating and looked over at Peggy and said, I still can't quite believe how lucky we were to get the three planners all together in one place and be able to talk so freely with them. It has saved us so much time and at the same time, kept us from being detected.

Can we trust them? Peggy shot the question at Savajic and it surprised him.

What makes you think we can't? he countered.

Well, if someone was threatening to kill my mother, I might do all kinds of things. I hope I wouldn't betray what I thought was right, but blood is thicker than water.

You are quite right of course, Peggy. Family loyalty and love are a strong combination and we must always take them into consideration. But then again, we can only deal with the facts as they present themselves to us. Let's recap what we learned with our trip to the quarry. One; George Buttress and his team are responsible for the supply of slate to the bridge. Two; the project is being managed by Brixun Mortah and Showvel Hanpix. Three; a quick collapse mechanism has been built into the bridge for the purpose of sabotage. Four; we have a comprehensive list of all the planners' families that are under threat.

I have known all three of them for most of my life and I would personally vouch for them. Consider this, Peggy; when we presented ourselves at the hut there was total surprise, but their relief at seeing us was spontaneous. And remember, they are putting their trust in us, even though they have no idea what we intend to do with the information they have given us.

And so, the answer to your question is yes, I know we can trust them. I will say this though, Peggy, I am so glad you asked the question because it means you are taking nothing for granted.

I think our first task today is to contact Enzebadier and set up a meeting with him. He knows all about you, Peggy, from what I have told him, and he has seen you on the screen, but you are both yet to meet in the flesh, so to speak. If you have finished with breakfast I suggest we should go to my study and contact him on the screen. They both stood up and Peggy followed Savajic over to his study.

They stood in front of the wall that was set up to reveal the screen. Would you like to do the honors, Peggy? Savajic said, smiling at her. You might as well get used to it.

Peggy said, Screen, and the wall changed immediately. Professor Enzebadier, please, she said, and he appeared life-size.

Good morning, Peggy. Good morning, Savajic.

Good morning, they both echoed.

I hope your visits to the quarry and the bridge were fruitful. I was not expecting to hear from you so soon.

We have good news, said Savajic. But I would like permission to bring Peggy and to meet you at the chamber, say, in an hour, is that possible?

Of course, said Enzebadier. And I will look forward to meeting Peggy. Until then, he said, and his picture faded and he was gone.

Peggy turned and looked at Savajic. I can't believe it, she said in an excited voice. I'm going to meet Professor Enzebadier, the elder in the chamber of wizards!

You will have to get used to it, Peggy, because there will be many more such visits to come before we overcome the evil that is Baldric Zealotte. Now let us both go and get ready for our visit. I will meet you on the terrace in thirty minutes.

When Peggy returned, Savajic was waiting for her. If you're ready, he said, we'll get going. He had already set the coordinates on his pendant. He took Peggy's hand, and they disappeared and just as quickly reappeared in the council chamber next to where Enzebadier was waiting.

Welcome to my chamber, Peggy! exclaimed Enzebadier. I have been looking forward to meeting you. Savajic has told me so much about you.

I am honored to meet you, Professor. Oh! I'm sorry, is that the right way to address you, sir?

Professor will do very nicely, said Enzebadier, and winked his eye. It made Peggy feel at ease.

I have assembled the war cabinet as you requested, Savajic, and I have enlarged the table and provided an extra place for our new member.

Peggy gave Savajic a puzzled look. He smiled at her and said, Yes, Peggy it's you. Come on, let's meet the other members.

Chapter 8
PEGGY'S NEW ROLE

Enzebadier led the way through the chamber and stopped when he came to the life-size painting of a wizard on the wall in a heavy golden frame. He turned to Peggy and said. This is a painting of Goodrick the Elder, a great and powerful wizard. He was the wizard that outwitted Baldric Zealotte and sent him spinning into space and saved the wizard world from disaster. He pointed his wand at the painting and said, Akko, and the painting slid sideways, revealing a door. He took a key from his robe and unlocked the door. Inside the room was a round table with seven chairs circling it, four of which were already occupied by wizards. As Enzebadier entered they all stood up, and after exchanging greetings, settled back down around the table.

Peggy, please let me introduce you to the war cabinet, said Enzebadier. Commander Churmill, head of the wizard army intelligence; Keymol Locke, warden of Lockstay Wizard Prison; Semach Siege, chief of the wizard police force; and Professor Gellit, astronomer at the Black Eagle School for Wizards. Peggy moved around the table, shaking hands as she went.

Peggy Goody! exclaimed Professor Gellit. Didn't Angus Fume bring you to see me on your first day at Black Eagle?

Yes, he did, Peggy answered. I'm very flattered you should remember me.

Quite so, quite so, said the professor, and sat down.

Enzebadier turned to Savajic and said. Would you please start the meeting?

Savajic stood up. He had four files, which he distributed between his four fellow wizards. These folders give you a full and detailed history of Peggy's progress in the wizard world up to date. You will find them quite extraordinary, and frankly, hard to believe. But I can assure you, every fact in true. I want you to read them very carefully and then destroy them. The contents are for your eyes only and must remain a secret. Peggy's ability to transfigure and to haze is our secret weapon and must remain so if we are to outwit the Black Watch. Now I will show you the progress Peggy and I have achieved thus far. He angled his camera at the wall and as the lights dimmed, an image of the bridge appeared, which showed wizards working alongside Hobgoblins and Trolls. There was a collective gasp in the room at the true scale of the bridge and the enormity of the deception the Black Watch had achieved successfully underneath their very noses. The image left the bridge and followed the road leading to the slate quarry. It showed the massive sheets of slate winding their way to the bridge, guided by Hobgoblins. Then the massive quarry came into view, showing the team of wizards working, slicing up the slate into plates. The image dimmed and the lights came back on. Savajic had been giving a commentary explaining the dimensions and the type of construction being applied. He had no need to name the planners because they were known to all of them. He then went into the meeting he and Peggy had with the planners; the revelation that the families of the planners were being held hostage shocked them all.

Savajic handed Commander Churmill a folder. Commander, this is the full list of the families being held under threat of death. I believe they are quite safe while the bridge is under construction, but as soon as it is completed, I believe the Death Riders will raise their ugly heads and eliminate any witnesses to their dirty secrets.

Commander, the timing of any action by you and Chief Siege will have to be coordinated to the second; every hostage taker must be targeted and eliminated at exactly the same time. There must be no mistakes and no mercy shown. It is imperative that no one on the bridge or elsewhere gets a signal anything has gone wrong. Then it is up to you to keep guard over the families and protect them.

Semach Siege spoke up. How long have we got to prepare, Savajic?

According to the planners, the bridge is about halfway completed and so we have at least nine months. The planners themselves can determine an actual date as they get closer to completion. Peggy and I will be in constant contact with the planners and will keep you informed along the way. It is our plan to observe the progress of the bridge and meet with the planners at various intervals and in the meantime, we will keep as low a profile as possible so the Black Watch spies have little or nothing to report about. And I strongly recommend we all do the same.

Savajic continued speaking. Keymol, I have reason to believe Sealin Belbur is the leader of the Black Watch, and it is his intention to break out of Lockstay just before the completion of the bridge. Can I ask you, when you arrested him, did you secure his wand?

It's strange you should ask, Savajic, but the answer to your question is no. We searched everywhere but we could not find it, and we all thought at the time it was an unbelievable piece of good fortune.

Maybe so, said Savajic. Or it may well have been part of a clever plan by a very evil criminal. Let's suppose his overall plan was to resurrect the Death Riders and then fall in league with the Hobgoblins and get them to think building a bridge and going to war with the Gnome nation was their idea. They would just have to work on the Hobgoblins' hatred for the Gnomes and give them a raft of false promises to secure their help. If you didn't want to raise suspicion and draw attention to yourself and you were planning something on such a massive scale, where better could you be than in prison?

Keymol stood up and stretched his tall and powerful body. He paced slowly around the room, holding his square jaw between his forefinger and thumb and was obviously thinking hard about something. He sat down and began to speak. Looking back to when Sealin Belbur was captured, it all seemed so easy. I can remember thinking how quiet he was when he arrived at Lockstay and how easy it was to settle him into his cell. He looked over to Semach and asked, Semach, how was the actual arrest? Was there much resistance?

Semach gave a knowing smile and said, It's all starting to make sense. It was easy. We had an anonymous tip-off Belbur was hiding in a log cabin on the edge of Lake Still and we were given the exact location. When we arrived, it was unnervingly quiet. There were no traps or alarms, we just simply walked in and there he was, slumped down on a chair, asleep. Beside him was an empty whisky bottle and a glass. We assumed he had been drinking and had passed out and we couldn't believe our luck. Now that we know what is going on, it seems we were being played all along by a very clever and elaborate plan to get Belbur safely tucked away in Lockstay Prison with no injury to himself. We were so relieved he hadn't put up a fight and killed any police we never for one moment thought it was all a set-up.

Keymol spoke up again. Belbur has been a model prisoner ever since he arrived at Lockstay and has surprised us all. He goes about his duty and never has a cross word for anyone. I have to admit, we all expected trouble and disruption from him knowing how powerful he is and the fact that he is a habitual killer. But since he has been at Lockstay, we have experienced just the opposite. All of the inmates follow his instructions because they fear him so much, so we have had quite a peaceful period since his arrival.

It all seems to be coming together as a carefully worked out plan, said Savajic. But what worries me greatly is the thought that all of this, plus the construction of the bridge, would take the help of some very high-ranking wizards and we have no idea who they are. The burning question is, whom can we trust? He looked across the table and said, Enzebadier, what are your thoughts about all of this?

Enzebadier cleared his throat with a gentle cough. Before I make my suggestions, I would like to have an update on the meteor's progress from Professor Gellit. If you would, Professor, please carry on.

Professor Gellit started by saying the meteor was travelling slightly faster than he first thought and could pass the earth some two months earlier than he first suspected. It would be some time in between next October to November. "I can be more accurate as it gets closer. I can also confirm it definitely has Zealotte in tow. Professor Snide is still plotting its course but how he knows of its existence baffles me greatly. I'm afraid I can't give you much more at this point."

Thank you, said Enzebadier. It seems to me the White Eagle School has somehow been taken over and is being used as a power base for the Black Watch movement. It is the only way I can think of that would allow them to have a hold on so many wizards all at one time. If they are holding the pupils under a threat of violence, then that amounts to hundreds of families possibly doing their bidding. Peggy,

I know you have left Black Eagle and I know your reasons for leaving, but I'm going to ask you to return there and before you give me your answer, let me explain why.

The annual wand speed championships this year are to be held at the end of January at White Eagle, and I happen to know that the Belbur twins are hot favorites to win the trophy. Owen Menglor won the trophy last year by a single point, as we know, and they are still fuming about it. Peggy, without taking anything away from Owen, with you on the team, we can guarantee the trophy coming back to Black Eagle. This I believe will anger Sealin Belbur and dent his ego. Then, in February, the Lightning Hawk Hunt Championships take place. As you may have learned last year, White Eagle took the trophy away from Black Eagle and it was widely believed Charlie Manders was cheated. Now again, with your special powers, Peggy, I think you could arrange for Charlie Manders to actually catch the Lightning Hawk, a feat that has eluded all comers thus far. I can imagine this would send Sealin Belbur into a rage. Then in May we have the Dragon Island Swimming Race Championships, again last year won by the Belbur twins. Peggy, with your unique powers I could see that helping Helda Scelda win would not be too difficult for you to arrange. All of this may not seem very important to you, but I can assure you it will have a big impact on Belbur's standing with his followers. Any sign of vulnerability on his behalf can throw doubt on his leadership and has to be to our advantage.

This is not the only reason for asking you to go back. It gives us the perfect chance to enter White Eagle, and for you and Savajic to have a good look around while hazing and undetected. Now Peggy, said Enzebadier, what do you think?

Peggy was amazed how quickly Enzebadier had come up with the plan and his knowledge of the schools. Her answer was just as quick. When do we start? It was effective, because all around the table they began to clap their hands. Savajic looked at her. He was amazed and proud both at the same time how quickly she had matured from a schoolgirl to a mature and confident young woman.

That's settled then, Peggy, said Enzebadier. Commander, you have the list. If you can link up with Semach and process it; and, Keymol, if you can keep a close eye on Sealin Belbur and his visitors; and, Professor Gellit, if you will keep on tracking the meteor; then

I think we can conclude our meeting. May I wish you all a happy holiday, and we will meet up again in the New Year. They all stood up, exchanging handshakes and goodwill wishes and began to go their separate ways.

Come on, Peggy, said Savajic. Let's get back home and make our plans for Christmas.

Chapter 9
INVITATIONS

For the next two days, Savajic and Peggy had the luxury of relaxing and making their plans for Christmas. Peggy had never been to a Black Eagle gala night before and was surprised to find that students put on various shows of their own. It was all kept a secret until the night of the gala, when the guests were all given a program of events. It sounds wonderful said Peggy. Could I do something?

Well yes, I suppose you could, Savajic said. What have you got in mind?

Well, if I am to be going back to Black Eagle, I could go back tomorrow and do something with Helda Scelda.

Savajic frowned. What have you got in mind?

Peggy began to laugh. Now that would be telling, wouldn't it? OK, said Savajic. But let's clear it with Professor Ableman first.

The invitations were all sent, and Peggy had the green light to return to Black Eagle in the morning. Peggy spent the afternoon getting her school things together. Over dinner, Savajic ran through the Christmas arrangements. The Gala Night was the first item, then Peggy and Owen would be home the next day and preparations were to be made to welcome Rose, Lily, and Charlie.

I think it's time for us to contact Professor Ableman, said Savajic. Let's go down to my workshop. Peggy stood up and followed him out of the dining room. When they had settled, Savajic commanded, Screen, and the wall changed instantly. Then he said, Professor Ableman.

Good evening Savajic, Peggy. I have been expecting your call. Professor Enzebadier has been in contact to discuss Peggy's return to Black Eagle in the morning, and may I say how delighted I am. He suggests that Peggy says she has been dealing with a problem in the human world and has concluded her business much sooner than she had anticipated. I will make sure this story is widely spread and hope it will allay any suspicion that she left Black Eagle for any other reason. I look forward to seeing her here tomorrow. Savajic, I would appreciate it if you could come as well, to go over a few points with me.

I would be delighted, Savajic replied. I will be there with Peggy. The screen disappeared and they both went back to Savajic's study, where he asked Cooper for two mugs of hot chocolate. They sat for a while, chatting things over, and when they had finished the chocolate they both retired for the night.

Chapter 10
Peggy's Welcome Return

Peggy was awake and up early. She showered and dressed for school. She looked at herself in the tall mirror and was feeling really excited about seeing her friends again. Her mind wandered back to the terrace outside the school gates and her awkward attempt at saying good-bye to Charlie, and their last kiss. She was smiling and thinking it was not good-bye, or at least not for a little while.

Her mind snapped back to the present. She picked up her wand belt and gazed into the large, square buckle. Her mother was smiling back at her. She held it to her lips and gently kissed it, then she fastened it around her waist and checked that her wand was secure. *Now time for some breakfast,* she thought.

Savajic was already down and tucking into his breakfast. Good morning, Peggy, he said, smiling at her. I trust you slept well?

Yes, thank you, never better, she replied. I can't wait to get started. I'm so excited!

Well, have yourself a good breakfast and we'll be on our way. I have a feeling you will have quite a reception waiting for you now that Professor Ableman has spread the word of your return.

Peggy downed her meal in ten minutes flat and was on her way up to her room for her cape and school books. When she returned, she was flushed and breathing heavily.

Savajic was waiting for her on the terrace and when he saw her he burst out laughing, I have not seen you so flustered since you smashed the crystal vase in my workshop, he said.

Peggy looked at him and started to laugh herself. I know, she said. I must look pathetic, but I can't help it! I'm so excited.

Savajic set the coordinates for Black Eagle and said, hold on tight, Peggy. She put her arm around his waist and they disappeared. They were on the terrace at Black Eagle in a second and began walking towards the massive gates. As they approached the gates swung open and the whole of the last-year class ran out to meet her. Charlie got there first and suddenly she was off her feet being twirled around and around. He put her down and hugged her and she hugged him back, tears of joy streaming down her cheeks.

I've missed you so much, said Charlie. Suddenly he was pulled away and Peggy felt the powerful arms of Helda Scelda wrap around her. Peggy! My best friend! I knew you would come back to us. Welcome!

It was a full twenty minutes before Peggy managed to get through the gates and the students had dispersed. A circle of four remained; Owen, Lilly, Charlie, and Peggy. They held hands, and the bond had never felt stronger.

They stood for a while quite still, savoring the moment, then Owen spoke up. It's good to have you back, Peggy.

Savajic had been standing there patiently watching. He was pleased to see Peggy have such a good reception. But now they needed to see the headmaster and discuss the schedule Professor Enzebadier had worked out for Peggy. Owen had gone over to him and was giving him a hug, obviously glad to see his father, and that Savajic had been missing his son was quite obvious too.

Owen said, I'd better get going or I'll be late for class. I'll see you at the Gala? Savajic waved as Owen shouted to Peggy, See you later! and disappeared into the school.

Savajic walked over to Peggy and said, Come on, let's go and see the headmaster.

As they approached the headmaster's room the door opened and they walked in. Welcome back, Peggy! The headmaster was genuinely happy to see her. Come and sit down and make yourself comfortable.

May I sit down? Savajic said with a big smile on his face.

Professor Ableman looked over at him and said, I'm sorry, Savajic, please take a seat. I'm so glad to see Peggy back I quite forgot you were there! They all laughed and sat down.

Peggy, I have talked at length with Professor Enzebadier and he has given me a glowing report on your contribution to our current problems. He has only given me the information he thinks I need to know, and of course that is understandable under the current circumstances. He has given me a list of various sporting occasions. He thinks that between us, we can work out how to beat White Eagle in each and every championship. And I think with my choice of competitor and your unique talents, we can comfortably accomplish his wishes. After the holidays will be the best time to start on our plans. And now, Peggy, is there anything you want to talk to me about?

Yes, Professor, there are a few things. For instance, do I go about my classes as if nothing has changed?

Yes, Peggy, you will take normal class lessons. There will not be any more special lessons for you from now on.

Savajic has told me that on Gala Night the last-year students put on a show for the school, and I was wondering if I could do something with Helda Scelda.

I have no objections, Peggy. What have you got in mind?

Well, it would mean I would have to use all my magic, but in a way no one would know how, not even Helda. Only the three of us and Professor Crie would have any idea.

The professor turned to Savajic and said, Can you see any problem there?

Savajic shook his head and said, no, it sounds quite interesting to me. I would look forward to it.

Then you have my blessing, Peggy. I would stress though that only you and those directly involved in the act can know anything about it until the night of the show, when a printed program will be given out containing all of the acts.

That's great, said Peggy. There's nothing else I need to know. Thank you, Professor.

Peggy was excused and made her way to the girls' dorm. When she went inside, she caught her breath. She still had the same bed, and all her things had been put away. It looked as if she had never been away. She lay on her bed and reflected on the past few weeks. So much had happened! Then her mind focused on the task ahead. *A magic show.* She couldn't wait to see the girls and play catch up; and wait until she told Helda what she had planned for them on Gala Night! She relaxed and just let her mind drift.

Suddenly the door burst open and the girls came rushing in. They circled Peggy's bed and all started asking questions at the same time. Peggy sat up on the bed with her legs crossed and began spinning a yarn about an aunt having an accident and her mother going to look after her, and while she was away she had to look after the laundry. It seemed to do the trick because the questions stopped, although Lilly looked like she needed more convincing. But then again, Lilly knew a lot more about Peggy than the other girls.

Peggy held Lilly's hand as the other girls went off to their own beds. I'll be able to talk to you later when you finish your lessons and tell you a bit more, she said.

Lilly smiled at Peggy and said, I guessed there was more to it than a sick aunt. And I've been having some really strange dreams about you since you left.

Like what? Peggy asked.

Well, in one dream I was standing next to you in a massive slate quarry and we were watching wizards cutting sheets of slate, and strange-looking creatures were taking them away. And in another dream, I was inside a room in the Council of Wizards building sitting next to you at a round table, with other wizards talking about a bridge.

Peggy looked concerned she realized she had a mental connection with Lilly, and probably the same with Charlie and Owen. Have you mentioned this to anyone else?

Only Owen, said Lilly.

We must keep it that way, Lilly. It is very important for the safety of our circle.

No problem, said Lilly.

Chapter 11
HELDA SCELDA, ILLUSIONIST

Helda was in the library studying potions, and Peggy thought it was the perfect opportunity to talk to her alone. She said, Hi, Helda, and made her jump.

Don't creep up on me like that! she said, and put her hand on her heart. She stood up and hugged her. It really is great to have you back, Peggy. Do you want to talk to me about something?

Yes, said Peggy, sitting down. Are you doing anything for Gala Night?

No, said Helda. Why do you ask?

Great, said Peggy. Would you like to do a magic act with me?

A magic act? How can I? I don't know any more magic than anyone else.

You would have to put your trust in me, said Peggy. But we can do it together. Are you willing to try?

Of course I am! said Helda. I would trust you with my life, you must know that.

Peggy smiled. Helda, this is going to be fun, I promise you. Can you meet me in the gym at 8:00 p.m. after dinner and we can go through it all?

At dinner, Charlie had a thousand questions, but Peggy was giving nothing away. Helda had mentioned to him about doing a show with her and he wanted to know all about it. Wait and see, Peggy said, and don't go all grumpy on me.

Charlie looked over at Owen for support. Don't look at me, said Owen. I don't know anything. And if I did, I wouldn't tell you. It's Peggy's surprise, so let's keep it that way.

Charlie pretended to be miserable and said, She never asked me. I could have done something with her.

Like what? Owen asked. What would be your great idea?

I don't know, said Charlie, looking up into space. Something.

Exactly, said Owen. And how do you know it's not Helda's idea anyway? She may have asked Peggy. Charlie looked at Peggy, but before he could say anything she did the impression of zipping her lips together and Owen burst out laughing.

Peggy had arranged to meet up with Lilly, Owen, and Charlie in the den at 9:00 p.m. after she had finished going over the act with Helda. Helda was waiting for her in the gym when she got there. I can't wait to hear what your idea is, she said excitedly.

OK, said Peggy, this is it. One, you will need to get a pair of black high-heeled shoes, black tights, a black leotard, and a black top hat. And if that doesn't show off your fabulous figure, nothing will. Two, we need to get a steel cage on a stand, and three, a large silk square big enough to cover up the cage. I have been told we can get anything we ask for if we go to Professor Trouper. The act will be called Helda Scelda, Illusionist.

But what about you? protested Helda. It's your idea.

Listen to me carefully, Helda. It is crucial there is no mention of my name at all so it looks like you are doing an illusion and not magic. The act will go like this. You will need a volunteer, so you call me up onto the stage from the audience. Then you open the door on the steel cage and ask me to go inside. When I'm inside you close the door, and lock it, and then invite two more up onto the stage from the audience to check that the door is locked and all the bars of the cage are solid steel. Then, when they have gone back to their seats, you can begin.

I suggest you enroll two of your swimming team girls to help you with the act because the steel cage will be ten feet tall and it needs to be covered with the silk square. If we have a set of steps on each side of the cage, they can each hold a corner and on your command, climb the steps, concealing the front of the cage from the audience. On your command they will let it go and expose the cage. You and your girls will have to be brave because when the silk square drops, inside the cage where I was standing will be a very fierce and angry polar bear some nine feet in height, roaring as loud as it can and rattling the cage. I hope this will get quite a reaction from the audience and I would expect quite a few screams from the younger students.

You will stand in front of the bear and gesture for it to calm down and then say, 'Lie down.'"

It won't be able to understand me, said Helda, looking very uneasy.

Don't worry, it will, Peggy assured her. This is where you have to have total trust in me. I promise I will not let you down. When the bear is calm and lying down you again ask the girls to hold the silk square and climb the steps, and when the cage is hidden from the audience, count to ten and on your command, they'll drop the silk square. The bear will have disappeared and a golden eagle will have taken its place. Then go over to the cage and unlock the door and on your command of 'fly' it will take off and circle the audience. Then on your command of 'home' it will fly back into the cage. Lock the door and for the last time cover the cage and on your command, the girls will drop the silk square and the cage will be empty. You will look surprised it is empty and walk around the cage so the audience can see you through it and then call out, 'Peggy where are you?' Then I will call back to you from behind the audience, 'I'm here, Helda!' and make my way back to the stage where you will take your bow and they will all think you have tricked them with an illusion, but they will not know how.

Helda was staring at Peggy and for a few moments, she couldn't speak. She snapped back and said, Do you really have that much magic? I can't believe it! How can it be?

It's a long story and it's also a closely guarded secret very few know of. Helda, you are a very special friend to me and I would not share this with anyone else, but before we go through with this I need you to promise me it will be our secret and our secret alone.

Helda held Peggy's hands and looked her directly in the eyes. I will never have another friend I will love like you and I will never betray your trust, on that you can rely. But, Peggy, how about the girls? They will see.

I've covered that problem, said Peggy. The top of the cage will be solid so the girls will only see what the audience sees. No one will see, not even you, Helda, so you have no need to worry.

I will sort out the cage and the steps and the silk square if you can sort out your costume and the girls and their costumes.

No problem, said Helda. I'll get started with the girls, and tomorrow we can get our costumes.

Now, said Peggy. We only have one day to rehearse, so let's all meet up here after breakfast tomorrow, let's say 10:00 a.m. Remember, we all have a day off to rehearse our acts.

Chapter 12
THE DEN

Peggy had to rush to get to the den for 9:00 p.m. but she made it on time. Lilly, Owen, and Charlie were already there. What you been up to this time? Charlie enquired.

I've been in the gym with Helda. She's asked me to help her with a show she's doing for Gala Night.

Helda, a show? they all echoed. Doing what?

An illusionist show, said Peggy. And it looks really good. Now no more questions. You already know more than you should; you know the rules.

I know I left school at short notice, but there was a good reason. As you know I have special powers; fairy speed and great strength just being two of them. But I've changed inasmuch I've grown very competitive. I can't help it, it's just happened to me. When I last played surf polo something happened to me that frightened me. I had been knocked off my board three times and it just came into my head enough was enough and I took off and smashed into Benjamin Fuller; you know the rest. It was then that I realized the next time it could be a lot worse, and with the attacks on me by the Black Watch becoming more frequent, one or more of the students may just be in the wrong place at the wrong time and get killed.

What I am about to tell you is for our ears only. I have been helping Savajic and the Council of Wizards to gather intelligence information about the Black Watch and the impending trouble that the return of Baldric Zealotte will bring. I cannot go into any detail with you and I must ask you not to press me with questions about it. But what I can tell you is, I am back for at least three months. I am coming back at the request of Enzebadier the Elder himself, and I have to work on a specific plan to do all I can to make sure Black Eagle wins all the championship events with White Eagle.

We have proof the Belbur Brothers are taking a potion that has been developed in the lab at White Eagle to make their reactions ten percent quicker than that of other wizards, giving them an unfair advantage in the speed events. We know they are already fast, and they were just beaten last year by Owen on the very last run. I am to partner you, Owen, in this year's speed championship and if they are cheating, I am to use my fairy speed to win.

Charlie, when you surf in the Lightning Hawk championships, Lilly and I will be in the forest in a haze watching and making sure you are not cheated out of it this year by the Belbur Brothers.

And I will team up with Helda in the lake swim and keep her safe and hopefully help her to win.

Can I ask you, Lilly and Charlie, if you had your holiday invitations to stay at Savajic's home? And can you make it?

Yes! they both shouted, and they all jumped up together and hugged each other.

Chapter 13
REHEARSALS

Breakfast was a noisy affair with everyone talking at the same time and trying to second guess just who was going to do what on Gala Night. But until the programs were handed out on the night, no one really knew, and all involved in the acts were keeping tight-lipped.

As soon as breakfast was over and cleared, away Peggy went and sat next to Helda. How far have you got? Peggy asked.

I have picked my girls and we are due to go and see Professor Frill about our costumes at 10:30 a.m., it should take about an hour.

Great, said Peggy. I am meeting Professor Grimlook at the zoo at the same time, and he is going to arrange for me to have a cage and the two sets of steps.

So, if I say we meet in the gym at 12.00 noon, will that give you enough time to get changed and be ready?

No problem, she replied.

OK, said Peggy. I'll see you later in the gym then.

Peggy went back to her dorm and picked up her board and then she made her way down to the rear bridge. She mounted and sped off towards the zoo. As she was surfing, she remembered the last time she had visited the zoo with Savajic, and the awful sight of the wizards being burned to death by the Arctic Dragon and how she had killed it with a rock. A cold shiver ran through her body at the thought of it and she wondered what Professor Grimlook might say to her.

She landed by the door that led to the bird aviary where the professor was waiting for her. Good morning, Peggy, I'm so pleased to see you. He was smiling and very welcoming. I think I have all of the things you need. But before we go and look, I would like to have a word with you in my rooms.

Of course, said Peggy, guessing what was coming. She entered the professor's room and sat down feeling a little bit uncomfortable.

I want to talk to you about the Arctic Snow Dragon, he began.

Peggy interrupted him. I'm so sorry! she blurted out. I wasn't thinking clearly.

The professor held up his hand. There is no need to be sorry, he said. The dragon still lives.

But how can it be? Peggy asked, shaking her head. I saw it lying on the ground, dead.

Ah, it wasn't quite dead, said the professor. But you did put it into a coma for two weeks. When Professor Gull and I examined the dragon, we noticed it blinked its one eye and with our combined knowledge of animal and bird potions, we were able to restore its heartbeat. Two weeks later, the dragon was back on its feet.

That's the best news anyone could possibly give me. Thank you so much for that, Professor!

My pleasure, said the professor. Now let's go and sort out the things you need. Thirty minutes later, the professor had sent her on her way to the gym.

Helda was busy with her girls down in Professor Frill's room. She had tweaked Peggy's idea, changing the top hat for a black cloak with a scarlet silk lining, and for the girls she had chosen emerald-green leotards with matching shoes, and when they were dressed they looked staggeringly beautiful. All three of them were tall and athletic, and with their long, blonde hair cascading down over their wide shoulders, they looked like three supermodels. Helda was so pleased, and she thought to herself, *the boys are going to love this.*

When Helda walked into the gym with her girls and Peggy saw their outfits, she clapped her hands with delight and said, Helda! You've done a fantastic job. You all look so beautiful and professional it's unbelievable!

The gym had been divided into several different sections by Parto spells, allowing the acts to rehearse in the privacy of their own space. Peggy had the cage in place and the stepladders erected on each side. The silk square was royal blue in color and had loops sewn onto one end and it had a lightweight pole running through them to make it easier for the girls to hold while climbing the steps, and when it was held up in large, golden letters it bore the legend "HELDA SCELDA, ILLUSIONIST." Helda loved it. Oh, Peggy, it's wonderful! she gushed, and gave her a hug.

Peggy went through the act step by step so the girls knew exactly what to expect and to assure them when the bear appeared they would be quite safe. Even so, it took three rehearsals before they could control their fear. The first rehearsal was a disaster because when they dropped the silk square, Peggy hit the cage so hard and let out such a deafening roar both the girls screamed and bolted down the steps and ran for cover. It was so funny they decided to make it part of the act. By 4:30 p.m. they were all happy with their parts and were ready for the big show on Gala Night. Peggy had been told the acts performing on the night would be given their programs with the act order and the times three hours before the rest of the school, to give them time to prepare.

At dinner, all the talk was about Gala Night and who was going to escort whom. Owen and Lilly seemed to be a couple now so that was sorted, and Charlie had asked Peggy; she had said yes, of course, and Angus, who had been teasing Helda about her act, had asked to be her escort and she had accepted. And so, it went on, from table to table.

Chapter 14
GALA NIGHT

Helda received her Gala Night program, and she and Peggy were looking through the list of acts.

Opening the show at 8:00 p.m. was Angus Fume, performing the Scottish Highland Sword Dance, accompanied on the bagpipes by Jimmy Squeezbe.

Second on the list were the Chow twins, performing a tumbling and balancing act.

Third was Helda Scelda, Illusionist.

And closing the show was Singh Machul, his sister Fatima, and the troupe performing a Bollywood Experience.

Helda was trembling with excitement. She said, I've never done anything like this before. Thank you for giving me this chance. But how about you, Peggy? You didn't even get a program.

I'm not supposed to, she replied. Remember, I'm not part of the act. I'm just someone you invite up to the stage to help you with your act.

I know, said Helda. It just seems a bit unfair.

Peggy smiled and said, it's not a problem for me, honestly, and I can't wait to see the boys' reactions when they see you and the girls in your costumes.

Dinner was early, at 6:00 p.m. This was to give time enough to clear away, and change the Great Hall into a theatre. Programs were handed out as the students left after dinner, and now they all knew what the acts were going to be on the night.

Lilly and Peggy were very fortunate with their outfits for the gala because unlike the other students who had had to pack their dresses and dinner suits before coming back to Black Eagle, they didn't have to because Savajic had worked his magic for them. He had taken notes from the girls and let their rooms in his house do the rest, and he had also done the same for Charlie and Owen.

Dinner was over, and the girls were getting ready for the big night. Lilly had chosen a figure-hugging cap-sleeve long Cheongsam with a fishtail design. It had a mandarin collar with a decorative Chinese floral frog and a back zip, and it had an embroidered floral pattern stitched with paillettes in shades of gold and brown. She had chosen gold high-heeled sandals to match. She had swept her beautiful, shiny, blue-black hair back and into French plait, and she looked wonderful.

Peggy was wearing a white A-line princess floor-length chiffon evening dress with a ruffle and front slit, and she had chosen white, high-heeled sandals. Lilly had brushed Peggy's hair and put it up in a bun with plaits circling it, and she looked stunning.

They stood and looked at each other. Come on, Peggy said. Let's knock 'em dead.

When they arrived at the Great Hall and went inside, it was amazing. They were in a full-size theatre with dozens of chandeliers hanging from the ceiling, and at one end was a large stage with its curtains closed.

Owen was inside waiting for them and when he saw them he shouted, wow! You both look great! Come on, Charlie's got us some seats at the front.

Charlie was waving to them and shouted, Come on, quick!

The boys looked very handsome in their dress suits and bow ties and the girls both felt proud to have them as their escorts.

Chapter 15
LET THE SHOW BEGIN

Everyone was seated and the lights dimmed. A spotlight sprang to life and focused on the center of the stage, and standing in its circle was Professor Ableman. Welcome to the Black Eagle Gala Night! he announced. May I welcome our first act for tonight, Jimmy Squeezbe playing the bagpipes and Angus Fume performing the Scottish Sword Dance!

The spotlight dimmed and the whole stage was lit up and transformed into a scene from the Scottish Highlands; it was beautiful! The sound of bagpipes filled the air and Jimmy walked onto the stage. He was wearing the full uniform of a Gordon Highlander and playing "Mull of Kintyre." The audience erupted and went wild. As the music ended and the applause died down, Angus Fume marched onto the stage, carrying two large swords. He wore the same uniform as Jimmy and he looked like a giant of a man. He laid the swords on the floor in a cross and stood in one corner of the cross, then he turned his head and nodded to Jimmy, who began playing.

Angus jumped into action with the agility of a seasoned dancer. His feet darted between the blades to the music and for a big man, he was surprisingly light on his feet. It was obvious he had practiced and danced it many times as a young boy.

The dance ended, and the audience clapped and whistled and shouted; the act was a great success. Jimmy and Angus stood on the stage and took their well-deserved bows. Then the curtains closed.

Professor Ableman walked onto the stage. And now it gives me great pleasure to present the Chow twins performing their tumbling and balancing act. The Chow twins! The curtains opened and the twins came onto the stage from opposite sides and as they neared the center they hit spring boards at the same time and shot up into the air, crossing each other and each grabbing a set of rings. They began to spin and twist, always in perfect synchronized timing. They dismounted with somersaults and went straight into their balancing routine.

They were wonderful, and the audience showed it with their applause at the end. The twins stood on the stage with big smiles on their faces and took their bows, and the curtains closed.

Once again, Professor Ableman walked onto the stage. Now, I introduce you to the strange world of Illusionist Helda Scelda! The curtains opened to a darkened stage, then a spotlight suddenly lit up a large silver cage with silver steps on each side. Standing in front of it were Helda and her two girls.

The audience gasped, and some of the boys whistled; they really did look beautiful in their costumes.

Helda walked to the front of the stage and threw her cloak over one shoulder; it flashed scarlet and looked very dramatic. Before I begin, I would like to ask my good friend, Peggy Goody, if she would be good enough to assist me. She pretended not to know where Peggy was sitting and put her hand to shield her eyes and peered out into the darkness of the theatre. A second spotlight sprang into action and found Peggy sitting in the front row. She pretended to be reluctant to go, and Charlie stood up and started to chant: Peggy, Peggy, Peggy, and then the audience took it up, so she stood up and made her way onto the stage.

Helda thanked Peggy and asked her to enter the cage, which she duly did, and Helda closed the door behind her and locked it. Helda turned to the audience and said, Could someone please come up onto the stage and check that Peggy is securely locked in and there is no way to leave the cage other than the door?

I'll do it! shouted Charlie, and bounded up onto the stage. He went all around and checked every single bar of the cage and the lock on the door; the spotlight was on him all the time. I'm satisfied, he said, and returned to his seat.

Helda signaled for the girls to lift the pole holding the silk square and to begin climbing the steps. When the cage was completely hidden from the audience, she slowly turned her back on the cage and lifted her arms. "Now!" she shouted, and let her arms fall to her side. The girls dropped the pole and standing there was a nine-foot polar bear. It gave out a terrifying roar and shook the cage, and its long claws came through the bars in a menacing way. As rehearsed, both the girls let out piercing screams and fled to the side of the stage. The effect on the audience was of total panic. Many of the students ran to the back of the theatre, screaming, and Charlie and Owen were on their feet; both had their wands out and were looking across the rows of seats. So did Professor Battell Crie.

Please be calm! Helda shouted. Everything is under my control! She turned around to the roaring bear and held up her arms; it instantly become calm and quiet, and then it lay down. Her two girls came back onto the stage and the audience returned to their seats. They were all talking and giving out nervous laughs; some of them were still shaking. Helda gave the signal to her girls, who picked up the pole and started to climb the steps. When the cage was covered, she turned and faced the audience. She slowly raised her arms. "Now!" she shouted, and her arms dropped to her side and the girls dropped the pole.

The audience let out a loud gasp. Perched in the center of the cage was a magnificent Golden Eagle. Helda walked up to the cage and opened the door and the eagle walked towards her. As it got to the door, Helda held out her arm and leaned in towards it and the eagle hopped on. Helda stood upright so the audience could see it perched on her arm. It was massive. Fly! she commanded, and the eagle took off into the air. It circled the theatre several times, its massive wings just skimming the students' heads and causing them to duck down. Back! commanded Helda, and the eagle landed back on her arm. She turned to the cage and put the eagle inside and locked the door.

Helda signaled for the girls to pick up the pole and climb the steps for the last time and when the cage was hidden, she raised her arms.

Now! she commanded, and the girls dropped the pole. The audience sat there in silence; the cage was completely empty. Helda looked concerned and began to pace up and down and around the cage. Of course, Peggy wasn't there. As soon as the silk square had covered the cage she had changed into a tiny sparrow and flown through the bars of the cage and up over the chandeliers to the back of the audience.

Helda was playing her part to the full and pretended to look worried. She walked to the front of the stage and shouted, Peggy, come back! Where are you?

I'm here! Peggy's voice came from the back of the theatre and she was picked up by a spotlight walking down the center aisle towards the stage. The students went wild, shouting and whistling, then they began to chant: Helda! Helda! Helda stood at the front of the stage holding hands with her girls and they took their bows. It took at least ten minutes for them to quiet down and for the curtains to close.

Once again, Professor Ableman was center stage with the spotlight on him. And now, to close our show, please put your hands together for the Bollywood Experience!

The curtains opened and the stage looked like the great hall of an Indian palace. The stage suddenly exploded in a blaze of color and music and the dancers poured onto the stage, it was unbelievable! The whole audience were on their feet dancing and cheering. The Machuls were leading the troupe, and boy oh boy could they dance! Their energy was amazing.

At the end of the show they stood on the stage in triumph. It was the perfect ending to a great show. A voice came from the stage: Please be seated. Everyone sat down and it went quiet. It was Professor Pike.

She began by saying what a wonderful show it had been and thanked all the participants on behalf of all the teaching staff. Now we need you all to make your way up to the front of the school. The gates will be open and tables laid out on the terrace with snacks and refreshments. In one hour, the ballroom will be ready for the gala. Please use both exits and retire to the terrace in an orderly fashion. Thank you.

Charlie held Peggy's hand and said, Come on, let's get a table on the terrace, then you can tell me how you did it.

Did what? Peggy said, shrugging her shoulders. Charlie was pulling her along the passage that led up to the terrace. Slow down, she said. I'm wearing high heels. Do you want me to twist my ankle?

Sorry, said Charlie. I just want to get away from the crowd.

As they reached the terrace, Charlie spotted a table with just two chairs next to the balustrade and overlooking the valley below. They walked over and sat down. It had been snowing, and the valley looked beautiful, coated in a perfectly smooth blanket of pure-white snow. I'm glad I'm not out there, said Charlie, rubbing his hands together. Of course the Black Eagle School for Wizards was insulated from the outside world, and happy to be so in wintertime.

OK, Peggy, now that we're alone, it's time to spill the beans. How did you do it? You know, the bear and the other stuff.

It was Helda's act, not mine, Peggy replied. You'll have to ask her.

I know it was you, I just know it! And I also know you're not going to tell me, are you?

There's nothing to tell, she said, giving Charlie a big smile.

Charlie pulled a large silk handkerchief from his inside pocket and pretended to wipe a tear from his eye, then he spread it out over the table. He held his hand above the handkerchief and began opening and closing his fingers and pulling it up from the table. The handkerchief rose up and when it stopped, Charlie pulled it off and in the center of the table was a bottle of pink champagne and two flutes. Peggy burst out laughing. How did you do that? she asked.

Charlie tapped the side of his nose and said, That's my little secret, isn't it? Then he pulled a funny face and started to grin at Peggy. She reached across the table and held his hand.

I love you, Charlie Manders. It just came out but she knew it was true and she meant it.

Charlie looked at Peggy, his face now serious. You know how I feel about you and it's something that will never change. Let's do a deal. if I promise to behave myself and be a good boy while you're at Black Eagle, can we be best mates?

It's a deal, said Peggy. But not too good, that's boring.

Charlie popped the cork and filled the flutes. Let's have a glass of bubbly on it. They clinked glasses and took a sip.

An hour and three flutes later they both had the giggles. The bell rang out and the ball was officially open. Come on, Peggy, let's see how good you are on the dance floor, said Charlie, rearing to go.

When they got there, the transformation was amazing. It was a full-size ballroom with tables and chairs all around and a stage with a twenty-piece dance band and three singers.

Over here! It was Angus. He had managed to get a table close to the band. Lilly and Owen, and Angus and Helda, and as Peggy looked around the table, she couldn't believe her eyes; sitting next to Sal Mendez was Kate Stringer! They both saw each other at the same time and met halfway across the dance floor. They flung their arms around each other and jumped up and down.

Sal came over to them and said to Peggy, "Surprise!" with his wonderful toothpaste smile.

Kate gushed, Sal invited me last week as a surprise, and I arrived about an hour ago.

I don't know what to say! said Peggy. I thought I might not ever see you again. It's just one of the best surprises ever!

They settled down and the band struck up. Come on, Helda, said Angus, and held out his hand and led her onto the dance floor. They were both unbelievable dancers and looked great together.

Blimey, said Charlie. "He makes me look like a 'roo.'" They all burst out laughing.

Come on, Charlie, show us what you can do, said Peggy, moving onto the dance floor, because Charlie was a great dancer and he knew it. The ball was a great success but everything has to come to an end, and Professor Ableman thanked all the students for coming and announced the last dance.

The next morning, breakfast was a noisy affair with everyone talking about their plans for the holidays. They were all packed and ready to go by 10:00 a.m. and made their way to the terrace; the Snake was due at Black Eagle at 10:30 a.m. Suddenly, a loud horn blared out. It's the Snake! someone shouted out, and a loud cheer went up.

The Snake came into view and pulled up level with the terrace; the balustrade disappeared and the doors opened. There was the usual rush to get a table, and as soon as they were all settled down the doors closed and they were on their way.

The Snake pulled up at the platform in the sky and the students poured out. There were various means of transport waiting to pick them up and take them home. Henry was waiting by the platform to pick up Lilly, Peggy, Charlie, and Owen. Over here! he called out. He had opened the boot, ready for them to pack away their cases and surf boards, and they all piled into the back of the limousine and started for home.

Chapter 16
THE HOLIDAYS

The car pulled up outside Savajic's home and they all got out. Henry popped the boot and they all took their cases and surf boards out. You all have the same rooms as before, said Henry, so if you will, please leave your luggage in the hall and I will have it put into your rooms. In the meantime, Master Savajic is waiting on the terrace to welcome you, so please make your way there. Thank you.

They started up the steps and the great doors opened as they approached. They placed their luggage down in the great hall and proceeded through to the terrace. When they got there, it was so strange! The gardens and grounds were covered in a blanket of snow but on the terrace it was warm and sunny, just like a summer's day. Another wonderful part of Savajic's enchanted home.

Welcome! said Savajic, standing up and walking towards them. Rose too was seated at the table and stood up when she saw Peggy. Peggy was already on her way over to her and they hugged each other.

I've missed you so much! said Rose.

And I've missed you too, said Peggy. How long are you staying? Peggy asked.

Christmas and New Year, replied Rose.

That's great, Peggy said. We can really do some catching up. She was secretly hoping that Savajic's powers to block Rose asking awkward questions would work.

They all sat down and tucked into the nibbles that were laid out on the table. Savajic broke the silence. We all have a treat for Christmas day he said. Rose has arranged a special Christmas lunch for us all at the Fox and Hounds Inn down in the village.

That sounds great! said Charlie. Are we going to have roast turkey with all the trimmings and Christmas pudding?

Yes, said Rose, and mince pies after, if you can manage them.

I'll do my best, said Charlie, and gave her a big grin.

Don't you ever think of anything but your stomach? said Lilly, and they all burst out laughing.

Because of Christmas lunch next day, they had decided to skip dinner and just snack in their rooms that evening. Lilly and Charlie needed to catch up with their families, so they were going to their rooms first to use the Mensorial net. The Mensorial network is run entirely by the power of the mind. Unlike humans, wizards have a unique DNA, and the Mensorial net allows wizards to contact and talk to their families anywhere in the world. It cannot be hacked into by anyone with a different DNA and needs no outside power source other than the power of the mind. And because of the Ailizium chemical in wizard blood, it is unique to wizards. Later they were going to catch up with Peggy and Owen in the pool. Rose and Savajic were only too happy to spend the evening together on their own.

Chapter 17
CHRISTMAS DINNER

Breakfast was over and done with and they had all gone to their rooms to get ready to go down to the Fox and Hounds for their Christmas lunch. Savajic had gone to his study because he had had an alert from Professor Enzebadier. As he strode into his study he commanded, Screen! and the wall changed into a screen and a very worried-looking Enzebadier was standing there.

Savajic, we've got big trouble, he said.

What's going on? Savajic asked, an uneasy feeling churning inside.

Enzebadier's words hit him like a sledge hammer. Keymol Locke is dead! Sealin Belbur has murdered him and escaped from Lockstay Prison and is on the run with five other prisoners.

Savajic sat down in his chair, scarcely believing what he was hearing. How can this be possible, Professor? Keymol was warned at our last meeting to be extra vigil.

I know, Enzebadier said. But it is Christmas day, and Keymol invited some of the sentries to his office for a seasonal drink. They must have gotten a little bit merry and dropped their guard. Sealin Belbur had requested a meeting with Keymol early in the morning and had been granted one, and when he entered his office he noticed Keymol had left his wand on his desk. Sealin seized his chance and snatched up the wand and stabbed Keymol through the eye and into his brain, and then stabbed him through the heart and snapped off the wand to make double sure he was dead. He stole Keymol's keys and proceeded to let out the other prisoners and when he disappeared, he left a full-scale riot going on behind him.

Semach Siege is on his way there now with his top units so there is very little for us to do, but I would like you and Peggy to come to a meeting here tomorrow at 11:00 a.m.

We will be there, Enzebadier. I assume I am at liberty to tell Peggy about the situation, Savajic said.

Of course, Enzebadier replied. Now I don't know what you have planned for the rest of the day, but please make sure you are wearing your wands and be aware of your surroundings. Savajic, I now believe you and Peggy are number one and two on the Black Watch death list, so please impress on Peggy to fire first and ask questions after. You are both going to have to hang tough, so until tomorrow, good-bye. The screen disappeared.

Savajic wasted no time. Within minutes he had Peggy, Lilly, Charlie, and Owen down from their rooms and into his study. He sat them down and told them of the prison break. When we go down to the village we will be leaving our exclusion zone; in other words, open to attack. I don't want to alarm you because I don't think anyone could possibly know we are booked in at the Fox and Hounds. But it is possible our front entrance gates are under surveillance. We can't just transfer there today because we have to play our parts as humans so we have to use the car in the conventional way and park up the same as everyone else. Now my whole attention will be given to Rose. She will have my sole protection, and that means you will all have to watch each other's back, is that crystal clear?

Yes, Savajic, they replied.

Good, Savajic said. So let's go and have some fun.

What are you all doing in here? It was Rose standing at the door of the study.

Savajic said, I'm just giving them a pep talk to behave themselves while they are in the village.

Doesn't sound like much fun, said Rose, and they all began to laugh.

Henry appeared in the great hall. I'm ready when you are, Master Savajic, he announced, and started back down to the limousine. They all followed down after him and got in, all chattering away, and the limo glided smoothly away down the drive. As it approached the large iron gates they opened majestically and closed behind them as they passed through.

Peggy's animal instinct was at its height, and she saw him hiding in the hedgerow. There was no doubt in her mind. Her eyes bored into the back of Savajic's head and he instinctively looked around at her. She gave him the smallest of nods but he knew what she meant. He had missed it, and was amazed at Peggy's ability.

The name of the game was to get everyone inside safely. It was fairly safe to gamble there hadn't been sufficient time for the Black Watch to set up an attack. But coming out would be a completely different proposition altogether. Savajic could put an exclusion spell on the limo, but only after everyone was inside, and there was fifty yards of no man's land across the car park to negotiate.

The transfer into the inn was without incident, and they were all ushered to their seats and were ready to go. Rose had arranged Bucks Fizz drinks to kick off with and they all clinked their glasses and wished each other a merry Christmas.

Rose picked up a cracker and held it out to Savajic. Make a wish, she said, and looked into his eyes. She had fallen hopelessly in love with him and couldn't help it. Savajic's dark eyes bored deeply into hers and as he held the other end her whole body felt electric. *Bang!* the cracker exploded and she came back down to earth.

The dinner was wonderful. Savajic was elected to carve the turkey and he did it with ease. Can I have a leg? Charlie called out, licking his lips.

Here we go again, said Lilly. Do you ever think of anything else other than your stomach?

Charlie looked at her. I know nobody likes the legs so I thought I'd help out, he lied. Charlie got his leg. It was massive, and he helped himself to all the trimmings.

Even Charlie was bloated by the time the mince pies and coffee came; it had been a wonderful meal. Peggy leaned over to Savajic, who was sitting to her left and said to him, Can I have a private word?

Savajic whispered something into Rose's ear and stood up and walked towards the cloakroom; Peggy stood up and followed. Peggy put her hand on Savajic's arm. You know there is probably a trap waiting for us to walk into outside.

Savajic looked at her and said, Yes, do you have a plan?

I've thought of one, said Peggy, but it's something I have to do alone. I need you to cover for my absence, about twenty minutes should do it. Say I am talking to someone I knew at school and ask them to excuse me for a few minutes.

I can do that, said Savajic. But please be careful.

You don't have to worry about me, she said. They won't even see me. And with that she opened the door and where she had been standing, there was a tiny sparrow. It took off, and Savajic closed the door.

When they had arrived at the Fox and Hounds, Peggy had noticed directly opposite the car park on the other side of the road there was a high bank covered with trees and ferns, a perfect cover for an ambush. She flew high and looked down through the trees. Her hunch was right, there being three wizards, each armed with a rifle that had telescopic sights fitted. They were there with one intention; to kill them as they walked to the car. And by using human weapons, it gave them accuracy over a greater distance. They knew getting into a face-to-face fight with Savajic would end up with them being on the losing side. They were about thirty feet apart and concentrating on the car park; some of the people had started to leave, so they were on full alert. Peggy dropped down behind the first one, changed back to normal and hazed. She tapped him on the shoulder and as he turned around in panic, she pulled off his head mask and rammed it into his mouth.

The next few minutes were pure agony for the wizard. Peggy systematically dislocated his fingers and thumbs, and his eyes were wide open in a look of terror and pain. What was happening to him? He couldn't see anyone or anything at all. Peggy looked down at him cowering on the floor; she felt nothing but contempt for him. He was just a coward hiding in wait ready to kill innocent people.

Well, he won't be using his hands for a while, she thought, and then she rendered him unconscious. The same fate befell the other two. She gathered up their weapons and relieved them of their wands and then she stood next to a large oak tree. Up, up, she said, and shot up to the top of the tree where she deposited the weapons and wands safely in between the crook of two branches. She said, Down, down, and came back to normal. She had a smile on her face and was thinking of all the new magic she had learned, yet she had just used the very first piece of magic she had been given by the fairies. Without delay, she transfigured back into a sparrow and flew back and landed by the door. She changed back to normal and went in.

Savajic looked over to her and she mimed the word *done*. Nothing else would be said until much later, in Savajic's study. Are we ready for the off? Savajic shouted, and they all shouted yes. They were all full of good cheer and just a little bit tipsy. Rose and Savajic went and thanked the landlord and his wife for looking after them so well and asked them to give the chef their compliments on an excellent meal. Savajic left the staff a very generous tip. Then they made their way to the car park and walked to the limo. They were completely oblivious to the danger they had avoided. Henry pulled smoothly away and headed for home and as they approached, the large iron gates swung open and they were all back safe and sound.

Chapter 18
Peggy's Report

The whole day had been a great success, and after they had retired for the night, Peggy left her room and made her way down to the study, where Savajic was waiting for her. They sat down in front of the log fire; it had burnt down low but was still giving off a warm glow, and Peggy began her report. She gave him every single detail, and after she finished, Savajic began asking her questions. He was amazed at how quickly Peggy had put her plan together but wanted to know the thinking behind her actions. He began by asking her why she had dislocated the wizard's fingers and thumbs.

Three reasons, she replied. Firstly, to give them lots of lasting pain, and secondly, to put them out of action without causing them too much injury. And last of all, they would not be able to get their head masks out of their mouths. Can you imagine what will happen to them when they get back and report their failure to whoever sent them? They didn't see or hear anything, and their weapons and wands have disappeared. And they will still be gagged and unable to use their hands. For me it is perfect justice against three renegade wizards attempting to kill the five most important people in my life. I really believe this will cause them quite a lot of concern.

Savajic said, Good, Peggy, I have to say I am really impressed. Do you remember the day at the quarry when you killed the Demodoms and you said to me you didn't have the knowhow to capture them and were very upset with yourself? Well, you have certainly come of age today. I don't know of anyone, including myself, who could have put such a plan together and execute it so well. You have kept a cool head and focused on the job at hand like a true professional. I'm very proud of you.

Peggy! Savajic looked at her and shifted a little nervously in his chair.

Is there something wrong? she asked, looking concerned.

No, said Savajic, it's something personal I need to talk to you about while we're alone. While you have been at Black Eagle, Rose and I have spent several weekends here together and we have grown very fond of each other. I know you do not remember your father, and how much you must have missed not having him to hold you and love you. Your mother has told me how much she loved your father and how much he loved you, and she thought she could never love anyone as much as she loved him. I felt the same way about Owen's mother. But fate has brought Rose and me together and we have fallen in love. Neither of us saw it coming, but it has. What I am trying to say, Peggy, is I would like to marry Rose and spend the rest of my life with her, and I would like to have your blessing. I have yet to speak to Owen, but I will when the time is right.

Peggy was surprised at first, and then she thought back to the summer holidays and how happy Rose had been, and how she and Savajic had enjoyed each other's company. She remembered thinking how she had never seen her mother laugh so much and how kind and gentle Savajic was with her. All the signs had been there.

Peggy looked at Savajic and said, You must know how much I love you. You have been to me the father I never had, and apart from my mother, there is no one on earth I respect more than you, and there never will be. Peggy stood up and crossed over to Savajic. He stood up and they held hands.

Peggy said, My mother has had so much tragedy and loss in her life and she has kept it hidden from me for all these years, never complaining. Make her happy, Savajic, that's all I ask of you. Tears ran down her face.

Thank you, Peggy, Savajic said, and squeezed her hands. Now this conversation must remain our secret for the time being. Until the situation with Baldric Zealotte is resolved, I can't risk putting Rose in any kind of danger.

Can I speak to mother about it?

Yes, of course, but not just yet, because I haven't asked Rose. So, when I do, I will tell her you know and she can give you the news herself.

Peggy thought, *Wow, this is some secret to keep.* But keep it she would.

Let's go and get some sleep, Savajic said. We have got to be at our best tomorrow when we have our meeting with Enzebadier.

Chapter 19
THE BLACK WATCH HQ

The Black Watch headquarters were deep down in the cellars of Ravens Claw Castle. The location was a secret, and unknown to the wizard world. It is the hub of all the Black Watch intelligence and is kept up to date by using the wizard's latest atomic holographic molecule transfer data gathering technology.

There was a flurry of activity and the wizards in charge were in a panic. There was a gap in the data they should have received from a unit out in the field, an unexplained blank in their communications, and it couldn't have happened at a worse time. Sealin Belbur had just arrived, and his first impression of their efficiency would not be good.

What do you mean? You've lost contact with a three-man unit? What was their mission? An elderly wizard stepped forward and said it was something operations had put together in a hurry. Apparently Savajic Menglor had been spotted leaving his home with several others and operations thought it would be a good chance to eliminate him for good. So, they put a team of three Death Riders in place to ambush him and his companions. They had been equipped with human firearms so they could make the kill from a safe distance, and they had with them more than adequate communications equipment. The gap in communications doesn't make sense. What action has been taken? Sealin snarled.

Cleaners are on their way as we speak, replied the elderly wizard, just in case something has gone badly wrong, and they should be reporting back at any minute.

Good, said Sealin. Now, what is the latest on the prison break? He was escorted to the hologram room and watched as Semach Siege turned up with his units and stormed the prison and he soon had everything back under control. A reporter for the *Wizard Daily Standard* was interviewing one of the prison guards and he was explaining how Sealin had murdered Keymol Locke with Keymol's own wand and then stolen his keys and had gone about releasing the other prisoners. Sealin had a wicked grin on his face, it had all been so easy, and he hadn't even had the use of his own wand. But now he was reunited with his wand and was back in control of all his power.

The elderly wizard from communications came into the room and Sealin turned to him and said, "Well! Not good news I'm afraid. The three Death Riders have been humiliated. They have been found unconscious with their head masks forced into their mouths, gagging them, and all the fingers and thumbs on their hands have been dislocated and their weapons and wands are nowhere to be found. They all swear they didn't see or hear a thing, it just happened to them.

That is ridiculous! They are lying to save their own skins. I will not stand for this level of incompetence! screamed Sealin. Send this message to the cleaners. Take the three of them to somewhere remote, kill them and bury them deep—and no trace, do you understand? And let this be a lesson to all; I will not tolerate failure. The stakes are far too high. Now get me Ivor Craktit at the bridge.

A wall in the cellar became a giant screen and standing in the middle of the bridge was a wizard. Greetings, Sealin. I trust the prison break went well?

I don't think it could have gone any smoother, boasted Sealin. How are we progressing with the bridge?

Better than we expected. So far there has not been one single hitch.

Great! roared Sealin. He was pleased with the news. Keep up the good work, Ivor, he said. I will be coming to see you soon and you can show me the progress. In the meantime, I will go and visit the Hobgoblins and talk to Petrid, their leader.

Chapter 20
The Death of Keymol Locke

Boxing Day breakfast was a quiet affair. Do I detect a few hangovers this morning? Savajic asked, looking around the table.

Not so loud, protested Charlie, who true to form had devoured everything that had been put in front of him, not to mention a couple of bottles of bubbly. Lilly and Owen hadn't fared much better, either. Owen suggested they go for a sauna and then have the rest of the morning in the pool.

Spot on, said Charlie, holding the top of his head.

Savajic had apologized to Rose in advance for having to take Peggy off to a meeting and promised to be back as soon as possible. Rose said she would join in and have a sauna and spend the morning by the pool. Just be careful and come back safely, she said.

Savajic held Peggy around the waist. Are you ready? he asked.

Yes, replied Peggy, and they disappeared. When they materialized on the chamber steps, Enzebadier was waiting for them.

There are just the three of us today, he said, and guided them through the chamber to his private rooms. Please come in and sit down and make yourselves comfortable, he said, gesturing towards two chairs. I'm sorry to pull you both away from your holidays, but the situation is grave, and I'm very concerned about the safety of you both. I do not have to tell you how dangerous and ruthless Sealin

Belbur is. And now that he is free and on the run, he will be able to give out his orders at will. I truly believe your safety will be put to the test as never before.

I have something to show you both. He waved his hand, and the back wall of his room turned into a screen. It is the murder of Keymol Locke, warden of Lockstay Prison; a close friend and colleague. Before we start, I must warn you that it is extremely violent and deeply upsetting. He waved his hand again and the inside of Keymol's office appeared.

Come in. It was Keymol's voice. The door opened, and the figure of Sealin Belbur appeared. Sit down, Sealin, I'll be with you in a minute, said Keymol, and turned to put a book back on the shelf. He reached up and put the book away and as he did, he heard a scuffling noise and turned around. He had no chance to protect himself. Sealin snatched up Keymol's wand from off his desk and stabbed him through his eye and into his brain. Then he pulled out the wand, and before Keymol could move he plunged the wand deep into his heart and snapped it off. Keymol fell to the ground in a pool of blood and Sealin bent down and calmly took a bunch of keys from Keymol's belt and rushed from the room. The picture faded and the screen went blank.

There was silence for a few moments, then Enzebadier spoke. I'm sorry to have put you through that but I want to impress upon you what a vile and vicious person we are dealing with. Remember, Keymol was a highly trained fighter and had very powerful combat magic, and Sealin didn't even have his wand.

I'm surprised Peggy said. Sealin looks so ordinary, not at all what I expected.

Don't be fooled by his good looks, said Savajic. I was at school with him for a while and he was a nasty piece of work. Fortunately, he transferred to White Eagle for his last two years. Enzebadier, please let me tell you how our Christmas day went. Savajic told him of the plot to ambush them by the Death Riders and how it was Peggy who had spotted the lookout. Then he told him of the outcome of their attempt, sparing no detail. And so, let me ask you; who do you think is the greatest threat? Our Peggy or their Sealin?

Enzebadier stroked his beard thoughtfully and said, Peggy, you are indeed a credit to all of your teachers. Your plan was unusual, to say the least. But I would not hold out much hope for the Death Riders' futures when Sealin Belbur is presented with the facts. And I can imagine he will try to make some sense of it. He will try to fathom what kind of magic you used, Savajic. He may well have heard of Peggy, but he has no idea of her powers so he will naturally think it's your doing. Oh! I have also been in contact with Professor Ableman at Black Eagle and put him on full alert, and to report directly to me the slightest incident, no matter how small.

Savajic stood up and stretched and paced the room in a thoughtful mood. He stopped and said, I think it's time for us to give Demodus another visit and lay our cards out on the table; tell him about our proposal before he joins forces with King Kelbot. In the meantime, I think we should all enjoy the remainder of the holiday. I have a feeling Sealin Belbur will be wanting to do the same with his family; remember, he has been away from them for quite some time now and in no particular rush.

I agree, said Enzebadier. Arrange for your meeting with Demodus when school resumes and keep me posted. His answer should be quite interesting. I won't keep you from your guests any longer. As always, it's been a pleasure to see you again, Peggy. Enjoy the rest of your holiday.

Hold on tight, Peggy, said Savajic, and held his pendant. They disappeared and materialized back home.

That was quick, said a voice; it was Rose. I didn't expect you back so soon. Did everything go well with your meeting?

Just routine, Savajic said. Did you enjoy your swim?

Yes, she said. The others are still there 'chilling out,' as Charlie has informed me.

Great, said Peggy. I think I'll go and join them if that's okay with you.

Of course it is, go and catch up. I want to talk with your mother anyway. Peggy disappeared upstairs to change.

Chapter 21
The Proposal

Savajic held Rose's hand and led her into his study. Is there something wrong? Rose asked.

On the contrary, answered Savajic. I want you to please sit down, Rose, and listen to what I have to say. As he began, his voice filled up with emotion. For many years now, since Owen's mother died, I have lived with an unhappy loneliness inside. We were very much in love, and when Owen was born, I truly believed life couldn't get any better. Her death devastated both my own and Owen's lives, and when Owen went to Black Eagle I was plunged into a period of unimaginable loneliness. Over the years, we have both dedicated ourselves to work. Owen has excelled at most things and has grown up to be a kind and loving young man. For myself, I have created much new magic and have worked hard to become part of our chamber of elders. I never thought someday I could have found love and happiness again, but I have.

Since I met you, Rose, the happiness I once knew has returned. I can only hope you have developed some kind of feelings for me. What I am desperately trying to say is that I have fallen in love with you, Rose, and I want to spend the rest of my life with you.

Rose had gone quite pale. She stood up and went over to where Savajic sat. If only you knew how many nights I have lain awake hoping someday I would hear you say those words. Savajic, I fell in love with you when I first came to stay here. I felt so guilty, as if somehow I was betraying Peggy's father. Like you I was very much in love, and gave up everything to be with him. When Peggy was born, we were both so proud. Then as you know, fate snatched it all away. But I had Peggy, and she was all that mattered in my life. Then by some miracle you and Peggy met, and because she is so special, I met you. I never dreamed I could ever love another man and have the love returned to me. If I could have a wish it would be to live with and love you for the rest of my life, and I know Peggy loves you and Owen just as much.

Savajic stood up and held Rose in his strong arms and their lips met in a passionate embrace. As they parted, Savajic said, Marry me, Rose, and she said, oh yes, and kissed him.

They say sat together in silence for a while and Savajic spoke. Rose, I have told Peggy and Owen about my feelings for you but they do not know I intended to propose to you. Can I leave it to you to tell Peggy?

I can't wait, she said.

Then there is just one more thing. He reached into his pocket and produced a box. Will you wear my ring? He opened it and inside was a beautiful sapphire ring. He took it out and slid it onto her finger. It was a perfect fit.

At dinner, Savajic announced he had asked Rose to marry him and she had accepted. They all clapped and gave their congratulations. I just want to ask one thing of you all, and that is to keep this a secret until we announce it officially. I don't envisage any problems, but Rose is human, and until I receive written permission from the elders, it is only right to say nothing. They all agreed, and Savajic lifted his glass in a toast. He said, To Rose, a remarkable woman and my future wife.

They raised their glasses and said, To Rose.

Peggy tapped her glass. Attention please. They stopped talking and looked over to her. I would like to make a toast of my own, she said. She raised her glass and said, I have been blessed with a wonderful mother, and now a future father and brother, two people who have shown me love and devotion. And they have taught me that with hard work and dedication, I can be anything I want to be. And one more thing is, I have always wanted a baby brother. Cheers. They all toasted and began to laugh.

Owen protested, What do you mean, baby? You're only three weeks older than me.

The holidays were over and Peggy, Lilly, Charlie, and Owen had loaded their cases and boards into the car, and now they were ready to go back to Black Eagle. Cooper was in the car and waiting, and after they had thanked Savajic for a great time and said their good-byes, they all got in and Cooper slowly pulled away.

I think that went well, said Savajic to Rose.

It was a wonderful Christmas, she said, and linked arms with him. Let's go in, it's cold out here, she whispered, and squeezed his arm. They sat in the study and looked into the log fire. Rose hadn't felt so secure for as long as she could remember and she loved it. How long have I got to make a decision on what I am going to do with the laundry? she asked.

Take as long as you like, Savajic said. Just make sure it's what you want. I know you would want to look after your people, that's true, she said, and snuggled up close.

Chapter 22

Savajic's Visit to Demodus

Savajic was alone again and his brain kicked back into gear. He had gone over in his mind what he was going to say to Demodus when they met, and now he was ready to go. He had no need to contact Bluebell this time because he had been given an open invitation to visit by Demodus himself on his last visit. He set his pendant and disappeared.

As he materialized in the clearing outside the entrance to the caves, Demodus came walking out. Savajic, this is a surprise. It's good to see you again. And to what do I owe this visit?

I've come to talk to you about a proposal I have and it's something I think will be of great interest to you.

Come in, said Demodus, and let me hear what you have to say. And he led Savajic into the caves. They walked deep into the mountain until it opened up into a gigantic cave and in the center was Demodus's magnificent, stately home. Savajic had seen it before on his first visit but it seemed even better this time. They entered and went straight to Demodus's study. Make yourself at home, he said, and they both settled down in the luxurious leather chairs.

Savajic began by saying to Demodus, I hope you will indulge me, but I want to tell you a story before I put forward my proposal to you.

Of course, said Demodus. Take all the time you need.

Thank you, Savajic replied. Some two thousand years ago, the wizard world was plunged into a vicious and bloody civil war, with wizards killing wizards. Whole bloodlines were completely wiped out, and all because of one evil wizard who had sold his soul to Kanzil. In return, Kanzil fashioned him an all-powerful sword, a sword that had the power of Kanzil himself, and it had no equal on earth.

The wizard was Baldric Zealotte, and he was winning the war. But because of his arrogance, the wizard leader, Goodrick the Elder, was able to separate Zealotte from the sword and trap him in a time bubble, and send him spinning out into space. It was hoped eventually the time bubble would land on some far distant planet and open, where he would spend the rest of his life. But alas, it has never happened, and while he is trapped in the time bubble he will keep healthy and not age even one second. We now know a meteor is heading for earth and has caught up the time bubble in its gravitational pull. We know the meteor will pass the earth at a safe distance, but we also believe the earth's gravitational pull will bring the time bubble back down to earth, where it will open and Zealotte will be free once more to roam the world and spread havoc.

An interesting story, Demodus said. But why should I be interested?

There is much more, said Savajic. If I may continue.

Be my guest, Demodus replied.

Savajic continued. On becoming free, the first thing Zealotte will seek is the sword, and he will go to any lengths to get his evil hands on it. Now it just happens to be the sword he will seek is the one that belongs to you, the Sword of Destiny.

What! Demodus raged. He will get it over my dead body.

That will be of little consequence to him. He will destroy anything that gets in his way to regain the power of the sword. But as long as you hold it in your hands and guard it closely, the power will be with you.

Demodus was standing now and pacing the room. He suddenly stopped. This doesn't make sense, he said. I know the sword has great powers because I have actually stood against Kanzil himself, and even he could not defeat me. But I have only ever used its power for good and the sword has always helped me and shown me the way.

This is good news, Savajic said, because it means the sword will do the bidding of he who wields it.

Demodus looked Savajic in the eye. You're right, he said. I found the sword buried deep in a cliff in the fjords. I was tunneling into the rock to make myself a new home when I broke into a large cave and in the center was a stone, holding the sword. It glowed and drew me to it. At first I wasn't interested, but at a later date I needed help with a problem. The sword came to me in a vision and helped me solve my problem, and I remember when I drew the sword from the stone words appeared, etched in flames. It is said that he who draws and wields this sword will be master of his own destiny. So, it must use its powers in equal measures for good or for evil.

Yes, Savajic said. It is certainly something Kanzil overlooked when he fashioned it from the magma.

To continue the story. Zealotte had a plan that involved the Hobgoblins. As you well know, they are a sworn enemy of the Gnome kingdom, and we believed he was planning, with the help of the Hobgoblins, to conquer the Gnome nation and use it for his seat of power. Fortunately, he never got the chance to carry out his evil plans and the Gnome nation has prospered over the centuries. Now as you know, the worm fields came into existence after the mines ran out of ore and became in itself a natural barrier between the two nations.

Zealotte's followers were called the Black Watch and his murderers were called Death Riders. All through the centuries they have kept a secret sect alive in the belief that one day Zealotte would return again and lead them to glory. And now, Demodus, the time has come when their prediction looks as if it is about to happen.

I have one more part of the story to tell before I come to my proposal, so please hear me out. The Black Watch have already contacted Petrid, the leader of the Hobgoblins, and they have convinced him that with their help he can defeat the Gnome nation and seize all of their assets and land, and enslave them. The Black Watch has captured the wizard's very best planners and are holding their families prisoner and threatening to kill them if they do not do exactly as they say. At this moment in time they have built an enormous bridge that reaches halfway across the worm fields and they plan to finish it before the return of Baldric Zealotte. As far as we know, the Hobgoblins are almost ready to march, and only the completion of the bridge will hold them back.

I have studied the history of the Gnome kingdom right from the date you left. King Igor never got over the feeling of guilt after he had banished you. You were his closest friend and his champion, and he loved you like a son. But he realized later that by revoking the death sentence, he had committed you to a fate far worse than death. As soon as you left he declared a week of mourning, and the whole nation mourned the loss of their greatest champion. He had your statue removed from the great square and erected in the grounds of your home next to the statue of Valyew Sellum, your father, and he made your home into a museum for the nation. And it still stands today for all to see. The king only lived for a short time after. People say he died of a broken heart. The Gnome nation believes you died in the wastes of the Arctic long ago and have no idea you are still alive, but your legend lives on and you are still their greatest champion. You have more than paid for your crime, and I have no doubt you would receive a full pardon from the king if you returned to Greco.

The Gnomes have had peace for centuries and because of this, they have grown weak and their army is a shadow of what it was. Your nation has never needed its champion more than now. Demodus, if I were able to set up a meeting with the king, would you come with me? The Gnome nation is on the brink of annihilation and is not even aware there is even a threat.

Demodus looked shell shocked. He had spent all his time for years planning and building an army strong enough to conquer Greco. And now he was being asked to save them. The truth hit him like a hammer blow. The power of the sword had given him all the tools he needed to do the job, and now they were in his hands it was up to him how he used them. "The one who wields the sword will be master of his own destiny." Now he understood. The day he had found the sword was not an accident, it was his destiny, and now the sword was giving him a chance to atone for his sins and save his nation.

Demodus walked over to his sword and touched it. It had been a good friend to him for so many years and had served him well.

A voice came into his head and spoke to him. It was the sword. *"Demodus, the time has come for you to make peace with yourself and free yourself from guilt. Go and meet with the king and become his champion, and save your people from the evil that is about to befall them. Fight your last battle with honor, and with my power, you will become the master of your own destiny."*

Demodus walked over to Savajic and held out his massive hand. You are a true friend. Meet with the king and if he agrees to see me, then I will gladly come immediately. I will not allow my people to become a nation of slaves.

Chapter 23
SAVAJIC VISITS GRECO

Savajic was back in his home. He was delighted with the outcome of his meeting with Demodus and went immediately to his study to inform Enzebadier. Screen! he demanded, and the wall was a screen, Enzebadier! Enzebadier appeared.

Greetings, Savajic. What news have you?

Good news, said Savajic. Demodus has agreed to come with me if I can arrange a meeting with King Kelbot, and he will offer him the services of himself and his army.

I don't know how you managed to pull it off, Savajic, but well done. Will you need my help for anything?

No thank you, said Savajic. I am going to ask the Fairy Queen to arrange the meeting. She has the king's ear, and he will trust her guidance.

Very well, said Enzebadier. Please let me know the outcome of your meeting on your return, and the screen faded.

Savajic wasted no time. Bluebell, help! he called. There was a flash of blue light and there was Bluebell, perched on his desk.

Savajic, how can I help you?

Bluebell, I'm so glad to see you again, he said, and went straight into his request.

I can't see a problem, said Bluebell. I'll let you know within the hour, and disappeared in a blue flash.

Savajic decided to have a shower and change his clothes, then he would eat and after, prepare his notes for his meeting with the king. With his hunger satisfied, Savajic retired to his study and settled himself down behind his desk. He now realized that the outcome of the meeting between Demodus and King Kelbot was crucial to the survival of the entire Gnome race, and he had to get his part as broker completely right; there would be no second chance.

There was a blue flash and Bluebell appeared. Greetings, Savajic. I bring you good news. The queen has arranged for you and Demodus to meet with King Kelbot at noon tomorrow. The king's guard will meet you at the city gates and escort you and Demodus to the palace, where the king will be waiting to greet you both. I have taken the liberty of sending word to Demodus of the arrangement.

Thank you, Bluebell. You are a true friend. And please give my best regards to the queen for her help.

I will, Bluebell said, and disappeared in a blue flash.

At ten minutes to noon, Savajic appeared in front of Demodus's cave entrance. Demodus was standing there waiting. He was wearing his sword and the tiger skin scabbard and belt the Scaleygills had made for him, and he looked like a fearsome warrior.

Greetings, Demodus, said Savajic. Are you ready to go?

Yes, said Demodus. I am ready. Savajic set the coordinates for Greco on his pendant and they held each other around the waist. Savajic said the words and they appeared outside the massive ancient wooden gates of the city. An imperial guard was waiting for them with two white stallions. He gave them one each and welcomed them in the name of the king. Please mount up and follow me. The king is waiting for you in the palace. They mounted their horses and began riding through the city towards the palace. Demodus was amazed so little had changed. The horse's hooves rang out as they struck the cobblestones, a sound that reminded Demodus of the days when he had ridden through the city as the king's champion to the cheers of the people.

When they reached the palace, they dismounted and followed the guard up the steps. Demodus had an overwhelming feeling of sorrow. The last time he had made this journey he was a prisoner charged with robbery and murder; it had been the worst day of his life. And now he was treading a path that would bring him full cycle, the last segment in the circle of his extraordinary life. The thought warmed him inside. And now he was ready to meet his king.

As they approached the throne room, King Kelbot came walking towards them. Greetings, Demodus, Savajic, he beamed. His happiness to see them was obvious.

Demodus fell to one knee and his head was bowed. Your Highness, he said, and as he lifted his head he was weeping. He had never dared to dream this day would come to pass, and his emotions had taken him over.

The king looked Demodus in the eyes. He could see the years of hurt, and his face gave him a story of a thousand years of hardship and battles. He had paid dearly for his crimes. Rise, Demodus, my champion, and welcome home, the king said, holding out his hands. Demodus stood up and thanked the king. He towered over him, but nevertheless he felt humbled.

They followed the king to his private rooms and sat down around his desk. I have been informed by the fairy queen of the Hobgoblins intentions, he said, but she had only a sparse knowledge of the actual situation. So perhaps, Savajic, you could give me the full story.

Savajic bent down and picked up a large bag he had brought with him. He had prepared a comprehensive presentation of all the information he had amassed over the last few months. He set up his camera on the king's desk and then waved his wand at the wall, which instantly became a blank screen. He then began his presentation.

I will not go into the circumstances that led me to find out about the bridge and of the Hobgoblins' plan to attack your nation, but I will give you all the information I have so far. An outlawed wizard movement called the Black Watch is behind this plan, and the plan is simply this. They have convinced the Hobgoblins that with their help, they can build a bridge across the worm fields and deliver their army safely to the gates of Greco unopposed. The pictures I am about to show you will give you a good perspective of how well advanced they are with their plans. The camera sprang to life and the screen became a 3-D picture of the bridge. It tracked along down the length of the bridge, showing its enormous proportions, and picked out those who were working there. As the end approached, the two massive Trolls that were working there suddenly came into view and the king gasped and said, Have we got to fight Trolls as well as Hobgoblins?

Savajic said, I think they are mercenaries and have been enlisted to carry a battering ram and break through the city gates, but I don't think there will be more than two of them.

The king turned to Demodus and said, Demodus, do you think we can defend ourselves against the Hobgoblins?

Demodus stood up and paced the room. He was a fearsome sight, as his warrior instincts had kicked in. Your Majesty, we will do much more than defend ourselves. I will need two things from you; complete control of your army, and one hundred of your best builders. If you grant me this, the Hobgoblins will never see past our city gates. I will make sure the Hobgoblin army will cease to exist for all time.

The king called for his guard, who came to him immediately. You called, Your Majesty? he asked, bowing.

The king said, Yes. Go and summon General Stingum to my rooms, and tell him it is urgent. Then he turned back to Demodus and said, General Stingum is the commander of my army. He will be instructed to give you anything you ask for. And the builders will be assembled for you in the next two days. Is there anything else I can help you with?

Yes, one more thing; open access to Greco City for Savajic and myself and for one other, Peggy Goody, a young wizard who is a crucial member of our plan, and Savajic's intelligence partner.

Granted, said the king.

I have nothing more for you at this stage Your Majesty.

Turning to Savajic he said, If you have finished, Savajic, I am ready to return. Your Majesty, we will be back in one week with a comprehensive plan of action, if that fits well with you.

I look forward to your next visit, said the king, and wish you both a safe journey back.

Savajic locked arms with Demodus and gave his pendant his command and they disappeared. They reappeared at the entrance to the cave.

Follow me, said Demodus. There is something I want you to see. You already know about my soldiers, but there is much more for you to see. At the entrance of the passage that led to the laboratory and the firing range, a large buggy was waiting with a driver seated at the wheel. Jump in, said Demodus. When they were seated Demodus said to the driver, "The hangar." They sped down the passage and passed the laboratory to the left.

As they passed through the firing range, Savajic noticed there must have been five hundred or more Demodom soldiers being drilled at various stages of their training program. You seem to be well up on your schedule, said Savajic.

Yes, replied Demodus. The professor and his team have done very well and will be rewarded for their efforts. We have a target of one thousand soldiers in six months' time, and hopefully I will have them all in place ready to face the Hobgoblins, who are in for quite a shock. But I have much more, as you will soon see.

They stopped outside an enormous hangar and the driver got off the buggy and pressed a large red button on the wall. A loud rumbling sound began and a sliding door began to move across, revealing a cavernous interior. Inside were rows of strange-looking flying crafts. What are they? Savajic asked, looking puzzled.

It's the latest secret weapon the British are working on.. The Hornet Drone. My team of scientists reckon that the British are about four years away from completion; we have ten completed and tested. It's amazing what can be achieved with enough money.

I'm impressed, said Savajic. How do they work?

Demodus beckoned over a man in a white coat and introduced him. This is Professor Fuelbank. He is in overall charge of our project. Professor, would you please give us a general picture of how the Hornet Drone works?

My pleasure, said the professor. The Hornet is unlike any other kind of drone. It only has one mission, and that is to seek out its target and totally destroy it and the area around it to a depth of three hundred meters. It is rocket propelled and has four rockets to the rear and four more rockets, two on either side of the craft that will swivel three hundred sixty degrees from front to back, and will swivel sideways one hundred eighty degrees. They are all fully synchronized and will change the direction of the craft instantly to prevent it from being shot out of the sky. It carries twenty missiles and will destroy anything that tries to prevent it from reaching its target. Once the Hornet has been programmed and it takes off, nothing will be able to stop it. And when it reaches its destination it will hone in on its target and self-destruct with devastating power, leaving no trace of anything.

Savajic looked at Demodus and asked him if he intended to build any more. No, said Demodus. Ten will be more than enough.

That's good, said Savajic. Because I dread to think what will happen when the humans get their hands on them. He looked around the vast hangar and saw hundreds of cross-country motorbikes. What's with the motorbikes?

Demodus smiled and said, How times have changed. They are for my cavalry. When I was young it was horses. I have decided to make half of my soldiers mobile, and hopefully panic the Hobgoblins and split them up. Now, Savajic, I have shared all of my secrets with you and I suggest that we go back to my house and have something to eat, and then put our heads together and work on a plan to defeat the Hobgoblins.

Chapter 24
BATTLE PLANS

Savajic and Demodus sat facing each other across the desk in Demodus' study. Before we start, I have something to tell you, said Demodus. For the past few years I have been building an army for the sole purpose of attacking Greco and dethroning the king, I wanted to exact my revenge on them for my exile into the wilderness. Thankfully you came along, Savajic, and changed my way of thinking, and stopped me from making a monumental mistake. Now I will do everything in my power to destroy the Hobgoblins and protect my king and my people.

Have you had any thoughts as to how you will defend Greco? Savajic inquired.

Well, I would like the battle to be over with before they could get as far as the city gates, replied Demodus. I realize after they have crossed the worm fields there is no great distance before they get to Greco, but the terrain benefits us inasmuch as there is virtually no cover until they can reach the great forest. And when they exit the forest, again there is little or no cover. That is where the battle will take place.

My soldiers will be placed behind fortifications I intend to build in front of Greco. On each end will be three machinegun stations angled so they will cover the open ground in crossfire. They will in turn create a nonstop curtain of bullets. A killing zone. Anything that should get through will face my soldiers' rifles, and they are all top snipers. I have no idea what the Hobgoblins have in their armory or whether they can get airborne and attack us from above. Therefore, my drones will be stationed at the rear, ready to take off and shoot down any enemy attacks from the sky. When the battle begins and most of the Hobgoblin army has crossed the bridge, I will send my cavalry out from the right and left flanks to go wide and get behind the Hobgoblins and trap them in the forest. Their mission will be to destroy as much of their fighting machine as possible before it can be used against us. These are my plans so far.

Savajic stood up and stretched. He motioned with his hand towards the decanter of brandy sitting on top of a priceless antique side table. May I? he asked.

Of course, said Demodus. And please pour one for me.

Savajic did the honors and sat down again. He sipped his brandy and let the full-bodied flavors race across his taste buds and then sat down, quietly studying his glass. After a few minutes, he looked over to Demodus and said, I'm impressed. You have not only employed human weapons but also human battle strategy, neither of which has ever been brought into our dimension before. It is such a pity we have to mimic the humans' destructive way of life to overcome our enemies, but so be it. And now, Demodus, how can I help you with your plans?

There are several things we will be struggling with, Demodus said. Our builders are few, and ill-equipped to deal with such a large-scale program I am about to ask of them. Do you think perhaps you could get a team of wizard planners to help us?

Savajic smiled. Wizards are building the bridge for the Hobgoblins. I would think helping you to build your fortifications would be the least we could do. Consider it done. Before we begin to build we will steal an idea from the enemy and we will put up a façade spell to work behind. It has worked for them, so let it work for us. Now what else can we help with?

Demodus drained his glass and stood up. Can I give you a refill? he asked Savajic.

Yes, please, he said and drained his glass. You have good taste, Demodus. Germain-Robin Alambic brandy, if I'm not mistaken.

Correct! said Demodus, and roared with laughter. With the compliments of the British aristocracy, from one of my visits to their cellars. He poured two generous refills and gave one to Savajic and then sat down again. I'll tell you what I would like the outcome of this battle to be, he said, and it is this.

I want to see the Hobgoblins totally defeated, not only on the battlefield, but right back into their homes. I want any survivors banished from Goblin territory, and the Goblin nation to re-establish itself and be self-governed once again and have lasting peace. Now I know you and Peggy have managed to penetrate their security and get behind their lines. So, this is what I think you and Peggy may be able to do. First, find out who the leader of the Goblins is and gain his or her confidence. Get them to give you the locations and coordinates of all the Hobgoblin army installations and store depots and any other important buildings. If I can get these, then as soon as their army has crossed the bridge, my drones will be programmed and sent to destroy them, and also the bridge. Any surviving army of theirs will be driven back into the worm fields.

I know you have wizards working on the bridge and they will be in danger, but I would like to think that when the time comes, you will have your own plans in place to help them escape. So, Savajic, what do you think?

I think it is all doable, Savajic replied. And I am sure Peggy and I will do our best to pull it all together. As soon as you have your ideas on paper, I will arrange for our planners to meet you in Greco and exchange ideas and begin building. Now, if that is all, I suggest we relax and enjoy your wonderful brandy.

Chapter 25

BELBUR CRACKS THE WHIP

Ravens Claw Castle was cloaked in a cloud and looked desolate and deserted, but underground in the cellars there was a frenzy of activity. Sealin Belbur was back, and barking out his orders. He ruled by fear and it worked. He had spent time with his family after his escape from Lockstay Prison, but his boys were back at White Eagle and it was back to business for him. He was still smarting from the bungled attempt they had made to kill Savajic Menglor when they had the chance. He and Savajic had been rivals from a very early age. At school, he had always come a close second to Savajic and he hated him for it. And when he had been transferred to White Eagle, he was glad to see the back of him. At White Eagle, Sealin had trained relentlessly to beat Savajic in the inter-schools trophies. He never did, but he came within a whisker of it and there was very little between them. Savajic had just had the edge on the day. But the bad blood continued between them after they both left school, and it was rumored Sealin was somehow involved in the attack on Savajic's father that had caused his death. In the years that followed, Sealin Belbur became a feared criminal gang leader and eliminated anyone who got in his way. And now here he was, head of the Black Watch and in control of the Death Riders. He owned Ravens Claw Castle, and now that he was back, he was going to control the operations personally in every aspect. He had used the story of Baldric

Zealotte's return to earth to great effect, both on the Hobgoblins and the outlaw wizards alike. He had no intention of giving up leadership to Zealotte. As far as he was concerned, without the Sword of Destiny, Zealotte was just another wizard, way behind the modern times, and he felt he was more than a match for him. His plans had no place for Zealotte, and he would be eliminated at the first opportunity.

He alone knew the real reason for the Hobgoblin war. He wasn't interested in grabbing Greco City for a power base; but what he did want desperately were the vast gold reserves the Gnomes had amassed over centuries of successful mining and trading. It was rumored they were even larger than the Rainbow Banks. And that would give him enormous power.

He was so confident his plans were faultless he was already building a vast underground complex to house his treasure. His ultimate plan was to use the gold to corrupt the wizard world and take control by stealth and fear. It would be pointless creating a wizard war and having the devastation that followed the last one, with whole blood lines of wizards lost forever. No, it would be very negative to take over the wizard world if half of the knowledge they had was wiped out by killing each other.

Now to the task at hand, he told himself. He must visit the bridge and get a first-hand appraisal of the progress made, and he also needed to talk to the planners about an addition to the plans he had made. He called for his transport officer and informed him to be ready to take him to the planners' cabin on the bridge site, and then he got Ivor Craktit on the wall screen.

Greetings, Ivor. I'm coming to see you in the next hour, so will you get together with Brixun and Showvel and meet me at their cabin?

Consider it done, Sealin, Ivor said. It will be good to see you again. It's been too long.

Sealin turned away from the screen and it faded away. Ivor Craktit and Sealin had been close friends from way back to their days at White Eagle. Ivor had gone on to become a top planner, and Sealin had joined the wizard army and successfully rose in the ranks. Unfortunately for Sealin, he was charged with unlawfully killing a prisoner, and although he protested his innocence and claimed it was self-defense, he was dishonorably discharged. It had taken him quite a while to come to terms with what had happened to him, but when he eventually recovered, he made a vow never to be under anyone else's command, ever. From now on, he would be his own boss.

When Sealin arrived at the planners' cabin they were there waiting for him. He greeted them one by one and went in. They sat around the table and Sealin began. First of all, before I get started, I would like to apologize to you, Brixun, and to you, Showvel, for the dramatic way in which you were both brought here. But unfortunately, I didn't have the time to argue with you both about my project. I knew you would both be against it, so I had to take the action I took. I want you to know and understand that your families and loved ones are in no danger from me or the Black Watch, and never will be.

I want to talk to you about the bridge, and after that, you can treat me to lunch and then show me around the quarry and the bridge. I don't know how much you know about the possibility of Baldric Zealotte returning to earth, and it is only a possibility; it is by no means etched in stone. But his coming or going is of little consequence to me because he has no bearing on the bridge or the impending battle. I have come here today for two reasons, and they are as follows: Number one, I want a definite completion date, no guesses no excuses, and the minute the Hobgoblins start to cross the bridge will be the moment you both go home and the Black Watch guards will disappear from your homes, and the same goes for the quarry crew. Number 2, I want you to build a Levita collapse spell into the first half of the bridge and give me and Ivor the spell command.

Brixun and Showvel looked at each other in disbelief. You want to collapse the bridge? Brixun said, pretending to be surprised.

That is exactly what I want, Sealin said with a wicked grin on his face, but in three stages. The Hobgoblin end first, and when the triumphant army are all on the bridge on the way home I want the other end down and then good-bye, Hobgoblins. The Snack Worms will do the rest. I don't want any Hobgoblins around to help Zealotte if by some miracle he should return to earth safely, and I want no way back for the Hobgoblins. I believe it is better for both of you if you know nothing else. And now perhaps we can have lunch.

Sealin was delighted with the bridge and was amazed by the progress that had been made. He was equally impressed by the size and scale of the bridge itself. It's perfect. It will hold the complete Hobgoblin army and all of their equipment. It's exactly what I wanted, he said. Well done. And then he asked the burning question. When do you think it can be completed?

Ivor said, What would be the best time for you, Sealin?

The end of August would be perfect, Sealin replied. Do you think that is possible?

Ivor turned to Brixun and Showvel. What do you think?

Brixun said, If we had an extra crew in the quarry and more workers, it's achievable. Yes, we could complete by the end of August.

That's good news, Sealin said. Ivor, can I leave this with you, Brixun, and Showvel?

Ivor said, Yes, leave it with us and consider it done.

I'm going to skip my visit to the quarry, Sealin said. I'm going back to Ravens Claw to prepare for a meeting with Petrid and his army leaders.

Chapter 26
Savajic and Peggy Get a Surprise

Peggy had settled back into school life after the Christmas holiday and was enjoying her trips to the aviary and her sessions with Professor Gull. She had been learning all about the different species of birds and their habitats and memorizing them for future reference. As she studied with the professor, she began to realize how wonderful the bird life was. For instance, most places in the world were accessible, and they were capable of travelling great distances. They were wonderful survivors in all kinds of climates and conditions. As she began to absorb all of these wonders, she began to understand what a wonderful gift Mother Earth had bestowed on her. And she was yet to go into the animal world and find out what powers she would gain from the bear world.

Professor Gull had devoted most of his life to the aviary and his birds and he had never married. When Professor Tweet had passed away some sixty years ago he had accepted the post at Black Eagle and had never regretted it for one moment. And now Peggy had come into his life and he adored her. She was bright and eager to learn, and there was something about her he couldn't quite understand. It was her ability to get up close and gain the confidence of the birds. It was almost as if they understood each other.

How's my favorite pupil today? he would say when she arrived for her lessons, and Peggy always gave him a kiss on the cheek and he would say, Oh, if only I was seventy years younger, and they would both burst out laughing. Peggy felt comfortable with the professor. He was like the grandfather she had never had.

She was finished for the day and said good-bye to the professor and started back to the school building. When she arrived back there was a note on her bed; it was from Savajic. It was short and to the point. "I will come and pick you up after breakfast tomorrow morning. I will tell you more when I see you. Savajic."

At dinner, all the talk was about the annual wand speed trophy to be held at White Eagle at the end of the month. The elimination rounds were well on their way, and both Owen and Charlie were safely through to the next round. It looked like they had found a new prospect, Ben Locke, from the year below. He had posted a score better than Charlie.

Why haven't you entered the competition, Peggy? Charlie asked.

I can answer, Owen interrupted. She has been made first reserve and has gone straight onto the list. Charlie didn't pursue it any further. It was Enzebadier's idea to make her first reserve so she didn't have to show how fast she was in the heats. A secret weapon to use only if it looked like the Belbur twins were going to win and topple Owen.

But if Owen could do it himself, all well and good. Peggy would not be used and her speed would remain a secret.

I have got to go out tomorrow, Peggy said to Owen. Savajic is coming to pick me up after breakfast, so don't be wondering where I am.

It's all right for some, said Charlie. We have to work while you go gallivanting all over the place. He puffed out his cheeks and pretended to be fed up.

Never mind, Peggy said, and reached over and patted his hand. I'll bring you some sweeties back, Bob-Bah. They all burst out laughing and Charlie dug his spoon into a banana split.

Next morning after breakfast, Peggy made her way to the headmaster's room and when she got there, Savajic was waiting for her.

Good morning, Peggy. Are you ready for some action?

Bring it on, she said, laughing out loud.

That's what I like to hear. Let's get going then. You don't need to bring anything other than your board. We have everything we need at home.

As soon as they arrived at Savajic's home they got down to business. I have drawn up a list of things to do, Savajic said, and handed Peggy the list. It's not in any particular order because I am not sure how to go about finding who is the leader of the Goblins, or even where to start looking.

I think I may be able to help there, Peggy said, because I think the fairies have close links to the Goblins and I could ask Bluebell to help us find out.

Good thinking, Peggy, Savajic said. Let's try.

Peggy called out, "Blue flash help!" There was a flash and there was Bluebell, standing next to her.

Peggy, Savajic, greetings! Is everything all right?

Yes, said Peggy. I'm sorry to trouble you, Bluebell, but I need some information I think you could help me with.

Tell me what you need to know and I will try, she replied.

I need to know who the leader of the Goblins is and where to go to talk to him or her. Is that possible?

It's more than possible. I can set up a meeting if you would like me to. The leader of the Goblins is Princess Sheiklin. She lives in the Yellow Mountains and is protected by powerful magic. The Hobgoblins have tried in vain to capture her but they have always failed. While she lives, the Hobgoblins will never truly reign over the Goblins. She has waited a very long time for an event like the Hobgoblin war to happen, and if the Goblins can help in any way to bring them down she will welcome you with open arms. Give me a few hours and I will get back to you with her decision.

Thank you, said Peggy, and Bluebell disappeared in a blue flash.

Demodus had asked Savajic for any locations that were strategic to the Hobgoblins' plans and he had listed army barracks, supply depots, communication centers, and any buildings that would shelter their leaders. He wanted the coordinates of each one and his drones would destroy them, leaving the Hobgoblins in total disarray. Then the Goblins themselves would be responsible for finishing the job and reclaiming their land.

Savajic handed the list to Peggy and asked her if she could think of anything else Demodus might need. She shook her head and said no. There is something I would really like to do, and that is to take a look at the bridge. Do you think we'll have the time?

We'll make time, Savajic said, because I want us to visit the planners and try to find out how much time we have before the Hobgoblins march on Greco. So, we can kill two birds with one stone.

There was a blue flash. Bluebell was back. Good news, she announced. Princess Sheiklin would be delighted to meet with you both. She will expect you at noon tomorrow. She handed Savajic a sheet of paper. These are the coordinates of her cave. Please memorize them and destroy the paper. And I also suggest you both travel there in full haze.

Thank you for all your help, Bluebell, Peggy said.

My pleasure, she replied, and there was a blue flash and she was gone. Savajic studied the coordinates and passed them to Peggy. Memorize this, he said, and destroy it when you have finished.

Peggy studied it for a few seconds and put it into her memory bank, then she folded the paper twice and put it into Savajic's large silver and crystal ash tray. She drew her wand and pointed it at the paper. It set itself on fire and burnt to ashes. Savajic studied her every move. He was pleased to see she hadn't given a verbal command but instead used her power of thought. Her magic was years ahead of any student in the land and indeed, well ahead of many wizards.

The next day after breakfast, they both went down to Savajic's workshop and set about getting their kit together for the trip. Savajic wanted to record the progress being made on the bridge so he could keep Enzebadier up to scratch with the latest events. He checked and double checked the cameras and packed them away when he was satisfied. When the last of the kit was safely stowed away, Savajic and Peggy took it up to the terrace, where it would be ready and waiting for them when they started. The table on the terrace had been laid out and there was tea and biscuits waiting for them. They had about an hour to kill, so Savajic went over his plan for the day with Peggy.

We will set up camp in the same place as before and from there we can visit Princess Sheiklin. Hopefully, when we have all the information we need for Demodus, we will come back to base and pick up our kit and visit the bridge. When we are finished on the bridge we can go to the quarry and contact George Buttress and let him know we will be visiting them at 7:00 p.m. and to expect us. After that we will come back to base and get some rest. You will need your energy to be at its maximum. Then we go and meet with the planners.

Right, Savajic said. Let's get our kit and make a move. Peggy, I want to get there early and set up camp and from there we'll go and meet the princess.

Peggy put her arm around Savajic's waist and went into haze. He set the pendant and gave the command. When they arrived, Savajic set up a 360-degree Parto spell that hid them from view and then Peggy came out of haze.

How long have we got before we go? Peggy asked.

About twenty minutes, replied Savajic. Why, are you feeling nervous?

No, Peggy said. I just thought I might as well use every chance that I get to top up my energy levels. And with that she lay on the ground and closed her eyes and let Mother Earth do the rest.

It's time to go, Peggy. Savajic's voice was quiet.

She opened her eyes and stood up and stretched. Let's go and meet the princess, she said.

Savajic smiled at her and said, come on, cheeky. They appeared opposite what looked like a rock fall.

Have we come to the right place? Peggy said, looking around. There was no sign of life anywhere around.

Be patient, Savajic said, and let's come out of haze. They won't know we're here yet. He was right, because as soon as they were visible the loose rocks started to move and magically formed themselves into a large entrance way. Standing in the center were three Goblins.

Greetings, said the Goblin in the center. I am Princess Sheiklin, and these are my guards, she said, gesturing to the Goblins on either side of her.

This is Peggy, and I am Savajic. We thank you for agreeing to meet with us, Princess, Savajic said, and bowed from the waist.

The princess was quite tiny, and Peggy was fascinated by her gentle way. She curtseyed and said, Princess.

The princess said, Will you please follow me? and turned and walked into the cave. As they followed, they heard the rumble of the entrance collapsing itself behind them. Please don't be alarmed by the noise. It's just our way of staying invisible to the Hobgoblins and so far, it has proved very effective.

The cave led up to an opening and through it was a green and fertile valley surrounded by mountains. The land had been cultivated and there were Goblins at work in the fields. This is an extinct volcano some fifty thousand years old, the princess said. The mountain is so high and steep no one ever comes near it, and so it's become a lost world, perfect for the Goblins to hide out in when the Hobgoblins have one of their persecution purges. They have ruled us by force for centuries. Our laws forbid us from going to war and fighting, and although we have much more powerful magic, we cannot use it for violent acts of any kind. Of course, we do use our magic to upset and confuse them, but we have to be careful how far we push them. They are natural killers and have murdered many Goblins.

She came to a stop at what looked like a large glass lantern, and one of her guards opened a glass door. The princess stepped inside and the guards followed. Please come in, she said. Savajic and Peggy followed. The guard closed the door behind them and the princess snapped her fingers. In the blink of an eye they were in a beautiful state room.

That's very impressive magic, Princess, Savajic said in genuine appreciation. Peggy stood there looking around in amazement.

Before you begin, the princess said, I want you to know we are fully aware of the bridge being built over the worm fields, and of the Hobgoblins' plans to invade the Gnome nation. We have waited a long, long time for a situation like this to arise and we are determined to make the most of it. We are at this very moment working on our plans to rid ourselves of the Hobgoblins forever. You need to know certain things about the Hobgoblins. Long ago in the distant past, Hobgoblins didn't exist. The Hoblis nation was a nation of proud warriors, but they made the fatal mistake of attacking the Beezac cave dwellers, an ancient tribe that practiced very powerful magic. They were taken by surprise and their queen was murdered.

The Beezacs repelled the Hoblis army and placed a curse on their women. They would never be able to give birth to a female child. This was to be the punishment for killing their queen. Over the passage of time, the population of the Hoblis nation shrank drastically. Then the unexpected happened; a Hoblis male and a female Goblin fell in love and mated, the result being the first Hobgoblin female. The consequences turned out to be devastating for the Goblins. As the word spread across the Hoblis nation, the Hoblis families realized this was a way to keep their bloodlines intact. Over time, many female Goblins were forced into marriages, and so the Hobgoblin race began to grow. The Hobgoblins are much larger physically than the Goblins and over time, had a population big enough to breed with their own kind. To the relief of the female Goblins, they have lost all interest in them. Now they are fierce warriors and will fight to the bitter end. When it comes to the battle, it will not just be the males that fight; the females and small ones will fight alongside them. They are born killers, and age and sex have no bearing at all. If they can walk, they will fight.

I have told you we cannot by virtue of our own laws use our magic to fight a war, but we can use our magic to destroy and collapse the bridge once they have crossed, and as they are terrified of the worm fields, there will be no way back for them. However, we have just found out they have enlisted the help of the flying Bull Hounds. They are dog-like creatures as big as a horse with horns and massive wings and can carry a Hobgoblin on its back quite easily. Fortunately, there are only about three hundred, and it is hoped the Gnome bowmen will bring them down. As a reward for their services, the Hobgoblins have promised them the Nectar Valley and all of the wine produced there. It's just another problem we have to face if indeed we have to.

Savajic began by saying he was pleased to know the Goblins were so well informed. It will possibly make my request to you a little easier, he said. Like you, we are aware of the bridge and of its purpose, and I can tell you that although the Hobgoblins think it is a secret, it is a secret that is shared by King Kelbot and ourselves. Extensive battle plans are being put into place as we speak, and certain aspects of it I think will be of particular interest to you. Peggy and I have come here today to ask you for the coordinates of every barracks, depot, and communication building, and any building or place Hobgoblins may use for safety. Unbelievably, the Gnomes have the same agenda as you have, and that is to leave no trace of the Hobgoblin race. But unlike you, they have in their possession frightening weapons of destruction, which they intend to use, and they will show no mercy.

If you can supply me with all of the coordinates you know of, then the weapons will be programmed to pinpoint accuracy and completely destroy whatever is there, leaving no trace it ever existed. They intend to destroy the bridge and they will take no prisoners. They intend to rid themselves of the Hobgoblin threat once and for all time.

The princess looked at Peggy and Savajic and said, You cannot even imagine what this will mean to my people. Your request is granted, of course. We know every bolt hole they will use and we log everything they do and where they go. There is nothing we do not know about them. You will have a dossier with all that you need. Give me fifteen minutes and I will be back. She turned to one of her guards and said, Make our guests comfortable and give them refreshments. She snapped her fingers and disappeared.

Fifteen minutes later, she was back with a bright-red folder. I think you will find everything you need in there, she said. How long have we got before it all starts, Savajic? the princess asked.

I can't give you a definite date yet, but it will be between the next six and nine months. We have many things still to do but as soon as I have a date, I will pass it on to you. One more thing, Princess. I have your coordinates, so can Peggy and I have your permission to turn up unannounced?

You will be more than welcome, the princess said, and thank you so much for bringing such wonderful news. She clicked her fingers and they were back in the glass room. My guards will escort you to the entrance of the cave, and I look forward to our next meeting. Then with a click of her fingers, she disappeared.

Chapter 27
Trouble on the Bridge

Back at base camp, Peggy was reflecting on their visit. I can't believe the Goblins plan to destroy the bridge as well. That's three ways it can go; the planners, Demodus, and now the Goblins.

Yes, Savajic said. Fate moves in mysterious ways. And talking of moving, get your camera and board and let's get moving to the bridge.

I am so looking forward to this, Peggy said. I can't wait.

We will be travelling along the bridge inside the Parto spell so we have to be very careful not to make a sound. You have taken your Anti-Oder liquid, haven't you, Peggy?

Yes, she replied. Before we left this morning. They mounted their boards and linked arms. Peggy went into haze, and they took off and began gliding smoothly towards the bridge entrance. As they approached, Savajic took out his anti-façade baton and pointed it at the concealed entrance. He didn't want to chance colliding with anything as they went blindly through the façade.

Peggy was amazed at the sight that greeted them as they went through the façade; it was so active! There was a continuous line of giant sheets of slate floating across the bridge in a perfectly straight line for as far as the eye could see. Some twenty yards in, a wizard was relieving the Hobgoblins of the sheets of slate and sending them across the bridge. The Hobgoblins then left the bridge and started back to the quarry for their next load. Peggy thought how it all resembled a line of worker ants.

They glided along six feet above the slates and it seemed to go on forever. This is massive, whispered Peggy.

I know, said Savajic. And when it's finished, it will be twenty miles long, a wonderful piece of building.

Suddenly Savajic squeezed Peggy's arm and said, No more talking. There was activity ahead, and they couldn't take the chance of being heard. They slowed down and started to hover. The two planners were there giving four massive Trolls instructions. The trolls were using their massive strength to maneuver the slabs of slate into position and the planners were using their wands to fix them in place. There were two other wizards present, and Peggy guessed they were Black Watch, there to keep an eye on them.

The pace was fast and furious and the slate was coming at a relentless pace. Suddenly, for some reason, one of the wizards shouted something at one of the Trolls. The Troll had stopped for a drink from a large water barrel. He looked at the wizard and let out a mighty roar. The wizard pulled out his wand and sent him a powerful sting. The troll leapt at the wizard, grabbed hold of him, and threw him off the bridge. The wizard screamed all the way down to the worm field and then it all went silent. The troll turned away and went back to work as if nothing had happened, and the relentless pace picked up again.

Savajic squeezed Peggy's arm and pointed up. They flew up and through the façade. Let's get back to base, Savajic said. I think we've seen enough.

They landed back at base camp and unloaded their gear. Well, Peggy said, that was an experience, to say the least, and a lesson learned.

And what lesson is that? asked Savajic, smiling at her.

Not to mess with Trolls unless you really mean it, said Peggy. They both burst out laughing.

OK, Savajic said. Our next stop is the quarry, and when we've finished there, we can come back and eat and get some rest, to be ready for tonight when we meet the planners. You've been hazing quite a bit today, Peggy. Are you good for another thirty minutes or so?

No problem, said Peggy. I'm ready if you are. They linked arms and Peggy went into haze, then they sped off towards the quarry where another surprise awaited them.

When they arrived, they found there was an extra slate cutting crew working there. Two crews, Savajic said. I wonder what this means. I thought the slate delivery had picked up when I saw how fast the Trolls were working. Let's get close in to George and see what he has to say.

They landed behind him and Savajic said, Don't turn around, George. It's Peggy and Savajic.

George pretended to cough and put his hand to his face. Can't talk, he said. You talk to me.

I understand Savajic said. It can wait for a few hours. We'll be back at 8:00 p.m. and follow you to the cabin. Don't say anything else. We're off.

They landed back at base and settled down behind the façade Savajic had put up. Are you hungry? he asked.

I am a bit, said Peggy. What have we got?

Savajic handed her an energy bar. Eat this, he said. It's packed with goodness and it will taste of anything you want it to. It's one of my special recipes.

Peggy munched away at it. It's really good! she said, and opened a bottle of still water. When she finished, she lay back on the ground. I'm going to rest now. Will you wake me when it's time to go?

Savajic replied, We have plenty of time, so just relax and recharge your energy.

She closed her eyes and became as one with Mother Earth. Savajic looked at her with pride. Without her by his side, he would not have been able to achieve a quarter of what he had. She seemed to take it all in her stride with a maturity well beyond her years. She would continue to experience things not many wizards would ever dream of. She was confident and powerful, and had a thirst for knowledge. But even so, each different experience she had seemed to fill her with wonder.

Wake up, Peggy. Savajic shook her shoulder gently.

She stirred and looked up at him. Is it time to go?

Savajic nodded and started to pack up their kit. He was meticulous, and there wouldn't be any trace they had ever been there.

Chapter 28
The Planners Are Excited

Peggy and Savajic landed silently behind George. We're behind you, George, Savajic whispered to him. George didn't speak, he just nodded his head. Five minutes later, George was opening the door of the cabin. He paused just long enough for Peggy and Savajic to slip past him and went in and closed the door behind him. Stay out of sight until Brixun and Showvel get here, he ordered, his voice sharp and edgy. Things are not the same as the last time you were here, he said.

The door opened and Brixun came in, followed closely by Showvel. They could tell something was up by the look on George's face. They quickly closed the door and drew their wands and put exclusion spells on the cabin. As soon as they were secure, Brixun asked George what the matter was.

OK, you can show, said George, and Savajic and Peggy came out of haze.

Brixun seemed overjoyed to see them and exclaimed, Aren't you both a sight for sore eyes! We have so much to tell you, so much has changed since we last met.

They all settled down around the table and Brixun began. Let me begin with our visit from Sealin Belbur. Until he came here, we all thought he was still in prison. We have no details of his escape from prison, but we imagine it would have been a very unpleasant affair.

It was, said Savajic. He murdered Keymol Locke in a vicious attack using Keymol's own wand as a dagger. He stabbed him twice, once in the eye and once in the heart, killing him instantly, then made his escape.

Keymol dead! exclaimed Brixun, and looked at Showvel and George. They all had a look of total shock on their faces. The room fell silent for a few moments. Brixun began to speak again. His voice was shaking, but he continued. It's hard to believe Keymol, of all wizards, would drop his guard in the company of Sealin Belbur. Now to continue with our news. When he called us together for a meeting he gave us new instructions. He wants us to bring forward the completion date of the bridge to the end of August, hence the extra crew in the quarry. The problem now is, who can we trust? There is no problem with George's crew, but the new crew, who knows?

George spoke up. To be honest, I've not told my crew anything of our meetings with Savajic and Peggy. I am sure I can trust them. But should they ever be interrogated by the Black Watch, they would have nothing of value to tell them.

That's good thinking, said Brixun.

Now we have a completion date for the bridge. He announced it is to be the last day of August. Can it be done? Savajic asked.

Yes, replied Brixun. With the extra crew in the quarry and all the extra workers Ivor Craktit has pulled together, we can do it.

Savajic looked puzzled. It doesn't add up, he said. Zealotte isn't expected back until December at the earliest. Why the rush?

Ah! said Brixun. Let me come to the best part of Belbur's narrative. He has no interest in Zealotte whatsoever. As far as he is concerned, without the Sword of Destiny in his possession, Zealotte is just another wizard and no match for him. Now back to Belbur's plan. He wants us to build a collapse spell into each end of the bridge and trap the Hobgoblin army on its way back home after defeating the Gnomes, and then feed them to the Snack Worms. He said he did not want any of the Hobgoblin army left alive that could help Zealotte, should he come back to Earth. He has also stated that the meteor pulling the Time Bubble holding Zealotte back to earth is being carefully monitored, and should it land and open, then he is to be killed immediately, on sight. And last but not least, Belbur has actually apologized to us for the way in which he brought us here and he has assured us we are free to go back to our families the moment the bridge is completed and the Hobgoblins are on the march. He has promised us that he intends us no harm, and by the time we get back home it will not matter who knows because it will be too late to stop the Hobgoblins from going to war.

For a few moments the room fell silent, while the information that had just been laid out before them was being digested.

Savajic was the first to speak. The sequel of the past few days' events has completely unsoldered the structure we had so far anticipated and turned our initial thoughts on their head. For instance, number one, we truly believed you and your families were in danger of being eliminated once the bridge was completed, and we were forming groups of specialist forces to deal with the Back Watch holding your families at risk. Number two, we believed the whole plan was to welcome Zealotte back and put him in command of the wizard world. Number three, we believed Greco was to be used for a power base from which Zealotte could operate. Number four, we believed Belbur was expecting to be Zealotte's second in command.

From what we know now, none of these four points apply, and everything has been turned on its head. I now believe that Sealin Belbur has no intention of causing needless bloodshed in the wizard world, and you will indeed be free to join your families after the completion of the bridge. And now we know that, as far as Belbur is concerned, Zealotte is a mere fly on the wall, to be swatted at the first opportunity. We thought Greco was to be used as a power base for Zealotte, but now it seems the true reason for the war is to eliminate the Hobgoblin race and prevent Zealotte from gaining a foothold should he return to Earth. And last but not least, we now know Belbur has not the slightest intention of sharing power with anyone, and intends to become the leader of the wizard world.

I have saved the best till last, because as clever as Sealin Belbur is, two loose words to you could be the undoing of him. They all looked surprised at Savajic.

What do you mean? George asked.

What indeed, said Savajic, with a broad smile on his face. Brixun, can you repeat what Belbur's parting words to you were?

Brixun thought for a while and said, He said he was going to skip his visit to the quarry and go back to Ravens Claw to arrange a meeting with Petrid. We all know who Petrid is, so what's so important about that?

Savajic laughed out loud. What's so important is he has unwittingly given us the secret location of his headquarters: Ravens Claw. Gentlemen, we have just struck gold.

Peggy listened quietly to everything that had been said and did her best to analyze what it all meant. But she could not bring herself to share Savajic's belief that Sealin Belbur, the cold-blooded murderer, would allow the planners and crews to have safe passage home; it just didn't add up. I can't understand why you put so much trust in Belbur's promises, Savajic, she said.

Well, Peggy, I do have an advantage over you when it comes to Sealin Belbur, Savajic countered. I have known him since we were both at school together, and over the years we have locked horns on more than one occasion. His specialty was mind over matter, and he was one of the best. When he joined the army, he was trained in brainwashing and memory wiping, and as far as I know, in these two skills he has no peers. I can guarantee you the planners and their crews will have no knowledge of the bridge or that they have even been away from home, and neither will their families. So, you see, they will prove no threat whatsoever to his plans. The deaths of several prominent planners and their families would cause a major investigation and be much more of a threat to him.

Brixun, Showvel, George, I would urge you not to try and resist Belbur when he wipes your memories. It will be safer for you all to just go along with his plans. Who knows; in the future, you may even have dreams of building such a bridge. Now that we have a completion date for the bridge, we can make our plans and be ready for what lies ahead. We won't have any contact with you again until ten days before completion of the bridge, and that will be just to make sure everything is on track and there are no sudden changes. Now, if you're ready, Peggy, we should start back home. Peggy linked arms and hazed and they were on their way.

Chapter 29

Peggy Makes a Brave Decision

As soon as they got back to Savajic's home they went down to his workshop. They put their kit away and retired to their rooms. Peggy undressed and laid her clothes on the bed. Clear! she commanded, and her clothes disappeared. Bathrobe! she commanded, and an array of bathrobes and slippers appeared on the bed. She chose a white terrycloth robe and slippers to match and headed for the bathroom. She lay in the warm, scented water of the bath going over and over in her mind the events that had unfolded before them in just the space of one day.

Sealin Belbur, the Goblins, and the Gnomes, were all intent on ridding the world of the Hobgoblins once and for all time. If the Hobgoblins had any idea of the odds stacked against them, instead of going to war, they would be running for cover.

Peggy stood up and stepped out of the bath. She was immediately dry, and she put on her robe and slippers and went back into the bedroom. There was a knock on the door and Peggy went over and opened it. Savajic was standing there. Peggy, I've had a message from Rose. She needs to see you at home and has asked me to go with you.

Peggy looked at Savajic. Has she had an accident? She fired the question at him with alarm in her voice.

No, nothing like that, replied Savajic, but Rose stressed it is urgent. I'm going to get changed and if you will do the same I will see you in the hall in ten minutes.

Peggy was there in seven minutes and Savajic was waiting for her. Come on, he said. Henry is waiting for us outside.

Couldn't we use your pendant? asked Peggy. It would be a lot quicker. Ah! Peggy, you must remember what I say now for future reference. When you arrive back home, you can only—and must only—act as a normal human. No one must ever know you are a wizard. This is why we will arrive at the cottage in my car, because we have no idea who will be there with Rose and we do not want to make ourselves conspicuous in any way. Peggy nodded in agreement and realized she still had a lot to learn.

Henry drove down the drive and gently took off up into the sky. Soon they were back down on the ground and heading towards the cottage. He pulled up and stopped. Peggy jumped out and ran to the door. Rose must have been watching and waiting for her because she flung open the door and held out her arms. Peggy embraced her and they hugged each other. When they parted, Rose looked at Savajic and said, Mr. Menglor, how nice it is to see you.

Savajic realized there was someone else in the room and replied, It's nice to see you again, Mrs. Goody.

Please come in, Rose said, holding open the door. Peggy and Savajic went in and Rose closed the door behind them. Rose seated them and herself around her kitchen table.

Already seated there was an immaculately dressed man. Let me introduce you to each other, said Rose. She held out her arm and gestured towards the man sitting opposite. May I introduce you to Sir David Blackstock from the home office, and Sir David, this Peggy, my daughter, and Savajic Menglor, a friend of the family. They shook hands and settled down.

Sir David looked at Peggy directly. Peggy, we have a situation of national importance; so important, that if we cannot bring it to a swift and successful conclusion, it could start an all-out war in the Middle East. I'm afraid I cannot go into any more detail at this time, but I am here on behalf of Her Majesty's government to ask you to accompany me back to London for a full and proper briefing. I'm sorry to be so sketchy, but all will be revealed at the appropriate time. Peggy, can you give me an answer within the next hour?

Peggy looked Savajic directly in the eyes; the mental link was made. A voice in Peggy's head said, *"Go, I can manage for the next few days."* Peggy blinked and turned to Sir David. When can we get started? she asked. Rose looked at Savajic and he gently squeezed her hand. She'll be all right, he said.

Savajic stood up and said, Before you go, Peggy, may I have a word with you in private? Peggy stood up and followed him outside. When they were out of earshot, Savajic said, Peggy, I want you to listen very carefully to what I am about to say to you. You are about to enter the most demanding and testing period of your life. By this I mean that you are a wizard with fairy magic and speed entering the human world. This is a unique situation that has never been tested before. The responsibility being placed on your shoulders is enormous. No matter what danger or threat you face, you cannot be seen to use magic in public view. Your self-control will have to be 100 percent in situations such as these. Is this understood?

Peggy nodded. Yes, I understand, Savajic, and I promise you I will only use my powers discreetly.

One other thing, Peggy. I must relieve you of your wand while you are in the human world. It is not permitted. By now you must have realized that a good part of your powers do not need the use of your wand, and holding out your hand will give you a powerful portal.

Peggy drew her wand and handed it to Savajic. Take good care of it, she said.

I will, Savajic assured, and slipped it into his belt. OK, he said. The rest is up to you. I need you back, so take care. They went back into the cottage where Sir David was waiting. Suddenly there was a loud roar of powerful engines, and Peggy realized she was about to take her first ride in a helicopter.

Rose and Savajic waved good-bye as the helicopter lifted into the air and disappeared into the distance. They held hands and walked back into the cottage. What do you make of all this? Rose asked.

Savajic shrugged his shoulders. Your guess is as good as mine, Rose, but I will say this; whatever service your government wants her to perform, she will be up to it.

I have got to get started back home, Rose, and tend to some rather urgent matters. But before I go, would you like to spend this weekend with me?

Yes, I would, she said. I'd love to.

Good, said Savajic. I'll send Henry for you, say, 10:00 a.m. Saturday?

Great, said Rose. I'll be waiting.

The engines of the helicopter droned as they sped through the sky towards London. One hour later, they touched down on the lawn of a large, private mansion. Welcome to Pine Needles, Peggy, Sir David said. This is the headquarters of SO5, the central brain of Special Operations. They walked across the lawn towards the impressive entrance. Peggy's instincts were on full alert, and she noticed the cameras tracking their movements and on the roof, she spotted two armed guards, both with their weapons pointed at them.

Peggy said, Sir David, I hope the two men on the roof pointing their weapons at us aren't trigger happy.

Sir David smiled and said, You're not supposed to be able to see them, well spotted.

When they were safely inside, Peggy was escorted to a large wood-paneled room with a large table in the center with sixteen chairs surrounding it, and the four at the far end were occupied. Sir David guided Peggy to a seat, then he addressed the man sitting at the head of the table as "General." This is Peggy Goody, he said, and sat down beside her.

The general stood up and walked towards Peggy. She stood up and stepped away from the table and as the general approached her, he held out his hand smiled and said, welcome, Peggy. I'm General French, head of operations here at SO5.

Peggy shook his hand and felt he had a firm grip. Pleased to meet you, General, she said, looking him in the eyes. His eyes were a clear, pale blue and he held her gaze steadily. She had the feeling she would be able to rely on him in a sticky situation.

The general went back and sat down. Peggy, I'm not going to beat around the bush. We have a situation of national importance, and we have no idea how to bring it to a satisfactory conclusion. We have heard of your unusual powers from the fire services and your local constabulary, and we hope you may be able to help us.

This is the situation we find ourselves in. Two days ago, a very important person was making a goodwill visit to Kabul, in Afghanistan. The helicopter transporting him never arrived at its destination, and we now know it was brought down over the desert. The helicopter has been recovered, and although it was badly damaged, the pilot had managed to land it. But sadly, the pilot and co-pilot were found dead, both shot through the head in an execution-style killing.

Yesterday, we received a video showing a masked man holding a sword and standing over his captive. His captive is our missing Mr. A. With it came a ransom demand for one hundred million pounds sterling and a threat to behead him if it is not paid in full. We have been given five days to pay. The British government has a policy on non-payment of ransoms and is non-negotiable. Peggy, if you think you can help us to affect his escape after learning all we know and where we think he is being held, only then will you be given his identity.

For the next thirty minutes, every scrap of up-to-date information was relayed to Peggy, and after they were finished, they all fell silent. Ten minutes of silence went by and then Peggy stood up. She cleared her throat and pronounced, I need an expert on the terrain and I need an explosives expert to make me a special type of bomb. Then I will need transport to a safe drop close to our target where we can be picked up again safely after our escape. If you can furnish me with these things, I will have Mr. A back safe and well within three days. But I will insist on one condition, and that is a promise from you personally, General French. That is, my identity will remain a secret between us in this room. I wish for no recognition whatsoever. As far as I am concerned, this meeting has never taken place. Now, General, do I have your word?

General French stood up, a look of amazement on his face and he scratched his head. Are you seriously suggesting you can free our captive singlehandedly, without backup?

Yes, said Peggy. It is crucial I go in alone. The only backup I will need is transportation in and out of our target area, and on that I must be able to rely one hundred percent.

What book of fairy stories is this coming from? A tall dark man with a black patch over one eye was standing up and gesturing towards Peggy.

Peggy smiled back at him. *If only you knew how close to the truth you were,* she thought. I'm sorry if I have offended you in any way, sir, she said politely. But if you have a better plan, then please be my guest.

General French said, Well, Major Mason, do you have an alternative plan?

Yes, I do, replied the major. Give me twenty crack SAS men and two choppers and let me go in and sort them out.

And while you're 'sorting them out,' what happens to our prisoner? The general was looking very annoyed. Our mission is to affect the escape of our prisoner, not to kill him or get him killed in some uncontrolled battle. Having said that, Major, I would be obliged if you would work on a Plan B should Peggy's plan fail.

Very well, said the major. But you have my thoughts on this.

Chapter 30
A Secret Plan

The general ended the meeting and began arranging for the specialists Peggy had requested to meet up with her later and furnish her with the items she would need. After a series of telephone calls, he sat back in his chair and looked over at Peggy. I've arranged for the specialists you asked for to meet us here in an hour, Peggy. I have also asked a translator to come over and teach you a few words that you may need.

Thank you, said Peggy. She didn't think it necessary to tell him of her ability to understand and speak any language on earth.

Could I get you some tea or coffee, Peggy? the general asked.

I would like tea please, Peggy replied.

The general motioned to a man in uniform standing at the door. Would you ask Mary to bring us a tray of tea in please, sergeant?

The sergeant came to attention. Yes, sir, he said, and disappeared from the room.

The tea was poured and they settled down to drink it. Now, said the general, what's your plan, Peggy?

It's fairly simple, she said. I intend to get up high above the camp and use the explosives to shock and confuse the terrorists, and in the resulting confusion and panic, relieve them of their prisoner, get him onto the helicopter and get him safely away. The rest is up to you. I will just add that when he is back with you he will not remember any of it. And that will be by design.

You haven't really told me anything, Peggy, have you? Is that also by design?

Peggy smiled and said, I'm sorry, General, but my methods must remain secret; that way, I have only myself to worry about.

So be it, said the general, and jokingly put up his hands in mock surrender.

There was a knock on the door and the sergeant came into the room followed by two men and a woman. Let me introduce you, Peggy. This is Major Speakman. She is fluent in nine languages and specializes in Middle Eastern dialects.

Peggy shook hands. Pleased to meet you, Peggy, she said in perfect Arabic. Peggy smiled and repeated the greeting, also in perfect Arabic. The general looked at Peggy in amazement and carried on with the introductions. Captain Blastby is our explosives expert, and Captain Fielding is our map and terrain specialist. They exchanged greetings, and all sat down around the end of the table.

Peggy, where would you like to start? the general asked.

With Captain Fielding, if I may. Captain, can you give me a fairly accurate idea of the area where we would land the helicopter? And how far it is to get to reasonable cover?

The captain was very well briefed on the area and had brought with him several aerial photographs of the terrain that had been taken by a low-flying drone. It also gave a good aerial view of the terrorists' camp. He proceeded to lay out a large map showing a much bigger area. He pointed to a circle with a cross inside on the map. This is where it would be safe for the helicopter to land. Unfortunately, it is a mile west of the camp. But it would be far too dangerous to land it any closer. Now, as you can see, the camp is nestled close to the base of the mountains and in a deep hollow. This means only one way in and one way out.

How steep are the mountains? Peggy asked.

They are very steep, almost sheer, so it would be very difficult to enter or exit the camp from the mountains.

Perfect, Peggy said. If it is one way in and out for me, it is exactly the same for the terrorists. She laid the photographs out and committed them to memory and then she said, That's all I need from you, Captain Fielding, thank you, and shook his hand.

Captain Blastby, can you help me with some explosives?

My pleasure, the captain said.

I need something that is very loud and very bright; not too powerful, possibly a ball shape, with a cord and ring attached to it so I could put my finger through it and dangle the ball. It would need to explode on contact with the ground or the first thing it touches, and weigh no more than a quarter-pound.

I think I might have just the thing, the captain said. We have been working on a new stun grenade containing phosphors. It is exceptionally bright and loud and has a low damage limit. I am certain I can adapt it for your purpose. Can I have about four hours to adapt it and give it an adequate test?

That would be great, Captain, but I will need twenty by tomorrow morning. Is that possible?

Yes, said the captain. I'll get right to it.

Major Speakman looked at Peggy and said, I have a feeling you will not be requiring my services, Peggy. It seems you have the same gift as me. She was speaking in Arabic, but this time in a different dialect. Peggy answered her fluently. I'm sorry, she said, but I can speak quite a few languages and I should manage quite well, but thank you very much for giving me your time. With that, the major said good-bye to the general and excused herself.

Peggy and the general were alone again. He looked at her and shook his head. You're quite an amazing young lady, Peggy, and your knowledge and understanding of military matters is surprising, to say the least. Have you any more requests before we end this meeting?

Yes, Peggy replied. Several, I'm afraid.

Carry on, the general said.

Good, Peggy began. I will need to be in constant contact with the helicopter pilot, and I will need him on 24/7 alert. Also, I will need a device that will enable me to signal him to scramble and pick us up. Maybe a warning light or an alarm; it must be something I can press. I do not want to talk into anything; I must remain silent. And one last thing; our man may be chained and manacled, so have you got something I can use to cut him free without making a noise?

The general was writing it all down and when he had finished, he made a telephone call to someone he called Pip and said he would be down to the lab in twenty minutes. Then he made a call to Mary, the housekeeper.

There was a knock on the door and the general said, come in.

Mary appeared and said, Everything is prepared, sir.

The general said, Peggy, I can take you home if you prefer, but I have taken the liberty of having a room prepared for you here. There is a telephone in your room to phone home, should you wish. It's just that I don't want to put you under any unnecessary pressure travelling to and fro.

That's very considerate of you, General. I would be happy to stay, Peggy said.

Excellent. Mary will show you to your room and give you the times for lunch and dinner tonight. Then, after lunch, I will take you to meet Professor Phillip Venter in his laboratory and workshop to see how your requested items are coming along.

As soon as Peggy was alone in her room she phoned Rose. Rose answered, and Peggy explained to her mother that she would be stopping in London for two or three days and for her not to worry about anything. Then she gave her a number to give to Savajic. Please ask him to call me as soon as he can on this number, she said, and rang off. As soon as she put the phone back she began to inspect the phone for bugs. She was right to do so; inside the mouthpiece was a tiny listening device. She deactivated it immediately and carried on looking. Sure enough, on the base of the phone was the backup, which she quickly deactivated as well.

Ten minutes later, the phone rang. It was Savajic. Is everything all right, Peggy? he asked.

Yes, everything is under control, she said. She quickly went over her plan with him to see if he could see any pitfalls. It sounds good to me, he said. By the way, have you checked the phone for bugs?

Yes, I have, she said. And I found two. They are not live now.

Good, said Savajic. I have only two things I would like to mention; one is to remember that you will be moving across sand, so don't leave a footprint trail, and two, make sure the helicopter pilot has enough fuel to get you back.

Don't even joke like that! Peggy shouted down the phone and they both burst out laughing.

By the way, Savajic said, I've located Ravens Claw Castle. It's in Northumberland, but the weather is terrible up there at the moment and there's no rush, so I won't be doing much until you get back. And besides, Rose is coming to keep me company. Wish you were here Ha! Ha! The phone went dead.

After lunch, the general came to pick Peggy up and take her to meet Professor Phillip Venter. On the way, he explained that the lab and workshop were where all the latest developments were tried and tested. It was top secret, and very few people knew what went on inside the building.

They pulled up outside what looked like a deserted warehouse and next to it was an enormous scrap yard full of rusting cars and vans piled up on top of each other. The driver opened the car door and they got out. They climbed six steps to the loading bay, crossed it, and went through a steel door. Inside, it was deserted. Peggy noticed there was a path through the dust on the floor that led to a large, round steel tank of some sort. Mounted on it was a square metal box that was locked, and again the dust on it had been disturbed, indicating someone had opened it recently.

The general took out a small bunch of keys from his coat pocket and unlocked the box. Inside was a list of numbers and letters and a small glass panel. He typed in several letters and numbers and pressed his thumb against the glass panel. The whole tank rose up into the air and inside was a lift. The general moved forward and this time looked into a round eyeglass. The lift door opened and they got in and it closed behind them at the same time the steel tank came back down and closed them in. Level two, the general commanded, and the lift began to descend. It stopped and they got off.

They were in a massive underground complex that stretched as far as Peggy could see. The ceiling was at least twenty feet high. The floor was painted gray and had a high-gloss finish, it was immaculately clean. The lighting was sharp and bright and cleverly designed not to cast shadows. To their right was a bank of four electric buggies.

Come on, the general said, and started walking towards them. He sat in the first one and said, grab a seat, Peggy. She climbed in and off they went. This is the firing range. We're driving down one side of it.

It's two hundred yards long and takes up the whole width of this end of the complex. We test every missile imaginable here.

They sped down past the range and came to a central block of glass enclosures where the activity was intense. Men and women in white coats were milling around in all directions, all working on their various projects. Come and meet the professor, said the general, and they entered one of the enclosures that were furnished as an office. Behind a large desk sat a tall, white-haired man. He looked up and motioned for them to sit down.

Hello, Frenchie. What brings you here?

Greetings, Pip. I would like you to meet Peggy Goody, the general said.

Pip stood up and moved from behind his desk. He was about six-three tall and slimly built. He walked over and shook Peggy's hand. Pleased to meet you, he said. Peggy noticed he had long, sinewy fingers and a powerful grip, and he also had a very slight Scottish accent.

I'm pleased to meet you too, Professor, she said.

Oh, please, call me Pip. Everybody else does.

What can I do for you, Frenchie?

I've come to check up on the items I requested earlier from Captain Blastby. And have you had time to talk to Ian Tickery about the multi-purpose wrist watch?

Give me a minute, said Pip, and he walked over to his desk. He flipped a switch on his telephone consul and punched in a number.

A voice said, Hello, Pip, what's up?

Nothing to worry about, I am just enquiring about how far away you are with the wrist watch.

I think you going to like this one, said Ian. I'm about half an hour away. I just want to run through the tests again to make absolutely sure everything is as it should be. As soon as I finish, I'll bring it over to you.

Good man, said Pip, and flicked the switch. Did you hear that? Pip asked.

Yes, they both said at the same time.

Right, said Pip. Let's jump in the buggy and go see how far Captain Blastby has got with his bombs. The bomb testing unit was at the far end of the complex and it had its own specially designed state-of-the-art enclosure built to withstand high explosions and deaden sound. Its extensive range of instruments could measure the smallest of details. As they arrived on site, a voice sounded out from a loudspeaker: Thirty seconds to detonation. Clear the area! They sat and waited for a few minutes and then climbed out of the buggy. Captain, how are things going? Pip called out.

Come and have a look! he called back. He was busy looking at a panel of instruments and taking notes. When he had finished writing, he looked up and noticed Peggy. He walked past the general and Pip as if they weren't there.

Peggy! he said, beaming at her. Come and see what I've got for you. The general looked at Pip and said, we will have to keep a close eye on the dashing captain, I think. Pip nodded in agreement and smiled.

Laid out on a stainless-steel bench were three sand-colored plastic balls, each with a thin chain and ring attached. They were just a bit smaller than a tennis ball.

They look pretty harmless, don't they? the captain said.

Can I pick one up? Peggy asked.

Be my guest, he said, flashing a smile at her. She picked one up and was surprised at how light it felt.

Is this complete? she asked.

Yes, said the captain. I'm rather pleased with the weight. It's less than I had anticipated. If you look carefully, you will see on each side of the chain there are two indents. These will allow you to prime the bombs by turning the top 90 degrees clockwise. As soon as they are primed, you will have to be very careful. You can pick them up and put them down with care, but should you bang them together or drop them, they will detonate.

The tests have given us very good readings. We have achieved 180 decibels of sound, loud enough to deafen humans, and a light flash of 5,000 Lumens. This is more than enough to temporarily blind anyone caught in the flash. The problem now being, if you are not wearing ear and eye protection, you will be affected exactly the same as your adversaries. And wearing a protective helmet and eye shield would make you somewhat stand out in the middle of the terrorist camp.

I have it covered, Captain, Peggy said. You have no need to be concerned. Now, can you have twenty of these ready for me to take with me tomorrow?

I will have them ready for you, Peggy, that's a promise. Is there anything else I can help you with?

Yes, said Peggy. A set of ear plugs would help.

The captain fished into his pocket and pulled out two sets in two separate plastic bags. Here you go. I always carry spares. Anything else?

No, that's great, said Peggy. Thank you very much.

They were back in the buggy and travelling back to the professor's office. When they arrived, Ian Tickery was waiting for them.

What you got for me? Pip asked him.

Ian held up a wrist watch. Have a look at this, he said. I think it will do the trick. I haven't wasted space with a compass because you told me Peggy had memorized the camps coordinates.

Quite so, the general said. She has.

The dial is ordinary, and has a second hand counting out seconds. On the side is a button to illuminate the face, and on the other side is the call button to alert the helicopter pilot you are ready to be picked up. It is recessed, so you cannot press it accidently. And when you press this, the dial will glow red. Now the technical bit. The whole of the strap is a very powerful battery. It's linked to a laser inside the body of the watch. The outside diameter of the watch turns; turn it 90 degrees, and it will release a telescopic antenna. This is a laser tube. Be very careful where you point it because it will cut through anything in its path. The beam is set to a depth of nine inches. To switch it on, twist the antennae anti-clockwise. It doesn't have any more tricks. I have purposely kept it simple and functional. I hope it's what you want, Peggy.

It's perfect, Peggy said. Can I put it on and try it?

Of course, Ian said. I was going to suggest you do, just to get the feel of it. You will notice there is no buckle. It has a Velcro strip so you can pull it tight. If you have to use the laser, the last thing you need is for your watch to be moving up and down and around.

Peggy put it on her wrist and secured it tightly with the Velcro. She made a fist and turned the outside of the watch 90 degrees. The antennae slowly unfolded and slid across the back of her hand and passed over her knuckles.

What can I test it on?

Ian produced a small section of steel bar, 1-inch in diameter, and held it out in front of him. Cut the end of this, he said. Peggy held her hand out away from her body and twisted the antennae. The laser beam shot out nine inches in front of her. Now pass it through the end of the bar in a slicing movement, Ian said. She held her hand steady and passed the laser beam through the steel, and the end of the bar fell to the floor. It was exactly what she wanted. She twisted the base of the antennae and the laser beam cut off, then she turned the outside of the watch 90 degrees back and the antennae retracted into the body of the watch.

Can I have another watch, Ian? Just a plain one, and synchronized with this one. And I want it easy to conceal. There is no need for a strap.

No problem, said Ian. How about a small, flat pocket watch?

That would be great, Peggy said. She turned to the professor and asked, Do you have a disguise department here?

An excellent one, he said. Why, who do you want to be?

A terrorist, she replied.

That's quite a transformation for someone as lovely as you, he said with a twinkle in his eye. But nonetheless, it is achievable. You will need to stay here for about another hour to get measured up for clothes and to sort out any facial changes, and a wig and skin color. Are you all right with that, Frenchie? he asked the general.

However long you need, Pip. We have got to get this right.

Chapter 31
OPERATION RESCUE

Peggy and the general left Pine Needles at 6:30 a.m. and made their way to the laboratory and workshop. When they stepped out of the lift, Professor Venter was waiting for them in a buggy. Good morning, Peggy. Good morning, Frenchie. Are you ready to go?

Good morning, Pip, they both replied. We certainly are, Peggy said. They climbed into the buggy and sped off. As they approached Pip's office, they could see quite a crowd of people all buzzing about. Peggy was introduced to the makeup team, and work on her began in earnest. She was seated in a reclining chair and they began by pinning up her hair and fitting it into a tight net. Then they tried on several tatty-looking dull black wigs, and when they had decided on which one they were going to use, they moved on to her face. They had various latex rubber parts. A few chins, noses, and ears. Their challenge was to make a lovely looking young lady into a weather-beaten terrorist.

By the time they had finished, the transformation was amazing. They had aged her face, her arms, legs, and feet. She was dressed in dirty clothes and looked every bit like someone who had been living rough in the desert.

Peggy was looking at herself in a long mirror, and staring back at her was a real, live terrorist. She could hardly believe it was herself.

What do you think? the general asked.

It's amazing, she said. How long will it last? I will need up to thirty-six hours.

That won't be a problem, just try your best to keep dry and don't be tempted to swill your face because it will probably get a bit itchy after a while.

Got it, Peggy said.

While all this had been going on, Captain Blastby had arrived at Pip's office with his bombs. They had been fitted tightly into a flat, hard suitcase, and standing next to him was Ian Tickery with the watches, and they were chatting. I can't believe the general is sending a young girl out on a mission as dangerous and delicate as this. I mean, what training could she possibly have had that puts her in front of our top agents?

I know, Ian said. I've been giving that some thought. Apparently, she can speak their language fluently. But how she intends to get into the camp and locate the hostage seems almost impossible. And even more impossible is how she intends to get out again with the hostage.

Well, said the captain, tapping the case he was holding, these little babies should cause some trouble. I can honestly say I've never been asked for anything like this before, and I'd love to be around to see how she uses them.

Good, Ian said. She certainly seems to know what she wants.

Suddenly the buggy carrying Peggy, the general, and Pip appeared. They all greeted each other and then got down to business. The captain was the first up. He placed his case carefully on Pip's desk and popped it open. Each side of the case was fitted with foam rubber molded to fit the bombs. Laid out neatly were twenty spherical bombs in four rows of five. What do you think of them, Peggy? the captain asked.

She walked over to the desk and took one out and dangled it on its chain. Perfect, she said, and replaced it in the case.

Next up was Ian. He produced a box containing the watches and opened it and offered it to Peggy. She took the wrist watch and secured it around her left wrist, then took the pocket watch and checked that the times on each watch were exactly the same. Thank you, Ian, they're just what I wanted, she said.

Well, General, I'm ready to go, she said. The general thanked Pip, and the captain and Ian walked over to the buggy, followed by Peggy. They headed off in the opposite direction of the lift where they had come in. Where are we going? Peggy asked.

We're heading for the monorail platform. It's at the entrance to the complex. It's where all the staff use to come in to work in the morning. The monorail leads to the basement of a block of government offices in the city. The warehouse entrance is used only by me and two others. Everyone else uses the monorail to get here.

Peggy was surprised at the size of the complex. It took six minutes of non-stop driving to reach the monorail platform. It resembled an airport terminal, with an x-ray walk-through. Obviously security had to be very tight with all the secretive and explorative work that went on there. They boarded and were whisked away. They were in a tunnel running directly under the center of London, a secret tunnel very few people knew existed.

After ten minutes, they emerged out onto another platform, but this time a much larger one. From where they were, Peggy could see other tunnels, all probably leading to other secret locations. She didn't bother to ask any questions. There were quite a few people milling around on the platform, some in foreign dress, some with beards, some with long hair, and some with no hair at all. Peggy couldn't help wondering to herself how many of them were for real; after all, she wasn't.

They were heading for a bank of four lifts and when they got there, the general pushed a down button. The door opened and they both got in. Again the general pushed a button marked ground floor and they began to rise. When it stopped, the doors opened and they entered what looked like a normal office with rows of desks and people busily working away. The general wasted no time. He led Peggy through the office and out into a car park where they walked over to a large black car that was waiting for them. The driver was wearing an RAF uniform and he saluted the general. The general saluted him back. They are all ready and waiting for you at the air strip, sir.

Well done, the general replied.

The air strip was very simple, just one very long tarmac runway with a very large airplane hangar at one end. The car came to a halt outside the hangar and they got out. A door opened, and two men appeared.

Hello, Frenchie, said a tall greying man. He turned to the second man, who was in uniform. This is Captain Taylor. He will be escorting our agent to her destination. The captain came to attention and saluted the general.

At ease, said the general. Now let me introduce you to our agent. She will be referred to as Chameleon in all communications, and it is of the utmost importance that no one learns of her true identity, is that quite clear?

Yes, message received and understood.

Now let's get inside, Minister, and sort things out, the general said. He held the door for Peggy and she walked in. It was nothing like she had expected. Three banks of computers, all with their screens on, were laid out in a "U" shape with a large screen at the bottom where each computer operator could see it, and on it was a map of Afghanistan.

The captain led the way down to the large screen.

We are able to zoom in and pick out the terrorists' camp while we have satellite connection, he said, and gave a signal to one of the operators. Immediately the map began to change and after several zooms, they could make out the camp.

That's pretty impressive, said Peggy. Is it possible 24/7?

Well, we do have small gaps as we change from one satellite to another, but nothing much. At night it's a different story because it's dark so, obviously, all we see is darkness, unless something is illuminated.

The captain turned to Peggy. Is there anything you would like to ask me before we get started?

No, I'm ready, said Peggy.

At the other end of the hangar, a massive door began to slide slowly open and powerful jet engines burst into life. Once the door was fully open, the jet began to taxi out onto the tarmac runway. The general held Peggy's hand and squeezed it.

Good luck, Peggy, and Godspeed. He watched as she walked away with the captain towards the jet, and silently prayed he would see her again.

The jet had come to a standstill and Peggy and the captain boarded it and the door was closed behind them. They took their seats and buckled themselves in. The engines roared and they began to move down the runway. The roar got louder, and suddenly they were airborne.

During the flight, the captain gave Peggy every scrap of local knowledge they had managed to gather over the last few weeks. He even explained to her how the temperature dropped dramatically at night. Now the hard bit, the captain said, looking quite concerned. If by some misfortune you should be captured and taken prisoner, our government will claim to have no knowledge of who you are, and you will not receive any support from us at all. When we land, you will be given the option of pulling out of the operation with no disgrace attached to you. But if you decide to carry on, then you will literally be out there on your own. Peggy logged everything the captain said and when he finished, he moved up front with the pilot to let Peggy get some rest.

She focused her mind back to Black Eagle and thought of Professor Gull in the aviary. An image of him appeared and she began to talk to him. Professor, I need your help. I want an Afghanistan bird that can carry ten balls each with a chain and ring attached and weighing eight ounces each, and then I want a common bird that everyone would expect to see. Can you help me?

The professor looked surprised and said, Peggy, I can hear you and yes, I can help you. Now let me see, he said, rubbing his beard. Oh yes. The bird you want to carry your balls is a steppe eagle; a female, he added. They're bigger than the male. They have a strong, hooked beak and strong yellow talons. Now the most common bird is the desert lark. You can find them almost everywhere, so they would not be a surprise to anyone who saw one.

Peggy logged every word the professor said and added it to her memory bank. She thanked the professor and said good-bye. She was relieved the professor hadn't asked her why she needed the information, or any other questions as to what she was doing. She closed her eyes and slowly drifted off to sleep.

The jet engine noise suddenly roared and Peggy opened her eyes. It had startled her. It was all new to her; she had never been in an airplane before today, and didn't realize they were about to land.

There was a sharp bump as the wheels touched down on the tarmac and they were in Afghanistan.

The captain had been sitting next to her for the last half-hour and he had let her sleep. He had been watching her sleep, and thinking, what the hell was she doing out here? Her task was almost impossible. She was going in alone, with no backup and he feared for her safety. It must mean she is a very special agent; or the defense minister was desperate. He hoped it wasn't the latter.

The jet had come to a halt and the door was opened. She picked up her case and holdall and stepped outside. As she walked down the steps, she could feel the sudden change in the temperature. It was a dry heat, but a welcome change to the cold air-conditioning on the airplane. They crossed the tarmac runway and entered a large concrete building. There were army personnel manning half a dozen desks on one side and what looked like some kind of store on the other side. The captain introduced Peggy to the camp commander. This is our agent, code name Chameleon.

Welcome, he said. I'm Major Phillips. We have everything ready for you he said. The helicopter pilot is on his way over to meet you. Would you like to eat before you go?

No thank you, replied Peggy. I have everything I need in my bag. But thank you for asking.

When the pilot came in, Peggy had to look twice. He was Charlie's double! That was, until he began to speak. He spoke in a clear, educated English accent. But in a strange way, he made her feel more relaxed.

He shook Peggy's hand and said, Piers Lambert, at your service. I will be your taxi driver into and out of the unknown.

Behave yourself, Lieutenant, the major said. Peggy laughed out loud; he really was like Charlie.

Piers reached for Peggy's hand and held it and looked into her eyes and said, The prisoner is a personal friend of mine. We have flown together on many occasions, and his rescue means the world to me. Indeed, the whole nation will owe you a debt of gratitude.

I'll get him out, I promise you. Just make sure you have enough fuel in the tank to get us back. They all began to laugh (Savajic's joke had gone down well).

Now, Piers, last but not least, have you got your alarm set up? Because we need to synchronize it with my watch and make sure it works.

Follow me over to the flight office, he said, and we can do just that. Inside the office there were three desks. One had a wooden block with his name printed on it. Next to it was what looked like a metal radio with dials and knobs, and on top was a red light bulb covered by a glass globe. This is it, said Piers.

Let's do it, Peggy said. He sat down and began to twist the knobs while Peggy was pressing on the watch. Suddenly the red light flashed and then stayed on.

Good, he said. Now let's fine-tune it. After trying it out in several different positions and they were satisfied with it, they locked the frequency in and relaxed.

Chapter 32
NO TURNING BACK

The engines cranked up and the blades began to turn. They were soon in the air and on their way. Forty-five minutes later, they were touching down. Piers had landed as close to the mountains as he could and the engines were idling. How long have I got before dark? Peggy asked.

Piers checked his watch and said, about two hours.

Right, she said. Then I'm off. See you soon, Piers. She grabbed her case and holdall and jumped out. She headed straight for the rocks and disappeared behind them. Piers watched her, and when she was out of sight, he climbed into the air and headed back to base. When he got back he would sit at his desk without moving until the red light came on.

Peggy needed to get up high and establish a camp that was out of sight, where she could relax and put her plan into action. The first part was going to be the trickiest, because she had to go into the terrorists' camp while it was still daylight, and she had to find the location of the prisoner and make contact with him.

She found a ledge about a hundred fifty feet up a sheer rock face. Perfect, she said to herself. She held onto her case and holdall and said. Up! Up! and when she got level with the ledge, she sat on the edge and said, Down! Down! and with her legs back to normal she set about sorting out her camp.

With everything in place, she opened her holdall and fished out a bottle of still water and one of Savajic's energy bars and her bottle of anti-Odor liquid. She didn't know what to expect when she entered their camp, and she was not going to take any unnecessary risks. After she had taken her anti-Odor liquid, eaten, and had a drink of water, she set about getting together the ear plugs and pocket watch and made sure they were tucked away safely in her pocket. She stood up closed her eyes and said to herself, Desert Lark. In the blink of an eye in her place was a small bird. She spread her wings and took to the sky. She circled high in the sky twice and chose her direction, then she flew directly over the mountains and was soon hovering high up over the terrorist camp. She was not the only bird in the sky, and avoided the other birds as much as she possibly could. She landed at the back of the camp next to a small stream that came down from high up in the mountain. It was a clever location for their camp, giving them a good supply of cold, clean water.

She decided to stay as a bird and fly around the camp and look for a place where there were guards posted; that would hopefully give her the location of their prisoner. It didn't take long. In the center of the camp was a large, black tent with two armed terrorists on guard. The back of the tent was directly against the rock face so made it impossible to gain entrance from the rear. *This is going to be tricky,* she thought. She flew up and perched on the mountain, overlooking the black tent. There were two guards about six feet apart. Taking them both out wouldn't be a problem, but if she did all hell would be let loose, and who knows what would happen to their hostage. She couldn't take the chance, as it would alert them to a possible rescue bid.

The solution came to her in a flash. Use one guard to put the other guard off guard. She took to the air and landed quietly behind one of the guards and transfigured back to herself, and immediately went into haze. She crept up behind the guard and in a lightning-fast move, dug her thumbs into the guard's jugular vein, which instantly stopped the flow of blood to his brain. She held it for five seconds and then let him go and he collapsed to the ground unconscious, without making a sound.

The other guard looked over and saw him fall and without thinking, rushed over to help. Peggy wasted no time. In seconds she was out of haze and inside the tent. The tent was divided in two by large curtains. The front of the tent was empty, and she hoped there would only be the hostage in the other half. She had luck on her side. The hostage was alone and lying on a camp bed, gazing into space.

Don't make a sound, she ordered. It made him jump and sit up.

You speak English. Who are you?

No questions, she said. Just listen to me and do exactly as I say. She produced the watch and the ear plugs. Take these, she said. At precisely 19:00 hours, push the ear plugs into your ears and bury your head into your pillow, then count up to five hundred. After you have finished counting, sit up and act as normal as you possibly can. At 20:00 hours repeat it, but this time get ready to move. Do you understand what you have to do?

Yes. The unwavering answer sounded assured. Peggy moved back through the curtain and went into haze.

She peered through the flaps of the tent. The guard was coming to and taking a drink of water, and the other guard was kneeling down beside him. Peggy slipped away unnoticed. Then she found a quiet spot and came out of haze and immediately transfigured back to a desert lark and took to the sky. When she landed back at her camp it was 18:00 hours. She had less than an hour to become an airborne steppe eagle carrying a cargo of ten deadly bombs. She reflected on her progress so far and was really pleased with the way the first phase had gone, and she felt sure now Mr. A wouldn't be injured by the bombs.

Chapter 33
PREPARATIONS

The sun was beginning to sink low in the sky and the temperature was beginning to drop. She hoped the terrorists would begin to relax too. She gave a wry smile and thought, *well, they won't be relaxed for very long, not when they get the taste of a Captain Blastby bomb.*

It was time to prepare the bombs. Peggy knew this was going to be the most awkward part of the mission. It was one thing for her to pick up the bombs, but quite another for an eagle, with its talons and beak. And before the eagle picked them up they'd have to be primed to go off on contact with the ground. There was no room for error.

Peggy opened her holdall and fished out two tubs of children's Play-Doh. She scooped a handful out of the tub and fashioned it into a disc, then repeated it. She laid the two Play-Doh discs on a flat rock that was protruding from the ledge. She had to make sure the eagle could reach them unhindered when her wings were spread.

Next she fashioned a fat cylinder shape and put it in front of the two discs. Now it was time for the bombs. She opened the case and took out ten of the bombs. She placed four bombs around each of the discs and two by the cylinder shape. *So far, so good,* she thought to herself. Now she took each ring one at a time and pressed them into the outside of the discs in a circle, and pointing up to the sky, then pressed the two front ones into the upstanding cylinder shape, also pointing up to the sky. She stood up and looked down at what she had done. She had created the footprint of a steppe eagle. The rings stood up precisely where the eagle's talons would open and close through the rings and the two in front would be held by its beak. *Should do it,* she thought, then she stepped down and relaxed for a few minutes.

Peggy looked at her watch; it was 18:50. She moved over to the bombs and began to prime them. She held each one firmly in one hand and turned the top with the other, working her way around until they were all primed. She looked at her watch again; it was 18:55. Perfect; she had given herself six minutes to transfigure and pick up the bombs and reach the terrorist camp for 19:01, thus making sure Mr. A had his head buried in his pillow and counting.

She stood up and transfigured into a magnificent female steppe eagle and immediately took to the sky. Then she hovered over the bombs and in one movement, her talons and her beak opened and closed and she took off with all the bombs safely secured. She soared up into the sky and headed directly for her target. It was easy to locate because the terrorists had lit several fires. She had decided to go in at about five hundred feet and she would be approaching them from a dark sky and gliding. They would have no idea of who or where the attack had come from and the bombs would disintegrate, leaving no trace.

Chapter 34
Time to Soften Them Up

She was gliding in and her speed was breathtaking. She was almost at the front of the camp and her one set of talons opened. The second set of talons opened almost immediately after the first, destined for the center of the camp, and her beak released the last two bombs at the back of the camp. On her first visit, Peggy had noticed a large tent where they seemed to congregate for their meals. She believed it would have quite a few of the terrorists eating and drinking in there. She was now soaring back high into the sky before the first bomb exploded, and now she was circling at three thousand feet in the sky above the camp. She gave it about five minutes for the dust to settle and dropped down to two hundred feet and began to circle above.

The terrorists were running around aimlessly. Some could see and some couldn't. Most of them couldn't hear, but there was still enough of them to obstruct a rescue. She had seen enough to satisfy herself and the whole operation had only taken ten minutes. She took off back to her camp, where she landed and transfigured back to normal.

She started preparing for the final run and everything had to be right. Mr. A had to come out of this alive or it would all have been for nothing. She checked the three pieces of Play-Doh, they had hardly been disturbed. She picked up the bomb case and carefully opened it up, then once again she began putting them out in exactly the same order as before.

Meanwhile, back at the terrorists' camp, chaos reigned, and those who could still see properly were looking around to find out what damage had been done to the camp. There wasn't any; it didn't make any sense! They had just gone through an horrendous bombing attack and yet there were no potholes and no damage to any of the tents, and apart from their brothers running around holding their heads, there weren't any casualties.

Outside the prisoner's tent, the two guards were on their hands and knees, their hands clasped over their ears, and both were screaming: I'm blind! I'm blind! One of Peggy's bombs had hit the ground just feet in front of them; they would probably never see again.

Mr. A could hear all the commotion outside. Wearing the ear plugs and burying his head in his pillow had worked. He had tucked the ear plugs and the watch safely away and was standing up and pretending to look bewildered as two of the terrorists rushed into his tent.

Can you hear me? one of them shouted at him in broken English.

Yes, Mr. A replied. The terrorist looked relieved. Mr. A was worth a lot of money and he didn't want him damaged. What's going on? Mr. A asked.

It's not your concern, growled the terrorist in English, and then in his own language he said, double the guards here tonight, and strode out of the tent.

Mr. A lay back down on the bed and began to wonder what was going to happen at the end of the next hour.

Peggy had taken a drink of water and was packing everything away in her holdall. After the next raid, she wouldn't be coming back, so she didn't want to leave any traces of her ever being there. The Play-Doh would disintegrate in a couple of days.

With everything packed away, she made her way down to the foot of the mountain and hid the holdall and bomb case out of sight. This was where she would bring Mr. A and wait for the helicopter.

Chapter 35
NOW OR NEVER

It was time to go, and Peggy was about to transfigure. She checked her watch. *It's now or never,* she thought. Once again she became a magnificent steppe eagle circling over the bombs. She dropped lower and hovered, then she locked onto the bombs and took off. She glided effortlessly through the air, and the terrorists' camp came into view. She lined herself up and went in exactly the same as before. The bombs were realized, and she was zooming back up into the sky. She circled the camp, looking for a place close to the captive's tent where it was safe to land, and dropped down just a few feet away, then she transfigured back.

There was even more chaos than before. The terrorists hadn't worked out what had happened the first time and now they were in total panic. There wasn't any warning; there wasn't any evidence of bombs and they were not fighting an enemy. It was as if Hell had come to visit them.

Peggy wasted no time. She moved towards the tent and as she drew level, two terrorists came running out, cupping their hands over their ears and screaming. She slipped in and made for the back of the tent and as she went through the dividing curtain, she realized Mr. A was not alone.

Who are you? the terrorist snarled.

I've come to help you, she replied in his own language. He relaxed when he heard her voice, and that was a mistake. Three seconds later he was lying on the floor, unconscious.

Mr. A had been knocked down and had blood running down his face.

Can you get up and walk? Peggy asked him.

Yes, I'm okay, he said. It was just a glancing blow.

Okay, Peggy said. She was already pulling the clothes off the terrorist. Put these on, she said, and let's get out of here while we can. He didn't need telling twice and was changed and ready to go.

Follow my lead, she said, and put her hands over her ears and began to moan out loud. Mr. A copied her every move and together they staggered through the camp unchallenged. As they got level with the guards at the entrance they could see they were in a state of shock and had been blinded from the bombs. It was a massive piece of luck for them and they passed by them without being challenged. Peggy was delighted because she desperately didn't want to go into haze. It was a secret she wanted to keep to herself and she had managed to do it.

As soon as they were clear of the camp and out of sight, Peggy stopped and activated the alarm on her watch. *I hope you haven't gone to sleep, Piers,* she thought to herself.

The light on Piers' desk flashed and he shot to his feet. He looked over to his co-pilot and shouted, Come on, let's go! They ran to the helicopter and jumped in. The blades began to turn and pick up speed. Clear for take

Off! shouted his co-pilot, and they lifted off. There was no way of them knowing what to expect when they got there because the only contact they had was the alarm. The name of the game was to get to them as soon as possible and pray everything had gone to plan.

Are you all right to run? Peggy asked.

Yes, replied Mr. A. I'm right behind you.

They covered the mile in seven minutes, which was pretty good running across the sand, and when they arrived at the pickup point they both fell to the floor exhausted.

What now? asked Mr. A. He was panting in between his words.

We wait for the helicopter and hope he gets here before the terrorists figure out what's happened and come after us.

Who are you? Mr. A asked. I guess you know who I am.

I do sir, said Peggy. I am Chameleon, and I'm afraid that is all I'm prepared to tell you. But I will say this much; this operation never took place, and you were never abducted, and there will be no paper record of it. It is and will remain a security secret, and so will my identity.

Peggy picked up the sound of the helicopter engines. They were still three or four miles away but with her instincts on full alert, she could hear the engine noise quite easily. She stood up and recovered her holdall and bomb case from behind the rocks.

Come on, she said. They're nearly here. A powerful downward light appeared in the sky and the roar of engines and as the helicopter descended, it blew up a great cloud of sand. They broke cover and ran to the open door.

After you, sir, Peggy said, and then jumped in after him. Seconds later, they were heading back to freedom.

Piers was overjoyed when he saw Mr. A. His close friend was safe and well. He turned to Peggy and said, thank you. We will never, ever be able to repay you for what you have done here today, and we don't even know who you are.

Tell me, Piers, have you got contact with the base?

Yes, said Piers. Why?

Has Major Phillips got any marines at the base? Because the terrorist camp at this moment in time is virtually defenseless, and a good squad of men could capture some of their leaders. It's just a thought.

Brilliant! Piers said, and was on the radio relaying that exact message to the major.

When they arrived back at the base, Mr. A shook Peggy's hand and thanked her for what she had done and then he was whisked away to a waiting car. Piers was grinning from ear to ear. What a great result! he said, and he grabbed Peggy and gave her a hug.

Peggy began to laugh. I bet you do this to all the terrorists, she said, and Piers joined in the laughter.

What do you really look like? Piers shot the question at her out of the blue.

Ah! That's for me to know and you to find out. Now when can I go home?

I'm not quite sure, Piers said. Apparently Major Phillips has taken your advice and taken a squad of men to raid the terrorists' camp. But I would imagine you will go back to England on the same plane as the— He pulled himself up short.

I know who Mr. A is, said Peggy. And when I get back home, I will deny any knowledge this mission ever happened.

Do you fancy a drink while we're waiting? Piers asked.

I could kill a mug of coffee, she said.

Piers looked at her and said, would you mind if I had a large Scotch on the rocks?

Be my guest, said Peggy. You're paying.

Piers looked at her and shook his head. You don't miss a trick, do you? As they both sipped their drinks, Peggy got to know a lot more of what was really going on there. Piers was on his fourth stint in Afghanistan, and so were most of the soldiers there. They were tired and battle hardened, and Peggy realized many of them were living on the edge. It was a brutal campaign, and they had given all they could for their country. They were all unsung heroes, and she hoped when they eventually got home they would be treated as such.

The sky was filled with the sound of powerful engines. Major Phillips was back safely with all of his men. They had captured six important terrorist leaders and had laid waste to the camp, and the terrorists had all fled in disarray. Major Phillips and his men were triumphant. It was the best thing that had happened for quite some time and it was just what the doctor ordered. Tonight they would be celebrating. Piers was up on his feet and on the way to the bar where he ordered two large whiskeys. The door opened and the major came in and he saw Piers standing at the bar and punched the air and shouted: "YES!"

Piers held up the whiskeys and said, Let's drink to it. The major took a glass from Piers and clinked it with his. "CHEERS!" he said, and they went and sat down with Peggy.

The major looked at Peggy and said, I don't know what you did to them and even less as to how, but whatever it was, it is was certainly effective. We went in without firing a single shot and they just surrendered or ran away. As I promised I won't ask you any questions, I just wish you weren't leaving us so soon.

Peggy had said her good-byes and was at last on her way home. The drone of the engines seemed to have a relaxing effect on her, and she drifted off to sleep.

A sudden change in the noise of the engines awoke her and she realized they had started their descent. A few minutes later she felt a bump, and they were back in England.

The door was opened and Peggy could feel the cool air on her face. She took a deep breath and realized how good it was to be home and as she walked down the steps, she saw two large, black cars parked on the tarmac. Mr. A had been whisked away and was getting into the first one when he suddenly stopped and looked back at her and raised his right hand high in the air with a thumbs up sign. Peggy did one back. It was a sign of mutual respect for each other. Mr. A and his car disappeared into the distance and Peggy was escorted to the other car. When she got inside, General French was waiting for her.

Congratulations, Peggy! A fantastic job, well done. Now let's get you back to the lab and the makeup team, and get you back to looking yourself, and then we can get you back home.

Peggy sat back in the same reclining chair she had sat in when the makeup team had originally worked their magic on her and transformed her into a terrorist, and bit by bit she was brought back to her normal self.

That's better, said General French. Now come with me, Peggy. We have a date with a helicopter. They left the lab and headed for Pine Needles, and as they got near she could hear the engines of the helicopter. Ten minutes later, she was on her way home. They hovered over the field next to Peggy's cottage, and Little Thatch had never looked so good to her. *Home at last,* she thought.

Chapter 36
Bad News on the Doorstep

As they touched down, Rose came out of the cottage and started running towards the helicopter. Peggy saw her and as soon as they had touched down she jumped out and ran towards her and they hugged each other. Peggy let go of her mother and turned to the pilot. She gave a thumbs up sign and waved. The pilot waved back and lifted off up into the sky and headed back to Pine Needles.

As Peggy and Rose entered the cottage, Peggy sensed something was wrong. Rose was physically shaking and began to cry and she held Peggy's hands and looked at her. Come and sit down, she said. They sat down and Rose was stammering. Savajic has been attacked and is fighting for his life . . . She could barely talk.

Peggy shot to her feet. Oh, my God! This is my fault. I should never have left him alone. Can you tell me what happened?

No, said Rose. I've only just found out. Cooper phoned and told me what had happened to him but he didn't go into any details. He said he had been calling out for Rose and Peggy and he has sent Henry to pick me up and take me to him. Thank God you came back when you did, Peggy; I need you by my side.

There was a loud rap on the door and Peggy went over and opened it. It was Henry. Come on, Mother, it's Henry. He's waiting outside for us. Rose stood up and looked shaky. Peggy picked up her coat and put it around her shoulders and put her arm around her. Let's go, she said. The car drove off and took to the sky and they were soon driving up to Savajic's home. Cooper was waiting for them as they approached; he looked grim faced. Master Savajic is in his room, he said. He has been asking for you both. Please try not to be alarmed because he keeps drifting in and out of consciousness. If you would be good enough to go straight up to his room, Miss Rose, I would like to have a word with Miss Peggy. Rose didn't need to be told twice, she was already running up the steps to the house.

Can we go to the study? Cooper asked.

Of course, Peggy replied, and without another word they walked to Savajic's study. They entered, and Cooper closed the door behind them.

I have been asked to bring you here and tell you to contact Enzebadier as soon as possible, he said. I'll leave you alone now. He turned and left the study, closing the door behind him.

Screen! commanded Peggy. The wall turned into a screen and Peggy said, Enzebadier! He appeared instantly on the screen.

Greetings, Peggy. I'm so sorry to bring you here to give you such tragic news, but you need to know what has happened right away.

Thank you, said Peggy.

Enzebadier began. I believe you are aware of Ravens Claw Castle and what it is being used for?

Yes, I am, Peggy said. It's the nerve center of the Black Watch movement.

Well, Savajic decided to pay them a visit and do a reconnaissance of the area. Unfortunately, he landed too close to the castle and six Black Watch wizards that were checking the area spotted him before he could put up a façade. They attacked him immediately from all directions, he didn't stand a chance. Fortunately, he had a built-in escape spell he used that brought him back home to his workshop, where he managed to raise the alarm. We have placed our best healers there with him but his wounds are severe and he is very weak, and only time will tell.

Thank you, Peggy said. I will keep you posted on any developments.

Peggy's mind was racing. She went back in her mind to when she was shot and what Savajic had done for her. She made her way down to his workshop and entered. She remembered the bottle of green liquid he had used to heal her that he kept in the glass cabinet. She went over and took it out. I have got to try it, she said to herself.

When she got up to Savajic's room, she entered and walked over to Savajic. Rose was leaning over him and talking to him. He seemed to be asleep.

She put her hand on Rose's shoulder and said, Mother, would you let me be on my own with Savajic, just for a few minutes?

Rose looked up in surprise. Why? she said.

I need to do something. Please trust me.

Rose stood up and said, Call me when you've finished, I'll be outside.

I will, Peggy said, and Rose left the room.

Can you hear me? Peggy asked. Savajic moved his hand, and that was enough for Peggy. She now knew his brain was working. She slowly pulled back the cover and looked at his wounds. There was nothing close to his heart or his head, and that was good news. Both legs were injured, his left shoulder, and his right side. She took the bottle of green liquid and poured a small amount on her hand and smoothed it on his shoulder. A mist appeared and covered his wound. Peggy closed her eyes and concentrated. Heal, heal, she repeated to herself. As the mist cleared she could see that the wound had healed, but this time it was different; there was a scar. Peggy pressed on and didn't stop until all the wounds were healed, and again each time it left a scar. Savajic was still lying unconscious, and Peggy knew what she had to do. She had had a torrid two days and she knew her energy level was low but she had no choice. She had to give Savajic what little she had left. She held his hands and concentrated. "Share, share," and she could feel the energy draining from her. She held Savajic for as long as she could, then shouted for her mother and collapsed onto the floor.

Rose came bursting through the door and when she saw Peggy lying on the floor she screamed for Cooper. He came dashing up to Savajic's room and kneeled down next to Peggy.

She looked up at him and said, Get me down into the garden and lay me on my back.

Cooper scooped her up in his powerful arms and carried her down into the garden and gently laid her down on the lawn, and then he rushed back indoors and returned with a blanket, which he carefully covered Peggy up with. Are you all right, Miss Peggy? He was looking very concerned.

I'm okay, she said. I just need to rest for a while. Please go and make sure Savajic is responding and Mother is all right.

Twenty minutes later, Peggy was back by Savajic's bedside. He had regained consciousness and was able to talk. He looked up at Peggy and said, Thank you, you saved my life. And how could I have been so stupid?

It was too much for Peggy. She burst into tears. Oh, Savajic, thank God you're all right! she sobbed. The wizard doctor had been watching carefully what Peggy had been doing and asked her to talk to him before he left. Of course, said Peggy. I'll see you in the study when you've finished up here.

Peggy was sitting in the study nursing a mug of hot chocolate when the doctor arrived. He sat down opposite her and said, Peggy, I've been a doctor for a long time, but in all of my years I can't remember seeing anything like what you did. Where did you learn such powerful healing skills?

Peggy said, Doctor, it's a long story, but I can tell you a large part of it is Savajic's own discovery. I'm sure he would be happy to discuss it with you when he is fully recovered.

The doctor said, Peggy, I want you to understand exactly what has happened to Savajic. He has lost a lot of blood, and wizards can't have blood transfusions. When wizard blood leaves the body, it deteriorates so quickly we can't store it for transfusions. So Savajic could take months or even years to get his blood levels back to normal.

Peggy was shocked but defiant. Savajic isn't a normal wizard when it comes to blood. His blood is mixed with my blood, and my human blood is mixed with his. Would you be prepared to take some of my blood and test it?

My answer to that is simple, the doctor said. I will be back tomorrow with a colleague and the necessary equipment.

That's a date, said Peggy. I'll meet you here tomorrow.

Chapter 37
A Surprise Result

By morning, Savajic had made positive progress through the night. He was sitting up in bed, although he was still very weak. Rose had been by his side all through the night holding his hand. She had had a lot of her religious beliefs knocked out of her because of all the things that had been dished out to her in life, but it didn't stop her from praying for Savajic long and hard.

Savajic looked at her with adoring eyes. Why don't you go and get some rest? he managed to say to her, and eat something. Then he closed his eyes and dropped off to sleep.

Peggy had been up early and had had her breakfast. She wanted to be ready when the doctor arrived so Savajic could have some of her blood; that is, if it passed the tests. She didn't have to wait long. Cooper found her in Savajic's study. The doctor has arrived, Miss Peggy, and has asked if you would join him in his mobile laboratory outside where he can carry out his tests.

Thank you, Peggy said, and followed Cooper down to the waiting doctor. Good morning, Doctor, she said. Thank you for coming so early.

Not at all, replied the doctor. I'm as eager to see the results as you are.

The doctor had prepared his instruments and was ready to start. He asked Peggy to sit in his chair and relax. She sat down and closed her eyes and relaxed. The doctor didn't take long before he had extracted enough of Peggy's blood to do all of his tests.

Thank you, Peggy, he said. Now if you will just sit there for a few minutes, I will have an answer for you. Peggy's mind drifted back to Savajic's workshop and to the time when they had mixed their blood. He had given her so much more than just his blood; he had given her the power to unlock the power of her brain, and it was awesome.

Peggy! The doctor's voice brought her back to the present.

Have you got a result? Peggy asked.

Yes, the doctor said, but not the one we wanted. As you know, part of your blood is wizard blood, and therefore the wizard part of your blood deteriorates as soon as it leaves your body.

Peggy felt devastated. So, that's it then, we're helpless.

Not necessarily so, the doctor said. Your human blood remained healthy, which suggests to me that your mother could give Savajic some of her pure human blood; that is, if she is the same group type as you are.

She is! Peggy gushed. She is!

Then let's get started, the doctor said.

Rose had taken Savajic's advice and had eaten a hearty breakfast and just as she laid down her knife and fork, Peggy came in. Mother, good news! The doctor thinks you can give Savajic some of your blood and help to make him well again.

That's wonderful news, Rose said. What do you want me to do?

The doctor is preparing things now, up in Savajic's room, Peggy said. Are you ready?

Yes, said Rose. Let's go and see what the doctor wants me to do.

When they entered Savajic's room he was still unconscious. Rose looked at the doctor. He was old and wise-looking and it gave her a feeling of confidence. Will it work if he is asleep? Rose posed the question to the doctor, hoping the answer would be yes.

You need not be concerned, said the doctor in a calming voice. I can assure you, your blood will flow quite freely into Savajic. But I'm afraid you will get nothing in return.

Rose smiled. You are so wrong, Doctor. I will have back the man I love dearly.

Rose lay quietly beside Savajic while her rich, healthy blood fed slowly into his body. Her mind was drifting off to another place, a place where she didn't want to go, but she couldn't stop it. George was lying on his deathbed and she was there next to him, holding his bloodied hand. He was looking up at her with his strong, handsome face. She remembered how clear and blue and honest his eyes were. His lips began to move. It was little more than a whisper. I'm sorry, Rose, I don't want to leave you. I love you both so much. Keep my little Peggy safe. Then his eyes closed and she had lost the love of her life and Peggy had lost her father. And now it seemed history was trying to repeat itself over again and she couldn't let this happen again to the man she loved so much.

Are you comfortable, Rose? The doctor's voice brought her back to Savajic's side.

Yes, I'm fine, she replied. Is everything all right?

Yes, everything has gone to plan, he said. Now I would like you to just relax for about ten minutes, and tonight have a hearty meal and an early night. Tomorrow we will need to repeat the procedure, so in the morning have your breakfast and relax and I will be back to give Savajic his second and hopefully his last transfusion.

The next day all went to plan and the doctor preformed his procedure and left. Rose was sitting by Savajic's bedside when he regained consciousness. How am I doing, Rose?

She smiled and said, I think you are going to pull through, tough guy. Savajic tried to laugh and winced. Are you in much pain? Rose asked.

Only when I laugh, replied Savajic.

I can see you're getting better, she said, glad to see his sense of humor was coming back.

Rose, will you ask Peggy to come up and see me please?

Rose began to protest. Savajic, please, you're not in any fit state to start working on anything yet, you need to rest.

I know, I don't intend to, he replied. I just need to ask her to do something for me, that's all.

Very well then, if that's a promise I'll go and tell her you want to see her. She smiled at him and left the room.

Chapter 38
PEGGY GOES IT ALONE

The door to Savajic's room opened and Peggy walked in. Savajic was sitting up in bed, and Peggy could see that the color was returning to his face. She walked over to the bed and kissed him on the cheek. You gave us quite a fright, she said. How are you feeling?

Pretty weak, he replied, but on the mend. Peggy, I want you to try and understand what my injuries are. Unlike the injuries you sustained in the shooting, my injuries are wizard magic injuries and can't be healed as yours were. Fortunately for me, I've had you and Rose to help me. It's never been known before for a wizard to have human blood given, and this was made possible because we had mixed our blood together and the fairy healing magic you possess enabled you to give me the strength to fight for my life. Now have no doubt, Peggy, I owe my life to you and Rose.

Peggy was choked for words. She looked deep into Savajic's eyes. Their minds were in tune with each other, as was their blood. Her lips didn't move but the message was sent and received. *"That's what close families do for each other, isn't it?"* Savajic smiled at her and nodded his head.

Peggy, what I am about to say stays within this room and is between the two of us. We cannot let anyone know. I cannot move my legs.

Peggy's hand shot up to her mouth to stifle a cry of anguish. She recovered her composure and said, What are we going to do? We can't just stop what we are doing and let this whole mess just get even worse.

No, we can't, Savajic replied, and this means you have to do all the field work on your own. Soon I will be operating from a wheelchair and I will be your coordinator. This will give me plenty of time to plan our moves. This is going to put enormous pressure on you, Peggy, but I cannot think of anyone more capable than you. You are about to put every scrap of training and magic and instinct into practice like never before.

I made a bad error of judgement when I transported to Ravens Claw Castle. I should have realized the area around the castle would be under surveillance constantly and checked for intruders. I can only hope I wasn't recognized. I was in and out so fast, I imagine they were as surprised as I was. They would have a hard time reporting my visit to Sealin Belbur without showing him a body, so I believe they will keep it to themselves out of fear of reprisals.

Peggy, this is what I want you to do. I need you to spend the next few days researching Ravens Claw and its surroundings. We need to find a way in without their knowledge. I know many of the old castles had tunnels that led out to the fields hundreds of yards from the castle walls so they could escape if it looked like they were going to be overrun by an enemy. If we were lucky enough to find one at Ravens Claw, it just might give us a way in undetected. It's just a possibility, that's all.

Peggy nodded. I'll get onto it right away, she said. Is there anything else you can think of?

Savajic said, Yes, there is one thing. When I went to Ravens Claw I was wearing my head camera. It's just a shot in the dark, but there might be something on it that might help. I'm sorry, Peggy, he said, I need to rest. His head fell back on his pillow, and he was asleep.

Peggy slipped quietly out of the room and made her way to the study. She wasted no time. Screen, she commanded, and as soon as it appeared she said, Professor Ableman.

The professor appeared immediately and greeted Peggy with a broad grin. It's so nice to see you, he said. How can I help you?

Professor, she began, is it possible for me to spend some time with Professor Gellit in the forbidden library? I need to do some research for Savajic and I think he would be able to help me.

I cannot see why not, Peggy, said the professor. Let me get him for you and you can ask him for yourself.

The screen faded and a minute later Professor Gellit appeared. It's good to see you, Peggy. How can I help you?

Is it possible to come and spend some time with you in the forbidden library, Professor?

Of course it is, he replied. Come to the library as soon as you return to Black Eagle.

Thank you, Professor, she said.

I'll see you soon. Good-bye, and the screen faded.

She sat down and the study door opened. Cooper appeared. Are you ready for lunch, Miss Peggy? he enquired.

Yes, she said. I'm famished. Is it possible to have a sandwich brought down to Savajic's workshop? I've got something that must be done.

Of course, Cooper replied. Would chicken be suitable, Miss Peggy? Perfect, said Peggy. And a glass of water would be good.

Peggy entered Savajic's workshop. It seemed a lifetime away from when she had first entered this magical place as a young, innocent schoolgirl, and now she was standing there a powerful wizard with a responsibility far greater than she could have ever imagined. To work, she told herself.

Savajic's clothes and belongings were scattered all around. Cooper had undressed him and got him up into his room and into bed before he had sent for the doctor. She began by retrieving Savajic's helmet camera. She set it up on the workbench and pressed the replay button. A picture flashed on the wall. It showed the ground coming up to meet him but within seconds there were several flashes and Savajic's voice screaming: "UNCAPTIVUS!" and that was it, nothing else until he was back in his workshop and it showed Cooper come dashing in and then it went blank.

It was bit of a letdown, but Savajic had said it was only a possibility. Just then Cooper came in with a tray and laid it on the workbench. Peggy put her hand on his arm and looked at his strong, honest face. Thank you for everything you've done, she said. Your quick actions saved Savajic's life.

Thank you, Miss Peggy, he said, but we all played our part. Let us all hope he makes a safe and speedy recovery. He turned and left the room.

Chapter 39
The Forbidden Library

Peggy contacted Black Eagle and secured the headmaster's permission to summon the Snake and return back to school. A time had been set for Henry to drop her off on the platform so she could board the Snake and gain entrance to the school. She had packed a bag and her board and as soon as she arrived at Black Eagle she went into haze. She didn't want to be seen and have to start answering questions about what she was doing back at school. She made her way down to the headmaster's room and knocked on the door.

Come in, Peggy, said the headmaster. She walked in and came out of haze. The headmaster looked at her with a grave face. These are very troublesome times, he said, shaking his head. How bad are Savajic's injuries?

Pretty severe, she said. He is going to need some time to heal, but he will be able to plan and coordinate from home so we will be able to manage for the time being.

I have informed Professor Gellit of your arrival so he will be expecting you. Is there anything you would like me to do for you while you are here, Peggy?

Not at the moment, Headmaster, she replied. But please remember it is very important that no one learns of Savajic's injuries. Peggy went into haze and left the headmaster's room and made her way outside, where she mounted her board and headed for the forbidden library. When she arrived she came out of haze, and Professor Gellit was standing on the platform jutting out from the building.

Welcome, Peggy, it's good to see you again. Come along in.

It was the first time Peggy had been inside and she was amazed. She had imagined it would be filled with old, dusty, glass door bookcases. It was just the opposite. A massive complex of bookshelves circled the entire perimeter of the building that went down from a balcony they were standing on and in turn the entire balcony went up and down so any book was within easy reach. The balcony itself was the observatory floor with a massive telescope taking up the center space. The professor's desk and various chairs were positioned around it and to one side was a large map table with what looked like star charts scattered on top of it. The dome roof was massive, and it had an opening slotted into it so the telescope could be pointed up into the sky.

What do you think of my little world, Peggy? the professor asked with a big grin on his face.

It's wonderful! she said. Absolutely wonderful.

I thought you'd like it, he said. Now down to business. How can I help you?

Peggy began, Before we start, Professor, could I ask you what progress Zealotte is making?

Of course, said the professor. I keep a daily log of the comet's path and I can tell you it is on schedule. I can't give you a precise day and time yet because it is still too far away.

Thank you, Peggy said. Now the reason for my visit. There is a remote, ruined castle in Northumberland called Ravens Claw Castle. It is rarely visited by humans because of its condition and remoteness. We know for certain it is being used by the Black Watch for its headquarters and is the nerve center of its operations. I need to know about the original building plans to find out if there are any secret passages that lead in and out of the castle and if so, are they still useable?

That shouldn't be too much of a problem, replied the professor. Our planners have been meticulous in recording every building of importance the humans have ever built right up to the present. Now let me see, planner's archives. He was holding a pad with numbers and letters on which he started to tap in various keys. He looked at Peggy and said, Here we go, and tapped one final key. The floor began to sink down like a giant lift and at the same time began to slowly revolve. It came to a standstill some way down from where they had started. This is the planner's archives, he announced, and began tapping his pad again. Suddenly a large volume dislodged itself from the shelves and flew through the air and landed on the professor's desk. Peggy gasped out loud, "WOW!" She couldn't help herself. The professor smiled and said, Well, Peggy, I'm far too old to spend all my time rummaging through millions of books, so I have made myself an enchanted library.

After spending some time poring through the plans, it was agreed there wasn't anything that could be of any real help to her. She would have to find her own way of gaining entry into the castle undetected. It was a disappointment, but Savajic had said it was just a shot in the dark, so nothing gained and nothing lost, in that respect. But she had gained quite a bit of knowledge as to the location and the lie of the land. But the best piece of luck was the fact that one of the towers of the castle was still standing, and a pair of red kites had nested in the top of the turret. They were incredibly rare for that part of the country, but most importantly for Peggy, they hadn't been disturbed by the Black Watch so she could be fairly certain they had been accepted as no threat. With Peggy's power to transfigure into any bird, it was her way into the castle. She was delighted, and she flung her arms around the professor and kissed him on the cheek.

The professor looked bemused. What was that for? he said.

Because you have shown me the way into Ravens Claw Castle! she gushed.

The professor shrugged his shoulders and thought to himself, *I don't know how,* but of course because he didn't know she could transfigure into a bird.

The professor tapped his pad and all the things they had been looking through folded themselves up and books closed, then they rose up from the desk and slotted themselves back into the bookshelves. Now, Peggy, is there anything else I can help you with?

Yes, there is, Professor, Peggy replied. It's a big ask.

Ask away, the professor said, and let's see if I can help.

Well, Peggy said, is it possible to have a look at the comet that's pulling Zealotte towards earth? I've never, ever looked through a telescope before.

That won't be a problem at all, the professor said, and was secretly pleased Peggy was showing such interest in his work. Once again the floor began to rise and this time it was rising high into the dome. It came to a stop and as it did, a large section of the dome opened up to the sky.

Oh, no, sighed Peggy. I forgot it was daytime.

The professor chuckled and looked at Peggy. The stars and planets don't disappear during the daytime, Peggy. Our world is of little consequence to the solar system. Now let's get a fix.

Ten minutes later, Peggy was watching a tiny speck speeding towards the earth. It's just a tiny speck, Professor, she said. How can you know it's pulling Zealotte's time bubble?

A very good question, Peggy, said the professor. But the answer is quite simple. From the moment the time bubble left earth all those years ago it has been closely monitored because of the threat that someday it might return. And now it looks like that day will soon be upon us.

Peggy could feel the professor's deep concern for the impending possibilities and didn't pursue it any further. Thank you, Professor, for giving me so much of your time. You have really helped me. It's been really productive and a privilege. The professor had taken a shine to Peggy right from the first time they had met when Angus Fume had introduced her to him on her first day at Black Eagle.

Peggy, you are always welcome here. I enjoy your company, and I hope you will come again soon.

I will she said. She looked at him and thought how humble he was for a person with such enormous knowledge. *If only there were just a few like him in the human world,* she thought, *how good life could be.*

Peggy knocked on the headmaster's door. Please come in, Peggy, the headmaster called out and the door opened. She walked in and the door closed behind her. I hope Professor Gellit was able to help you, Peggy, he said. Please take a seat.

Peggy sat down and looked over to the headmaster. Professor Gellit has been a tremendous help to me and has given me a possible way into Ravens Claw Castle. Now I need to get back to Savajic and report to him, she said. I'm sure he will be pleased with what I have found out.

Do you need me to arrange for your transport back, Peggy?

No, she said. I have a quick way back. So if you will please excuse me, Headmaster, I will be on my way. Uncaptivus!" She gave the command and there was a flash and she was back in Savajic's workshop.

Chapter 40

A Night To Remember

She wasted no time and headed for Savajic's room. She knocked on the door and walked in. What met her stopped her dead in her tracks. Sitting at a small round bedroom table were Savajic and Rose, both drinking a glass of champagne.

What? How? Peggy couldn't find words to describe her feelings. Rose put her glass down on the table and ran over to Peggy. She was so excited she hugged her and turned around to Savajic.

Show her, Savajic, show her!

Savajic slowly got to his feet. He gripped tightly onto the end of the bed and then he took three wobbly steps and collapsed onto the bed. He looked around at Peggy and smiled and said, What do you think?

Peggy was across the room in a second and she scooped him up in her arms as if he was weightless and she spun him round and round. You wonderful, wonderful man! she said, and tears ran down her cheeks.

Don't you dare hurt him again! shouted Rose, and they all began to laugh. Peggy set Savajic down in his chair.

Have a glass of champagne, Peggy, and let me tell you the good news. When the doctor carried out the blood transfusions from Rose to me, he took back with him samples of our blood for further tests in his lab. He discovered that when our blood was mixed together, the red corpuscles more than quadrupled, and somehow it has enabled my nerve ends to regenerate and join back up together. He said if I continue to progress at the same rate I could be back to normal within a month from now.

I can't believe it! Peggy said. It's the best news ever. I'm so excited and so relieved. I have news for you too, Savajic, but it is going to have to wait until tonight at dinner. I think we're entitled to celebrate now. Cheers!" She held out her glass. Here's to Savajic's continued progress.

Peggy finished her drink and stood up and said, I hope you don't mind, but I feel like going for a swim before dinner, and I've got a feeling you won't object to being left alone together.

Savajic raised his glass. Be my guest, he said, and laughed out loud.

Peggy loved it in the pool. It was twenty-five meters long and she could really let it rip. She was a powerful swimmer and had good technique. She swam ten lengths and got out of the pool. She dried off instantly, and when she lay back on a lounger an artificial sun came out. Savajic's magic was so creative and powerful. She closed her eyes and drifted off to sleep.

Up in Savajic's room, the last of the champagne had been consumed and Savajic looked Rose in the eyes. Something is bothering you, Rose. What is it?

Rose held his gaze. There is something I need to tell you, and I need to find the right words. I don't want it to sound all wrong.

Savajic smiled. Why don't you start with your love affair with James in London before you married George?

Rose was shocked. How could you possibly know about James? How could anyone know?

Savajic began, Well, when I went in search of your mother's silver dressing table set, I managed to locate everything except her silver-backed comb, and as luck would have it, the dealer remembered querying it with your father, who told him your mother had given it to her maid, Tilly. With a little bit of research, I managed to locate her, and she still had it. I obviously made her a good offer for it but she said she would not part with it for any amount of money. I had no alternative but to tell her who I wanted it for and about George's death just after Peggy was born. She broke down and cried. She said, 'My poor Rose, she didn't marry for love. She married to give her child a father.' She told me that when you were staying at your father's house in London you had met and fallen in love with a government secret agent called James, and you and he had had an affair. One day he had been called up to take on a mission abroad. He could not tell you anything about it or how long it would take, but he promised to be back. That day was to be the last time you would see him. Four weeks later you were informed he had been killed on some secret mission for his country. When you came back home you found out you were pregnant.

She said you and George had known each other for years, and George was head over heels in love with you. After you told George what had happened and James had been killed, George proposed, and the rest is history.

Rose reached out and held Savajic's powerful hands. Please don't think ill of me for not telling you of this before. I'm not ashamed of what I did, but in my own way I came to love George for his strength and kindness, and for a short time he was a wonderful father to Peggy.

Savajic gently squeezed Rose's hand and said, We have both known another love and have both lost our dear ones, but this does not diminish my love for you. We have both been given a second chance to love, and for me it will be until I draw my last breath.

I feel the same way too, said Rose. We have both had so much heartache in the past, surely we are due a measure of happiness.

There is something else you need to know, Rose, so brace yourself. James isn't dead.

At first Rose couldn't take in what Savajic had said to her and then it hit her. Oh, my God! What am I going to do?

Nothing, said Savajic, and I'll tell you why. During my investigations, I found out James was somewhere in South America and had been flying in a cargo plane carrying a large quantity of drugs bound for the USA. He had managed to overcome the crew somehow and had cut the engines and sent the plane spiraling down to the ground. It crashed in a ball of flames. There was no contact from James, and it was assumed he had gone down with the plane and died. Three months later, James turned up in London, a little worse for wear but all in one piece. He had been living in Brazil with family all that time. When he returned he was put into a physical training program, and as soon as he was fit he was put back into the field. I also found out James is the department's top agent, and has been for years. His disappearance was nothing new; it had happened before, more than once.

To set your mind at ease, James did try to contact you but he found out you had married and moved on, and so has he. He has no knowledge Peggy is his child.

Rose was still in a state of shock. You knew all of this and never said anything? I can't believe it.

Savajic just smiled and said, Rose, this is something you needed to tell me, and I knew you would when the time was right.

Rose stood up and walked up behind Savajic and wrapped her arms around him and kissed him on the head. I love you, Mr. Menglor, she whispered in his ear, and always will. I still have one concern though, she said. You know Peggy has just been on a secret mission for the government and it was a complete success. And so you know it will not stop there. From what I can gather, she has already been offered a position in the Secret Service when she is ready, and to be quite honest, I think it is in her blood.

Why should that concern you, Rose? You've just hit the nail on the head when you said it is in her blood. Just think what that means. Let's start with James, a top agent and a planner, a survivor, a killer, and a charmer. Then there is you, a competitor, a lady's upbringing with all the social graces, and a determination never to give in, whatever the odds. And then there is me, a wizard with battle experience, not afraid to kill and with considerable magic. Put them all together and you have Peggy Goody. I for one would not like her as a foe.

That's not really my concern, Rose said. I was thinking if indeed Peggy does take up a position with the Secret Service, one day her path must lead to James, and they may even be put together on some mission, maybe a mission impossible.

Look, said Savajic. James has proved over and over he is a survivor, but even he will eventually have to retire. And can you imagine a safer pair of hands to hand over to than Peggy's? Now seriously, Rose, you know about James and so do I. Please let it remain our secret. Do we agree?

I agree, said Rose.

Then that is the end of it.

At dinner, Peggy was feeling wonderful. Savajic had walked into the dining room on Rose's arm. He seemed to be getting stronger by the hour. Over dinner, she told Savajic all about her visit to the forbidden library and what she had discovered about Ravens Claw Castle, and they all had a great night laughing and joking about all kinds of things.

Chapter 41
THE LIGHTNING HAWK HUNT

Peggy had missed the wand speed champion competition at White Eagle because of her mission in the desert. But the outcome couldn't have been better. Owen had won it with the slenderest of margins; in fact, just one point between first and second position. It would have the desired effect on Sealin Belbur, who would be fuming because his sons hadn't won. First blood to us, Savajic had said to Peggy.

A week later, Savajic was walking around unaided, and he had been using his time at home in his workshop. He had developed a transfer bracelet for Peggy and had packed it in a box to give it to her for a present. *I think she will like this,* he said to himself, and put it away in his glass cabinet.

Peggy was back at the Black Eagle School in secret and was hiding out in the aviary. Tomorrow was the Lightning Hawk Hunt. She had to pay Professor Gull a visit. The professor was always pleased to see her. He liked the way she showed so much interest in his birds, and the way the birds themselves were comfortable around her. She wanted to know all about the number of lightning hawks that were being used on the day and how the races were run and how the birds knew what to do.

Let me explain, said the professor. There are four chasers from White Eagle and four chasers from Black Eagle. The races will be one on one. Four races in the first round will produce four winners. The four winners will race one on one in two races, and will produce our two finalists. The chasers that lost will race against each other for third and fourth place, and the final race will be for first and second place. The lightning hawks are trained to fly back to the aviary on release, and so altogether there will be sixteen. Now is that a good enough explanation, Peggy?

That's great, Peggy said. Have you selected them yet?

Yes, replied the professor. They are all together and ready for tomorrow.

Is it possible for me to see them? Peggy asked.

Of course you can, he said. Follow me. He took her to a large cage where they were all perched. I'll have to leave you now, Peggy. Will you be able to find your way back without me?

No problem, replied Peggy.

As soon as the professor was out of sight, Peggy transfigured into a lightning hawk. Can you hear me? she said.

The hawks began fluttering around inside the cage. We can hear you, came the answer from inside the cage.

Good, Peggy said. Early tomorrow morning I will come and change places with one of you. I wish you no harm, so don't be afraid.

The next morning, Peggy was up early and on her way to the bird aviary. She let herself in and went straight to the cage where the lightning hawks were. She selected two bars on the cage and pulled them apart, and then she put her hand inside the cage and against the feet of one of the lightning hawks. The bird jumped onto her hand and she drew it out of the cage. As soon as it was out of the cage, it flew away. Next Peggy transfigured into a lightning hawk and flew into the cage. She perched onto a branch and began to speak. The birds fluttered about the cage and then came to rest around her.

I am joining you today for the chase, and this is what I want you to do. As each race comes up, I want you to push up to the door of the cage and make sure you are picked before me, because I need to be in the last race.

We all understand, said one of the hawks. Peggy assumed it was the senior hawk.

That's great, Peggy said. So, let's get some rest before the races.

As the cage approached the forest, a loud voice roared out, Good morning, Professor Gull! I hope you are in good spirits and your birds are ready to go!

Good morning, Polonius, replied the professor. My birds are all present and correct, and raring to go. Now how about your trees, are they all in their positions?

Of course! Polonius roared.

Wonderful, the professor said. May I proceed into your forest and set up the stations and the cage on the starting platform?

Be my guest! roared Polonius.

Professor Gull always liked to get set up on the platform in the forest at least an hour before any of the students arrived, as this would give the lightning hawks time to adjust to the dappled shade of the forest.

One hour later, the racers began to arrive and they all looked splendid in their team colors. Professor Gull came to check that all was well with his birds and he was dressed in his full robes. His job for the day was to select the hawks and put them into their individual starting traps, and as soon as the flap doors dropped, the race was on. The chasers would be already on their boards and in the air and ready to go. All that was needed now were the marshals to be in place.

The first race was always a scramble and the most dangerous because no one wanted to be the first out of the running, so all caution was pushed to one side. But it was very important not to hit a tree and get knocked off your board because you would be automatically eliminated. Eight separate lines of trees were lined up in a straight line, and when the hawks were released, they would weave in and out of the trees and the chasers would have to fly in the exact same path as the hawks. Any missed moves would attract a ten-second penalty that would be added to their overall time, so skill was as important as speed.

Polonius had created a massive clear space for race day, and Professors Ableman and Battell Crie had both been busy working their magic. They had created a magnificent amphitheater, with banners and flags representing both schools. As the seats began to fill, the tension and excitement began to reach fever pitch, with each school trying to out-shout and scream each other with their chanting.

The chasers took their places on the platform and Professor Gill introduced them. From the White Eagle School for Wizards, in position one, Leo Mello. In position two, Jed Belbur. In position three, Shuvan Pooshe. And in position four, Guy Belbur. Black Eagle School for Wizards is represented by, in position five, Sal Mendez. In position six, Lilly Wong. In position seven, Helda Scelda. And in position eight is Charlie Manders.

As the names were announced, the crowd got louder and louder. It was almost impossible to hear the starter's orders.

Professor Gull had loaded the first hawks to race and was calling the chasers to order. Take to your boards and get ready! The doors on the traps dropped, the hawks were released, and the chase was on. The speed of the hawks was frightening. They took to the air and headed for the trees. The chasers all anticipated what would happen and also headed for the trees. In and out they weaved. The chasers were all up for it and pushed their abilities to the limit. Leading the field was Lilly Wong, followed closely by Jed Belbur and Charlie Manders. Their skill was amazing, but halfway through the lead kept on changing. Then suddenly the race was turned upside down. Jed Belbur, who was leading, glanced a tree branch and lost his balance. It was enough to send him crashing down to the forest floor. For him, the race was over. Guy Belbur was now in second place behind Charlie Manders and going well, totally oblivious of his brother's fate, which was just as well because Lilly Wong was only one board length behind him and Helda Scelda was level with her. Behind them was a fierce battle going on between Sal Mendez and Leo Mello. With six trees remaining, the picture changed again dramatically, Helda Scelda realizing that because they were so close to Charlie Manders, there was a good chance they could be in the semi-final. She made the mistake of looking over towards Lilly Wong and missed a maneuver. She screamed out loud as soon as she realized what she had done; a ten-second penalty. Sal Mendez heard her scream and looked over and did exactly the same; a ten-second penalty. As they all crossed the finishing line and the times were checked, it became clear to all that because of the time penalties, Helda Scelda and Sal Mendez had ruled themselves out of the semi-finals, along with Shuvan Pooshe and Jed Belbur.

The semi-finalists were announced. Lilly Wong was to race against Guy Belbur, and Charlie Manders was to race against Leo Mello. And now there was to be a fifteen-minute break before the next race.

The hawks had done their job well. Peggy was as far away from the cage door as possible and the remaining five were perched as close to the door as possible. Peggy had to gamble now that she could get into a Black Eagle trap, should one from Black Eagle be in the final. Nothing could be taken for granted. All the four chasers were on top of their game. If both White Eagle chasers won their semi-finals, then it didn't matter which trap she went into, and the same went if both Black Eagle chasers won.

The fifteen minutes were up and Professor Gull began placing the hawks in the traps. When the last hawk was in place, the professor stood back. Chasers, mount your boards! he commanded. Ready! The trap doors dropped and the chase was on. They all took off as one, bobbing and weaving their way through the trees, four streaks of color moving at almost identical speeds. At the end of the race it was a dead heat for first place between Guy Belbur and Charlie Manders, and third and fourth were also too close to call, both finishing five one hundredths of a second behind. It was the closest semi-final ever recorded. This time there was to be a thirty-minute rest period so the chasers could have a snack and a drink before the last two races.

There were refreshments being served in the amphitheater and the noise and excitement was almost at fever pitch, with each school chanting the names of their chasers. The rest period was over and Professor announced the chasers who would race for third place. Lilly Wong from Black Eagle and Leo Mello from White Eagle. They both mounted their boards and waited for the doors on the traps to drop and drop they did, and they were off. Unknown to the chasers, Polonius had been asked if his trees could put out a few extra branches to make the race a more skillful run for the last two races. Polonius had put the thirty-minute recess to good use, and his trees were now a much more difficult proposition.

Once again the chasers were neck and neck when suddenly they both encountered the extra branches and were both too late to avoid them. They both lost their footing and fell, but all was not lost. Somehow Lilly was holding onto her board with one hand and trying to pull herself back up onto her board and with her last bit of energy, she scrambled back on. Lilly looked down and saw poor Leo lying on the forest floor. All she had to do was finish the race; the time didn't really matter now.

The final race was here at last. The winner would be this year's champion and would win the cup for his school. As they lined up against each other, Guy Belbur looked over to Charlie and shouted: "HEY!" Charlie looked over and Belbur, who had a leering grin on his face, ran his finger across his neck in a cut throat motion. He was a nasty piece of work, but Charlie knew he was a great chaser and on this day, was quite able to win the race. But having said that, he wasn't going to fall for his mind games. Bring it on! he shouted back.

Peggy had been listening to all of this and it made her even more determined than ever to help Charlie win. But first she was relying on Professor Gull being the consummate gentleman and loading the visitor's trap first. He didn't let her down and now she was in Charlie's trap.

The amphitheater fell quiet and Professor Gull's voice rang out: "MOUNT YOUR BOARDS!" The trap doors dropped and they were off. The wall of silence turned into a wall of noise, shouting and screaming their chaser's name. Charlie just went for it and so did Guy, in and out, up and down, they matched each other move for move. There were three trees left and it was too close to call. Peggy had to act. She purposely flew into the leaves of a branch that halted her just for a moment. Charlie saw it and reacted with breathtaking speed. His hand shot out and caught her.

He emerged from the trees in triumph. He was the first chaser in the history of the race ever to catch a lightning hawk and as he flew back to the amphitheater gently holding the lightning hawk high above his head, the crowd went berserk.

At the presentation of the cup, Charlie held the cup and said, I want to dedicate this cup to an absent friend, Peggy Goody. If only he knew just how close he was to her and how much she loved him.

Then something very strange happened that day. Both of the Belbur twins came up onto the stage and shook Charlie's hand and congratulated him on his victory. It was an unexpected act of sportsmanship from the twins, and both Black Eagle and White Eagle joined in together chanting: Bel-bur! Bel-bur! Bel-bur! It was definitely another first.

Charlie released his hold on the lightning hawk and it flew away and landed well out of sight of the forest, and Peggy transfigured back to normal. She would have loved to say something to Charlie, anything! But it had to be a secret; her secret and hers alone.

Chapter 42
PLANS TO VISIT RAVENS CLAW CASTLE

Savajic was waiting for Peggy when she returned from Black Eagle and greeted her with a hug. It's good to be home, she said.

And, Savajic said, at last.

What? Peggy said, looking puzzled.

Savajic looked her in the eyes and said, you've just called this home.

I guess I have, she replied. And I mean it.

They walked towards the study and Savajic said, Now come and tell me what you've been up to, young lady, while you've been at Black Eagle. After Peggy had finished her story, Savajic said, What a great result! I would never have thought of that in a million years. And so, it's second blood to us. Sealin Belbur will be seething, especially with his two sons publically congratulating Charlie. While you've been away, Peggy, I've been going over and over my arrival at Ravens Claw Castle and how quickly I was attacked. It was instantaneous, which brings me to the conclusion they have some sort of permanent barrier set up that screens anything that comes into the area of the castle, and if it is something they do not recognize that enters, it's attacked by guards on a twenty-four-hour watch. I turned up out of nowhere and must have given them quite a fright. They probably attacked me out of pure reaction, and then I disappeared just as quickly. I doubt if they even reported it to Sealin Belbur.

This leads me to our next visit, said Savajic. We have got to find a way of getting past the guards.

Peggy looked at Savajic and said, there isn't a next we. I've got to do this on my own and before you say no, please listen to my plan. As you have probably rightly guessed, they have some kind of security shield in place, and if you remember when we were going over all the information we obtained from the forbidden library, there was a nest of birds living in the old tower. That's my way in. They have probably just got used to them flying in and out and leave them alone, so another bird won't give them any suspicions.

What about humans? Peggy fired the question at Savajic.

I've given some thought, he replied. I don't really think it matters because the Black Watch will have a secret entrance they use and it is completely invisible to humans. The castle is so remote, probably only a handful of bird spotters would go there anyway, just to monitor the kites. When you looked at the plans, Peggy, did the castle have a moat around it?

Yes, it did, she said. And a draw bridge. Why?

Well then, another possibility is the drawbridge is long gone, and it would be easy for the Black Watch to make sure it was full up with water. And if that were the case, the bird spotters would only be watching the kites through binoculars. As you are aware, crossing water poses no problem for wizards. Peggy nodded in agreement.

The plan to investigate Ravens Claw Castle was to be in seven days' time and was now complete. Savajic had convinced Peggy it was essential they both went, and set up a camp ten miles away from the castle, just in case Peggy had to make several visits, and a camp in the close vicinity would save time. Peggy knew how much it meant to Savajic to get back into the field and active again so she didn't protest, much to Savajic's relief. In the next seven days, Savajic wanted to spend time with Peggy on the range and get himself back into shape. Peggy was wearing her transference arm bracelet and loved it, and Savajic wanted to make sure she could use it correctly. He also wanted to show her how to work out coordinates accurately. Peggy hadn't realized how complicated it would be to use it. Savajic had to teach her new techniques in brain concentration because this was crucial in transference, and only a trained and powerful mind could achieve it. Savajic worked on this for two years before he perfected it. Now all the building blocks were in place and had been proven and tested, and he could pass on his knowledge to Peggy. He warned Peggy how dangerous this new power could be she now possessed, reminding her of what had happened to himself at Ravens Claw Castle. Peggy promised him she would measure twice and cut once.

The seven days passed by and it had been both successful and productive. Peggy was delighted with her transference bracelet and had memorized every aspect of it while Savajic was back to his normal self. His recovery was amazing and most welcome.

They were both kitted up and ready to go. The chosen campsite was ten miles south of the castle. Savajic wanted to make sure that this time there would be no unwanted surprises and of course, this time they would arrive in haze mode. The coordinates were set and they were on their way. As soon as they were on solid ground, Savajic set up a façade to conceal them from any prying eyes, and they went about setting up camp.

The first visit was for Peggy to fly in as a kite and settle herself in the tower. If it didn't cause any kind of alarm, she would determine the best positions as to where to put concealed cameras and record the comings and goings of the Black Watch wizards. She transfigured into a kite and started her journey across the moors.

As soon as she got to the castle, she settled herself in the tower and waited. Fortunately, there was no adverse reaction from the other kites, so Peggy could move around and work out her camera positions. She had been there for about an hour and there had been no sign of activity so she decided to head back to camp and organize the cameras and how best to get them to the castle and in place.

When she landed back at camp, she briefed Savajic on what had happened and they set about sorting out what cameras they would use and how best Peggy could carry them. The cameras themselves were a wonder of miniature engineering, each no bigger than a coat button, and with a powerful fish eye lens. They had built-in intelligence and would pick up and follow any movement within four hundred meters. This would be recorded and transmitted to a full-size screen in Savajic's workshop so as soon as they were in place, Savajic and Peggy could go back and view proceedings at their leisure.

The cameras were in place, and Peggy was on her way back to camp. She landed and signaled her success, and they both breathed a sigh of relief.

When all their gear was stowed away and they were ready to go, Savajic turned to Peggy and said, Go on then, use your bracelet. Practice makes perfect.

Peggy smiled. OK, she said, and went into concentration mode and disappeared. In the blink of an eye she was back in Savajic's workshop. Wow! That's awesome, she said out loud, and seconds later Savajic was standing next to her.

I'm proud of you, Peggy, he said.

Thank you, she said a little sheepishly, and they both burst out laughing.

After Savajic and Peggy had both showered and changed into something more comfortable, they had lunch and discussed what they would do next. I think we should leave the cameras in place for the next week and view once a day. After all, we're not in any rush because the cameras don't self-destruct for three weeks, and we have most things in hand. So, Peggy, would you like to spend some time at home with your mother? I need to go there myself and we could perhaps go together.

I'd love to, Peggy said. When can we go?

I'll have a word with Rose and ask if we can go in the morning. How does that sound?

That sounds great, said Peggy.

I think you're in for a few surprises, said Savajic.

How do you mean? Peggy asked.

You will have to wait and see, said Savajic with a big grin on his face. Now let me go and arrange it.

Chapter 43
JIM SMILEY

When Savajic and Peggy arrived at the cottage, Rose was waiting for them. Peggy gave her mother a hug and kissed her on the cheek. My turn, said Savajic, and embraced Rose. I've missed you already, he whispered to her, and Rose whispered, me too.

How is Jim Smiley getting on? Savajic asked Rose.

You can see for yourself when we visit the laundry this afternoon, she replied.

Peggy looked concerned. Has Jimmy been poorly? she asked.

No, said Rose. On the contrary. He's looking great, and went on to explain how Savajic had arranged for a wizard doctor to have a look at Jimmy's arm and leg, and with the help of some very clever wizard magic, Jimmy's arm and leg had returned to normal.

Wow! Peggy said. I can't wait to see him.

He has done us all proud, said Rose. Since his early days with us he has taken his work very seriously and has worked hard with all of his studies. He has passed all of his business management exams with honors and is now a director of the company.

That's great news, said Peggy. He deserves all the success that comes his way.

Chapter 44
BACK TO BUSINESS

A week had flown by, and Peggy was back with Savajic. He had been studying all the footage of the comings and goings at Ravens Claw and had condensed it all down to the relevant parts that were needed to find a way in. There didn't seem to be any special checks being made for entering the headquarters. The wizards made straight for an old fireplace that had seen better days and had passed right through the back wall. The wall was obviously a façade.

That's our way in, he said to Peggy, holding up his hand as he said it. He was expecting her to object to him going.

That's OK, she said in a casual way and gave a little shrug, then added, "I'll be holding your hand this time." Savajic made a grab for her and they both began to laugh.

All the preparations had been made and they were ready to go. Savajic looked Peggy in the eyes and said, I know I don't really have to say this but I'm going to anyway. These wizards are on full alert. We cannot touch anything or make the slightest noise. We've both taken our anti-odor liquid, so that's covered. Now, Peggy, if any sort of alarm sounds off we must leave immediately, and if we have to, we must use our Uncaptivus spell. Under no circumstances can we compromise our position and let them know we're on to them.

Peggy nodded in agreement. I understand, she said.

Then let's get started, said Savajic. They linked arms, and Peggy went into haze.

They left all their equipment behind this time and were wearing tight-fitting Lycra suits that would allow them freedom to move about and not touch anything. They both had two loops on the back of their suits so either one could loop up and make sure they kept in contact with each other and didn't break the haze. This time they landed silently in the middle of the castle ruins. Savajic led the way and motioned for them to move towards the large fireplace.

They both took a deep breath and walked through the wall. On the other side, they were greeted by a brightly lit staircase and they began their descent. At the bottom was a wide passage with a wizard sitting behind a desk at the far end.

They must check visitors in and out, Peggy whispered to Savajic.

He nodded his head in agreement and said, we must risk slipping past without being noticed. Before we try, Peggy, if we get the slightest reaction or sign of danger, we use the Uncaptivus spell. Is that understood?

Yes, she whispered.

They crept quietly down the passage and passed the wizard sitting at the desk and to their relief, there was no reaction. From there they passed through an archway that led them into the heart of the operations room. It was enormous, with banks of screens each showing different government departments. They were literally monitoring the wizard government departments, and Savajic was amazed at how they had managed to compromise government security without being detected.

Savajic's eyes searched for any of the departments that knew about his knowledge of the bridge but couldn't find any. At one end of the room was an enormous screen showing the progress of the bridge. The building was going on at a frantic pace. He suddenly stiffened. Standing in front of the screen was Sealin Belbur. He looked lean and mean, and Savajic knew he was a match for any wizard. He motioned to Peggy and pointed towards him; she had already recognized him because his image was burned into her memory after watching the recording of his murderous attack on Keymol Locke. He was talking into his pager, which told Savajic there must be other rooms, so the complex must be quite large.

Suddenly, Belbur was on the move. Let's follow him, said Savajic. They began to follow close behind. A few minutes later, they were standing in front of an enormous vault door. Belbur drew his wand and pointed at the door and it began to swing slowly open. As soon as the door was fully opened, he walked through and into the vault.

Quick! Savajic whispered, and they followed him in. It was an enormous room that stretched way out of sight. There were what looked like hundreds of wooden crates stacked up. They were stenciled with the word *GOLD* and an identification number.

Suddenly the vault door closed behind them and Belbur walked over to a table and picked something up. He put it on his head and turned around. It was a pair of infrared goggles.

He smiled and said, Welcome to my gold reserve, and as he did, ten wizards with their wands drawn appeared from behind the crates, all wearing the same goggles. Belbur laughed out loud and said, I can't believe you would be so naïve as to think you could gain entry without my knowledge. It doesn't really matter anyway, because you are going nowhere. Now show yourselves before you die.

There was a blinding flash, and Savajic and Peggy were gone.

Safely back in Savajic's workshop, Peggy was hugging Savajic. He was shaking uncontrollably. She had never seen him in this state before, and it proved to her he hadn't gotten over his attack and was pushing himself far above and beyond the call of duty.

When he had stopped shaking they went up to the library, and Peggy organized some hot drinks. They sat for a while, not saying anything, mulling over what they had just seen and witnessed.

Savajic was the first to speak. Peggy, please forgive me for my reactions.

Peggy shrugged her shoulders and said, There's nothing to forgive. You kept it all together when it really mattered. But I beg you to consider this as a warning; you need a lot more rest.

I know, Savajic said. And I promise to listen to my body. But I am so very worried what might happen if I am out of action.

You will never be out of action. With all your magic and planning, and my abilities, we still make a formidable team. And you're forgetting Demodus and the Sword of Destiny and the reception being planned for the Hobgoblins.

You're right, said Savajic. There's just one more thing. Rose doesn't have to know about what's happened, does she?

Peggy began to laugh. Not from me, she won't.

Savajic sipped his hot sweet tea and looked a lot more relaxed. Do you realize what we discovered today, Peggy?

Yes, said Peggy. Sealin Belbur is a very wealthy man with a large amount of gold.

And what do's that lead you to suspect?

Peggy shrugged her shoulders. I don't know what you mean, she replied.

Well, I think I know what the building of the bridge and the Hobgoblin war is all about. GOLD. There are three main concentrations of gold in the world. The Gnome Treasury, the Rainbow Bank, and Fort Knox, and the biggest by far is the Gnome Treasury. Belbur isn't really interested in Greco, he's after the gold.

If he could manage to transfer all of the Gnomes' gold to his vaults, it would make him the richest man in our world and the human world both put together. Can you even begin to realize the power that would give him and the chaos he could cause? I now believe his true plan is to take over both of our worlds—wizards, and humans—all fueled by gold and greed.

What's our next move? Peggy asked. The realization of what lay ahead was beginning to sink in. And without Savajic at her side, she was going to have to be at her best and make use of every scrap of training she had received and all her powers she now possessed.

Savajic picked up on Peggy's thoughts he was staring directly into her eyes. She realized what he was doing and stood up and broke his gaze.

Before you say anything, Savajic, she said, no matter what you have to say to me, there is no way I am going to back out of any of this. Savajic smiled. He was so proud of her. What I was going to say was that we have both got to be at our best, and I suggest we both spend some time going over everything we have learned so far and work on our plans going forward. And over the next few weeks, spend time on the range honing our combat skills. No visits and no interruptions.

That won't be possible, said Peggy. You're forgetting the Dragon Island Swim Championships. I need to be there to make sure the

Belbur brothers don't cheat their way to the trophy, and it's next week, the first week in May.

That's all taken care of, Savajic replied. The brothers aren't going to compete this year, they have dropped out. So it will be a fair contest. Peggy looked disappointed; she would like to have seen her friends again. But still, the holidays would be soon and she could do all the catching up that she wanted.

Chapter 45

Devastating News from Black Eagle

Saturday the 9th of May, 2016, would be etched on Peggy's heart for the rest of her life. That evening at dinner came the devastating news that in the Dragon Island Swim, six students had lost their lives. Three from White Eagle and three from Black Eagle. The three from Black Eagle were Helda Scelda, Lilly Wong, and Charlie Manders. When Savajic broke the news to Peggy she stood up and screamed and screamed and screamed some more and then passed out and fell to the floor.

When Peggy came to she was lying in bed. Savajic had got her there and had given her a sleeping potion, then he had sent Henry to pick up Rose so she could be next to her when she woke up from her sleep. Rose was holding Peggy's hand and looking at her and when she opened her eyes, she leaned over and kissed her.

Savajic told me what happened to your friends, and I am so sorry. Peggy's chest was heaving and she was sobbing quietly. Take your time and let the hurt out, I'm not going to leave your side.

Peggy's lips moved. Is Owen all right?

Yes, said Rose. He wasn't taking part this year so he wasn't involved. The headmaster has asked Savajic to go to Black Eagle and try to make some sort of sense to it all, and he has already gone.

Will you stay with me tonight? Peggy asked.

Of course, said Rose. We will have a night together.

Peggy squeezed Rose's hand. We were all so very close. The girls were like sisters rather than just friends, and Charlie was my first love. I broke it off with him because I was afraid I would hurt him. I will regret that decision for the rest of my life. I would give anything just to see him again, just for a few moments.

Savajic arrived back home the following lunchtime and the three of them sat around the table on the terrace. He gave them a picture of what had happened and said the parents of all the victims had been contacted and were visiting Black Eagle the following day to sort out their individual family arrangements. Peggy was shaking her head. It doesn't make any kind of sense. Six champion swimmers all getting into trouble at the same time? How could it be possible?

Savajic said they didn't make any mistakes or misjudgments, the trouble came to them.

The race was being fiercely contested and they were swimming the final leg when a twenty-meter vortex appeared from nowhere and dragged them all down to the bottom of the lake. They were down there for about ten minutes and then the vortex disappeared, and slowly the bodies had floated back up to the surface of the lake. By that time, it was too late to save them. Army divers have searched the bottom of the lake but could find no evidence to support such an occurrence. I'm afraid that at this moment in time, it remains a mystery.

What is Owen going to do now? Peggy asked. He must be devastated. Lilly meant everything to him.

He intends to wait at Black Eagle and meet with Lilly's father. As you probably know, she lost her mother when she was quite young, and she was an only child. Owen wishes to tell her father how close he was to her and try to help console him. Then he intends to end his studies and come back home. At this moment, he is feeling very bitter.

Is this another attempt to distract us from the bridge? Peggy fired the question at Savajic and took him by surprise.

What do you mean? he asked, looking at her.

Well, said Peggy, I can't help wondering why shortly after the episode at Ravens Claw, with Belbur wondering who may be onto him, why his sons suddenly pulled out of the race. It was an ideal time and place for a major distraction. A lot of parents are going to be demanding answers, aren't they? With all your magic, Savajic, is it possible for you to create such a vortex?

He thought for a moment and said, Yes, it is. But are you seriously suggesting Belbur would murder six innocent students? Surely not.

I am doing just that, replied Peggy. Remember, it was you who told me not to underestimate Belbur, and never be surprised at the lengths he would go to achieve his goal.

Savajic's mind was racing. He sat with his eyes closed, concentrating hard, trying to figure out how it was done. He opened his eyes and said, It is not too hard to spin a body of water, but to create a vortex of that scale and speed it would take three or maybe even four wizards. They would have to be equally spaced in a circle, each one feeding their power simultaneously and accelerating each other's magic, and then as soon as the right speed was obtained, the vortex would appear and drag down anything in its path.

The worrying thing is that the wizards performing such a vile deed would have to be the parents of some of our students, and a major worry is how Belbur has gained the power to make them stoop so low. I will have to report our suspicions to Enzebadier so if you will excuse me, I will talk to him in the library.

Chapter 46
BACK AT GRECO

Demodus had been busy with the building of the outer city defenses. They were mostly built and in place, and the help he had from the wizard planners had been an enormous advantage in his preparations. He once again called upon Hawcas to ask his family and friends to transport all the equipment from his kingdom to Greco, and now everything was there. He paid off all the humans the money he had promised them, and now they would all wake up back at home, not knowing where they had been but all of them very happy and considerably richer.

The final task for the soldiers had been to lay explosives so that when Demodus finally left his kingdom, it would be sealed forever. Demodus thanked Hawcas and his family, and he asked Hawcas for one final mission. He was about to say good-bye to the Scaleygills and to his underground kingdom. He was wearing his leopard skin scabbard and the Sword of Destiny and he climbed up onto Hawcas and said, Let's go, my friend.

Hawcas circled and landed in the clearing by the cave and settled down. I'll get back as soon as I have finalized a bit of unfinished business, Demodus said to Hawcas, and headed off towards Furnusabal and his fire pit.

When he arrived, Furnusabal was sitting in his black granite seat. Welcome, Demodus! he roared. Demodus walked up to him, drew his sword, and plunged it into his heart. Fernusabal's eyes bulged out and he held his chest as Demodus withdrew the sword. Why? He was choking as his foul blood flowed from his hideous mouth.

Why? Demodus let out a loud roar and said, That is for my wife and son, and all of my people Kanzil murdered while my back was turned. Now it's his turn to lose his family. Did you really think I didn't know why you were here? You wanted my sword and now you have it. Through your evil heart! He sheathed his sword and heaved Furnusabal up out of his seat, carried him over to his fire pit and threw him in. His fire imps jumped in after him. Demodus looked down into the pit and pointed his sword. Seal! he commanded, and the fire pit disappeared without a trace.

Demodus had detonated the explosive charges and was on his way back to Greco. Hawcas circled and landed outside the city gates and Demodus jumped off his back. This is our final good-bye, said Demodus, and hugged Hawcas around his massive neck. You have been the best and most faithful friend a man could ever have, and I will never be able to thank you enough for what you and your family have done for me and my family. Now go, my friend, and live in peace. We will never meet again. Hawcas took to the sky and circled above three times in a salute to his master, then he disappeared high into the sky, gone forever. As he disappeared, Demodus felt a part of himself had disappeared with him too.

Demodus now knew there was no turning back. He shook himself and began barking out orders. He was going to make sure everything would be ready for when the Hobgoblins mounted their assault on Greco.

He had been given a large room where he kept his plans and had spent long hours going over the information Savajic managed to obtain from Princess Sheiklin, giving all the coordinates of the Hobgoblin strongholds. In the near future, they would be set into the drones' computers and sent on their way to destroy their targets, and on his signal, Princess Sheiklin would move all of the goblins away to safety.

Chapter 47
Owen Returns Home

Henry brought the car to a halt and Owen got out. Peggy and Savajic were waiting to welcome him home. They were in for quite a shock. Gone was the smile and the hug for Peggy. Instead there was a curt, Peggy, Father, and he was on his way up the steps.

Peggy was about to say something to him but Savajic put his finger to his mouth and said, Shush.

Peggy glared at him and said, He's not the only one to lose a loved one, is he?

I beg you to give him some time to mourn. Remember how you felt when you learned about Charlie. He has no mother to comfort him and it will take all our love to bring him back to us.

I'm sorry, Peggy said, but I was so looking forward to holding him close. You know how much I love him and I miss him all the time we are apart.

I know, Savajic said. And we must let him know just that, but it's going to take time and patience. When he is eventually ready, I am sure he will unload all his feelings to you.

It took a full week for Owen to unleash his feelings. Peggy was in the pool when Owen came down. She got out immediately, and Owen came to her. He threw his arms around her and said, I'm so sorry, and began to sob. Peggy clung to him and began to sob with him. Neither would let go, for they were lost in an endless wave of grief.

Peggy broke the spell. Let's get these monsters, she said with a venom that surprised both of them. It was the first time Peggy had ever felt this kind of hatred, and she knew revenge was the only thing that would set them both free to get on with their lives. They sat down and held hands. Peggy looked into Owen's eyes. She could see the hurt, and then she saw something else; a steel-hard stare told her he wanted to get even no matter what the cost.

Owen, welcome back, she said. Now let's go and tell Savajic we are ready for business.

Savajic was in his workshop when Peggy and Owen found him. Come in, he said, without looking up. He knew his son was ready to take his place in the field and was preparing a transference pendant for him. Sit down, Owen, he said, motioning over to his chair. We need to talk.

Owen sat down and looked up at his father. I'm sorry, he said, but I really thought Lilly and I were going to spend the rest of our lives together. It felt as bad as losing Mother all over again. Why do things like this have to happen?

Savajic took a deep breath and said, Unfortunately, there is much evil in our world at the present time. And it looks like a major part of cleaning it up is going to rest on our shoulders. Owen, I have prepared a transference pendant for you to wear and use. Peggy and I will teach you how to use it and how to work out coordinates. Then I will prepare you for the Uncaptivus spell. So let's get started right away.

One week later, Owen was working the transference pendant with ease, and Savajic had implanted a small chip of stone from his workshop wall into his skin behind his ear. When Savajic was satisfied Owen had mastered both of the spells, he said they were all going to spend time on the range so they could work on their speed and skills. That evening after dinner, Savajic announced he was no longer going to work in the field. From now on it's going to be down to both of you to be my eyes and ears. Owen, I want you to follow Peggy's lead. There is so much you have to learn from what we have both been working on while you were at Black Eagle. You will now realize why Peggy cut short her schoolwork to join me in our fight against Sealin Belbur and his Death Riders.

Over the next few weeks, Peggy and Owen entered into an entirely different kind of relationship than they had been used to in the past. Owen had always been the teacher, and he had given his time willingly to help Peggy learn correctly many of the basic magic skills she had eventually mastered. Now he realized their roles had been reversed, and Peggy was now the teacher. He was both amazed and thrilled by how much her magical powers had increased, and how confident she was. She seemed to have matured ten years in as many months. It also spoke volumes of Savajic's ability to bring out the very best in Peggy.

The partnership they formed was amazing. They became telepathic with each other to such an extent they could communicate to each other without actually speaking, and the more they practiced, the better they got. They spent hours in different rooms of the house testing each other by writing down what came into their heads and comparing each other's notes later, and they had become almost word perfect.

It gave great satisfaction to Savajic to see them both blossom into two mature wizards and an unbreakable partnership that would prove to be a challenge to anyone getting in their way.

Chapter 48
ALARMING NEWS

Savajic had called Peggy and Owen into his study. I have had some very disturbing news from Professor Gellit. Apparently, the meteor pulling Baldric Zealotte towards Earth has somehow begun to accelerate its speed, and now his calculations as to the time of arrival have drastically altered. He has asked us to go and visit him as soon as possible so he can go over all the different permutations he's been working on. I suggest we get ourselves ready and get there post haste.

When they arrived at Black Eagle, they made their way to the headmaster's rooms. Please come in, said Professor Ableman, and when they entered, Professor Gellit was waiting for them.

Thank you for coming so promptly, he said. We really do need to get our heads together on this one because it certainly has me puzzled. Let me explain. Meteors travelling through space, in general, have a constant speed that varies very little. But for some unexplained reason, this meteor has accelerated its speed by some fifty percent. Very, very strange, to say the least.

Peggy spoke up first. Do you think Kanzil has anything to do with it? After all, he has a vested interest in getting Zealotte back to Earth and must be getting impatient with the waiting.

They all turned and looked at her. Professor Gellit said, it is more than likely Kanzil could be using his gravitational powers to help it on its way. He has to be painted into this picture; to ignore him would be a grave mistake. Well done, Peggy. I think by putting Kanzil into the equation I can adjust my speed calculations. By the by, I am almost certain Professor Snide at White Eagle will not be able to work out the new speed of the meteor; he doesn't have the knowledge. He was one of my pupils, but limited. I think this will give us an advantage, and I imagine it will throw them into turmoil. In the meantime, please give me some time to recalculate the speed. And I would suggest that any plans you might have, to seriously consider bringing them forward.

Savajic stood up and said, Peggy, Owen, we need to get back and start making our plans. Professor Gellit, if you would furnish the headmaster with the new speed and estimated time of arrival, he will pass them on to me. Thank you both for your time, we must go. They set their coordinates and disappeared. When they got back, Savajic suggested they have lunch and then spend the afternoon in his study and make out a list of things to do.

Chapter 49

THE RAGE OF SEALIN BELBUR

It was a pity the cameras set up by Peggy at Ravens Claw Castle had self-destructed. They would have been able to watch the flurry of activity suddenly going on. Word of the sudden change in speed of the meteor pulling Zealotte back to Earth had been transmitted to Sealin Belbur. He had ordered a meeting of all his main players and they were arriving from all directions.

As the last of the wizards arrived, the meeting got under way. They sat around a thirty-seat oblong highly polished table in a private room Sealin had built for his briefings. He stood up and began. It seems we may have a problem. The meteor pulling the time bubble with Baldric Zealotte trapped inside has gained speed. This means our plans have to be revised and brought forward; by how much, I'm not certain. But I'm sure Professor Snide will tell us. Professor Snide, if you will enlighten us, said Sealin, and sat down.

Professor Snide slowly stood up and nervously straightened his robe. We have a situation that is unprecedented. Meteors travel through space at a constant speed, thus giving us the means of tracking them and predicting their predetermined destinations. But now with this meteor, we have no means of saying precisely when it will pass by Earth. Because of this, I have no idea how much sooner it will arrive.

Sealin jumped to his feet and banged the table. What do you mean you don't know?

I-I-I just don't know, stammered Professor Snide.

Sealin drew his wand and shouted, You useless fool! There was a blinding flash from his wand and Professor Snide fell across the table, dead. Am I surrounded by idiots? he screamed. All the wizards were looking down at the table, afraid of catching the crazed stare of their leader.

This alters everything, said Sealin. The best laid plans and all that rubbish. This brought a lot of nodding in agreement from the wizards, all desperately trying to get in line with him.

Has anyone got a suggestion? he snapped.

One of the younger wizards stood up and said, Is it possible Professor Gellit would know? Because I think I'm right in saying Professor Snide was a pupil of Professor Gellit, and he probably has much more knowledge about these things. But how we would be able to get to him I have no idea.

That's good thinking, said Sealin. Certainly gives me food for thought. I need time to think this one through. He stood up and said, Meeting over. I'll contact you all when I have a plan.

Chapter 50
KANZIL TAKES CONTROL

When Fernusabal's dead body fell down into the magma, Kanzil knew immediately that Demodus was responsible for his death, because the only thing on Earth that could kill him was the sword he himself had fashioned from the magma. The Sword of Destiny—and Demodus possessed it.

His angry reactions were immediately felt on Earth; two severe earthquakes and three volcano eruptions followed in quick succession. Once again, the human race would suffer his evil violence.

As his anger settled down, he realized he would have more than enough time to settle his account with Demodus, but for now he must put all his effort into the task ahead. He had so far managed to influence the speed of the meteor, but that was not his main objective. As soon as the meteor was well into his gravitational power, he would try to detach the time bubble and bring it down to earth and guide it to the landing place of his choice. His choice of landing had been carefully chosen; it was in the center of a long extinct and dormant volcano on an uninhabited island. He had waited a long time to see Zealotte again, and didn't want anyone else to witness his return. He knew if he could detach the time bubble and bring it down safely, he could then reverse his gravitational pull on the meteor and send it safely on its way back into space. He also knew any prying eyes that were following the path of the meteor would be fixed on the meteor and they would temporarily lose sight of the time bubble. By the time they realized what had happened he would have landed the time bubble safely, it would have opened, and he would have Zealotte all to himself.

Kanzil had plans for Zealotte. His first move would be to let Sealin Belbur know where he could find and eliminate Zealotte. Kanzil had entered Sealin Belbur's mind many years ago and turned him into the evil monster he was today, so it would be easy to point him in the right direction. Kanzil knew very well that Belbur was no match for Zealotte and his Black Magic, and Zealotte would dispatch him to the history books before he realized what happened to him, and from there on Zealotte would take control of the Black Watch and the Death Riders. And as soon as that had been achieved, he would contact Petrid and mobilize the Hobgoblins. From there he would lead them across the bridge and attack the Gnomes and gain possession of the Sword of Destiny, then return it to him, where it belonged. After that he could do whatever he wished, because it would only be a matter of time when, without the power of the sword, someone, somewhere, would kill him, and then he would at long last have his soul. Then he would turn his attention to Demodus, who would not have the protection of the sword and he would pay the price for killing Furnusabal.

Chapter 51
Sealin Has a Capture Plan

Sealin had an ace up his sleeve; the four wizards that had created the vortex in the lake at Black Eagle were still there hiding in the forest, and they were under Sealin's strict instructions to wait for any further orders he may give them. Four cold-blooded murderers of innocent students who were more than keen to follow his orders. Sealin had a wicked smirk on his face. It had been a master stroke to leave the Death Riders concealed at Black Eagle, and no one would ever suspect a kidnap was about to take place; he held all the aces.

Savajic had asked Peggy to go to Black Eagle and visit the headmaster and see if there was anything at all he or she could do to help with the ongoing investigation into the lake tragedy.

Of course I'll go, she said. Would you mind if I ask Owen to come with me?

By all means, Savajic replied. If he feels up to it.

Owen didn't have any second thoughts when Peggy asked him. Try and keep me away, he said.

Then that's a go, said Peggy. Let's get started.

The headmaster was more than pleased to see them both when they arrived. Come in, please, and take a seat. Would you like something to drink? he said. They both declined his offer. The past week has been a very dark chapter in Black Eagle's history, he began.

And worst of all, I am convinced that four wizards were involved in creating the vortex that killed our students, which in turn probably means four of the visiting families were involved. Professor Crie has taken charge of a search party to scour the school grounds and see if any wizards stayed behind in all the confusion in the aftermath of the tragedy. It has turned out to be an unfruitful search. But I for one am not convinced they are not somewhere in hiding, waiting to strike again. How right he was because as he spoke, Belbur was contacting the four wizards who were hiding out in the forest. The message was to position themselves around the forbidden library, concealed under a PARTO spell, and wait for Professor Gellit to appear. As soon as he was a safe distance from the building they would stun him and capture him, and then report back.

Headmaster, what would you like us to do to help? Peggy asked.

The headmaster stood up and paced the room, stroking his beard. He stopped and said, Owen, if you were hiding out, what would you do?

I'd set up a 360-degree PARTO spell somewhere out of the way, just off a well-used path and hide there. That way I could watch what was going on without being detected. Owen gave his answer in an instant.

Precisely! exclaimed the headmaster. And if a search party came into the area, they would simply keep their position and watch as they passed by.

He looked at Peggy and said, How good have your senses improved since we last met?

They are very strong now, she said in answer to his question. Why?

If you and Owen took all the well-trodden paths in haze, do you think you might sense the whereabouts of someone hiding behind a PARTO spell?

I can do much better than that, Peggy said. Let me demonstrate. Owen, would you go and stand by the headmaster's bookshelves and throw a PARTO spell?

No problem, replied Owen, and he walked over to the bookshelves, turned and faced them, and drew his wand. His lips moved and he disappeared.

Excellent! said the headmaster, and turned to Peggy. What now?

Peggy withdrew her hand from her pocket. She was holding Savajic's anti-façade baton. She pointed it at the bookshelves and squeezed the center section. Immediately, Owen came into view, and when she loosened her grip, he disappeared again.

The headmaster was amazed. What have you got there? he asked.

It belongs to Savajic. It's an anti-façade baton he invented, and the one we used to record the progress on the bridge.

We are so fortunate to have someone with Savajic's inventive magic genius on our side, said the headmaster.

I agree, Peggy echoed.

Owen lifted the PARTO spell and came back into view. What's our next move? he asked.

The headmaster slowly shook his head in a kind of disbelief. What next, indeed, he said.

Peggy took it up. This is what I suggest; see what you think. Owen and I will travel the main routes in haze, using the baton, and if we see anyone hiding, they won't know we have seen them. We will stun them and leave them under their PARTO spell and carry on searching, then we can go back for them later. We keep moving, just in case there are more of them. From what you have said, Headmaster, there should be at least four.

Well, that is my theory, the headmaster said. I'm reasonably certain there would be four.

Chapter 52
Sweet Revenge

They had decided to do a "Round Robin" trip, starting at the forbidden library. It turned out to be the right choice. The first wizard came into view twenty yards away from the building. Peggy nodded at Owen and pointed down to a spot behind the wizard, who was sitting on the ground with his eyes fixed on the building. They landed quietly behind him, and Peggy put him out of action. Owen bound and gagged him.

One hour later they had four wizards lined up in front of them and they were out of haze, asking questions. Let's start with the vortex, said Peggy. She pointed her wand at the chest of one of the wizards. You, did you create the vortex in the lake? You'd better start talking.

The wizard laughed at her. What makes you think I'm going to talk to a slip of a girl? Peggy's eyes flared and the wizard's chest began to smoke.

Let's apply a bit of heat, she growled. Now I'll ask you again; did you create the vortex in the lake? I suggest this time we have the truth.

Yes, stammered the wizard. We all did it together. We had no choice! Sealin Belbur said he would kill our families if we didn't follow his instructions to the letter.

Liar! shouted Owen. You're all dirty rotten Death Riders and you're proud to be. You're murderous cowards, the four of you. You are all responsible for the deaths of the ones we loved and others, and you're going to pay for it!

One of the wizards spoke up. He had a sickly smirk on his face. You talk big when you're talking to someone with his hands tied behind his back, but if they weren't, would you still be as brave? I don't think so.

Peggy whispered to Owen, Can you handle the one on your right with a FLECTA spell?

Yes, no problem, he answered.

OK then, leave the other three to me. Now if you would, go and untie one of them and come back and get ready to do battle.

Owen moved quickly. He walked over and untied one of the wizards and moved back into position, facing the four.

Now you, Peggy said in a calm and menacing voice, pointing at the wizard Owen had just released. Untie the others. The wizard wasted no time and went about his task untying the others.

Done, he said.

Good, said Peggy. Now check your wands. They all looked down and checked that their wands were ready to draw and looked up and nodded to her. When you're ready, she said. Let's see how good you murderers are in a fair fight.

The wizards looked at each other in bewilderment. They couldn't believe these two crazy students were giving them the chance to kill them. How stupid could they get? The four Death Riders squared up against Peggy and Owen and drew as one, and their wands flashed. Peggy and Owen had waited until the wands were out and pointing, watching for their mouths to move, and at the first twitch their wands responded and in a flash. Four Death Riders lay dead, killed by their own spells. Peggy and Owen looked at each other and nodded. Justice had been done. It wouldn't bring back their loved ones but at least they had been avenged.

We have to finish the job now, Peggy said. We need to dispose of the bodies.

How are we going to do that without someone finding out? Owen asked.

I know just the place, she said with a smile on her face. Being as they like to make a good vortex. Let's put them into one that has no return. They set about securing the wizards to their boards and then began floating them down towards the Death Swamp. As they arrived there they could smell the evil; it was horrible.

Let them go, said Peggy, and slowly the wizards drifted towards the Worm Hole and they were sucked down into oblivion. Peggy shivered; it was a frightening sight. Let's get back to the headmaster, she said, and off they flew.

Chapter 53
ZEALOTTE HAS LANDED

Peggy and Owen were back with the headmaster and she was reporting to him in detail what had happened. The professor was seated behind his desk, leaning forward, with his head resting in his hands. His mind was digesting what he had just been told. He didn't really condone what had happened; he thought they would hopefully locate the wizards and report back with their positions. He never dreamt they would seek them out and eliminate them. Then again, they had given the wizards the opportunity to surrender and not fight, which they had obviously declined, thinking they could overcome and kill the two young students. He sat in silence for a few minutes, a little confused by his own argument. Then he looked up and leaned back in his chair and gazed across the room at Peggy and Owen. He saw before him two brave, cool, calm, and collected young wizards with a combined power that was awesome. In a sense, it was frightening, and yet really rather reassuring.

He stood up and said, I think perhaps we should all go over to the forbidden library and check to see if Professor Gellit is all right, don't you?

They both nodded. Good idea, said Owen. When they arrived at the library, the professor was waiting for them and welcomed them. Headmaster, this is very good timing because I was about to contact you. Please come in and take a look at my findings, he said, finding it hard to conceal the excitement in his voice.

That morning the meteor had suddenly veered away from Earth. It didn't make sense, and Professor Gellit couldn't put forward any logical explanation for its sudden erratic path. After two hours of intense brainstorming, the professor had suddenly clapped his hands together. "GOT IT!" he'd shouted.

The professor led them up into the observatory where they sat down around his desk, and the professor began to explain to them the meteor's erratic path change. For hours, I've been trying to make sense of it, and then I remembered something Peggy had said. And that was, it would be a mistake to leave Kanzil out of the equation, with his power over the Earth's gravitational pull. Now with this in mind, I calculated the distance from Earth the meteor was when it changed direction, and if at that precise moment the time bubble with Zealotte inside had been detached and pulled down to Earth, it would mean as we talk that Zealotte is back with us on Earth. I do have a rough idea of where he would have come down but it would be, in my opinion, quite fruitless to search for him because he will be long gone by now.

What now? said Professor Ableman, stroking his beard.

Well, replied Professor Gellit, astronomically there isn't much more I can help you with. Except to say that Zealotte has landed. I would suggest you take my findings and present them to Savajic and see what he makes of it all. The professor gave Owen his findings and they all parted.

The time bubble had indeed found its target and landed in the center of the dead crater, and as soon as it touched the ground it opened. Zealotte stretched out his arms and took in a deep gulp of the oxygen-rich atmosphere Earth provided. At last! he shouted. I'm back! And now they will pay the price for what they did to me!

There was a loud rumbling and the ground shook, and over the rim of the volcano came a massive figure of a man made of fire. It was Kanzil. Welcome back, Zealotte! he roared, and Zealotte fell to his knees.

Thank you, master! he screamed. Thank you for bringing me back! Kanzil spoke. I want you to listen carefully to what I have to say, and follow my instructions to the letter. You will not realize it, but you have been away for about two thousand years and in time, many changes have occurred. The world has changed in so many ways you will not recognize most of it as it is today. So, this is what I want you to do. You will dress like all the other wizards and mingle with them and observe; you will not display any of your powers to anyone. No one must have any inclination of who you are. Then when the time is right, you will show your true identity. There are those who know you are on your way back to Earth and have strict instructions to kill you on sight, but more of later.

Over the next few weeks, I will show you what is happening in today's wizard world. I am sure you will like what I show you. Now I will transport you to a dwelling where it is safe for you to stay.

Zealotte was suddenly standing in the bedroom of a small house in the wizard town of Ozmil, and lying on the bed was a change of clothes. A voice came into Zealotte's head, it was Kanzil. *"Change into the clothes I have provided. There is money in your coat pocket. Go into town and eat a meal and observe your surroundings. I will contact you tomorrow and bring you up to date. Once again, make sure you keep your wand in your belt. I do not want any slip-ups."* The voice disappeared from Zealotte's head and he began to change his clothes.

As Zealotte walked around the busy little town, he couldn't help noticing the wizards were no longer using broomsticks to travel about, but they were standing on some strange sort of flat wooden platform. And although he could easily understand what they were saying, the language sounded unfamiliar.

He found a quiet inn and sat down and ordered a meal. The food was good and the ale very pleasant, and when he was finished, he paid the innkeeper and thanked him and left. He walked around, observing the wizards as they went about their daily business, and as he walked around a smile came on his face. He realized he had just eaten his first meal for the best part of two thousand years. He decided to walk around and look in the various shop windows and see what sort of things were being sold and then go back to his house and while away the time and see what Kanzil had in store for him in the morning.

Chapter 54

PROFESSOR GELLIT'S PAPERS

Peggy and Owen were back with Savajic. They were all seated in his study, and Owen had passed Professor Gellit's papers to him and had given him a full account of what the professor told them. Savajic studied them and put them down on his desk. He was pacing the room in deep thought. Peggy and Owen sat quietly, watching him.

Suddenly Peggy blurted out, "There's something else."

Savajic stopped dead in his tracks. Something else? he echoed. What?

Peggy told him in detail about the four wizards they had captured outside the forbidden library, and that they had confessed to the murder of the six students in the lake. She told him they were all killed and they had disposed of them in the Worm Hole. Unfortunately, she also told him they had lined them up and used a Flecta spell to make them kill themselves.

You did what? You used a Flecta spell against four hardened killers? How stupid can you get? he was shaking with temper.

Owen stood up and glared at his father. Their eyes met in a cold, hard stare as they faced each other. It wasn't stupid, he growled. It was personal, and I'd do it again in a heartbeat.

Peggy broke the tension. She just simply said, And how stupid was it to go to Ravens Claw Castle on your own and nearly get yourself killed?

Savajic threw his hands up in the air and sat down heavily in his chair. Owen turned to Peggy. What do you mean, nearly got himself killed? And what's Ravens Claw Castle?

Peggy gestured over to Savajic and said, Ask your father.

Savajic looked over to Peggy and said, You promised to keep the incident at Ravens Claw between the two of us. You've broken your word.

Peggy was just as fired up as Owen and responded with, Yes, I did, but that was before you decided to move the goal posts. What's good for the goose is good for the gander. Lilly was the world to Owen, as was Charlie to me. We did what we felt we needed to do. We gave these evil murderers a chance because we wanted to wipe the sickly grins off their faces. It may have been reckless, but we didn't want to jump into the same filthy trough as them. We went in clean and we came out clean, and hopefully we can now both move on.

Savajic had calmed down and said he was sorry for his outburst, then said, Do you honestly think I love you two any less? The Death Riders are determined killers. They are highly trained and will take no prisoners. You cannot afford to give them any kind of advantage. The thought of losing you both makes my blood run cold. But through it all, a massive positive has been gained because can you imagine what this will do to Sealin Belbur when he can't contact his four Death Riders. He will have no idea as to what has happened, and hopefully no way of finding out. And I genuinely believe he will begin to unravel. Now please, let us draw a line under all of this and concentrate on the problem of Zealotte. And, Owen, I promise I will tell you all about Ravens Claw at dinner tonight.

Before we go, Peggy said to Savajic, if Zealotte is back, what do you think his first move will be?

If Kanzil has brought him back then he will surely have told him of Sealin Belbur's plans and will have given him a hiding place, and from there I think Zealotte will seek out Belbur and try to eliminate him. Yes, I think the next few days will be quite exciting.

Chapter 55
KANZIL'S MESSENGER

Zealotte was up early and had bathed and dressed and was anxiously waiting for Kanzil to make contact with him. He didn't have to wait long. There was a knock on the door, and Zealotte jumped to his feet and went over. Who's there? he asked.

I've been sent by Kanzil, came the answer.

Zealotte slowly opened the door with one hand on the door and his other hand was on his wand. When he opened the door, standing there was an ordinary-looking wizard. My name is Mibbs, he said. May I come in?

Zealotte stepped aside and gestured towards a table with two chairs. Please come in and sit with me, he said.

They both sat down facing each other across the table and Mibbs began by saying he was Kanzil's messenger, and his mission was to show him everything that was currently happening. Let us begin with Sealin Belbur. He is a very powerful and ruthless wizard, and he has taken on the role of leader of the Black Watch and has reformed the Death Riders. It is now common knowledge that you were heading back towards Earth and had a good chance landing back in the wizard world, and Sealin Belbur has used your name to rally the Black Watch and all of its members together again.

Baldric, I want you to look over to the wall and I will show you what he has planned for the future. The wall lit up with a picture of the bridge stretching out over the worm fields and all of the activity going on with the building work.

Mibbs began, As you know, before Goodrick the Elder tricked you and sent you spinning out into space, your control center was in Hobgoblin territory and you had formed an alliance with the Hobgoblins and were working on a plan to attack Greco and overthrow the Gnomes and use Greco as your base and to repay the Hobgoblins with Gnome gold.

That is correct, Zealotte said.

Sealin Belbur somehow found out what your plan was and is using it to fulfil his own plans. And this is what he is planning. He has no intention of giving the Hobgoblins anything but death. As soon as the bridge is completed, he will give the signal for the Hobgoblins to attack Greco; but unlike you, he will not be leading them, and after they have defeated the Gnomes he will convince them to go home, while he and the Death Riders locate the gold and then ship it over to them across the bridge.

The bridge is twenty miles long, and will quite easily hold all of the Hobgoblin army. As soon as they are all a safe distance on their way, he will collapse the bridge and leave it to the Snack Worms to do the rest. Then this is how his plan differs from yours, Baldric. He intends to use the Gnome gold to corrupt the wizard world and take control by stealth. It has nothing to do with him being afraid of a fight because he is a natural killer who has murdered any wizard that has opposed him so far, and he is as powerful as any known wizard. He has, however, reasoned it is better to corrupt the wizard world and use their various skills to his advantage rather than kill them out of hand.

Zealotte was nodding his head in agreement. He sounds like someone who is very clever and calculating, and of course, very dangerous. I will have to tread around him with great caution.

Mibbs took it up again and the picture on the wall changed to Ravens Claw Castle. This is the center of Sealin Belbur's operations. Everything that happens has to pass through here, and he has already amassed a large fortune in gold, which he keeps in a well-guarded vault below the castle.

This is what the next few days have in store for you. Kanzil will arrange for Sealin Belbur to find out where you are living, but he has no idea what you look like. So until you reveal yourself, he will be alert and on edge and very dangerous. It will be entirely up to you how much of a chance you give him before you kill him. But kill him you will.

After he is dead, you will be able to use your wand whenever you feel the need. Kanzil wants you to leave Belbur's body in a public place but leave no clue as to who killed him, and then you will go to Ravens Claw Castle and take charge. On arrival, you will announce yourself and tell them Sealin Belbur is dead. Here are the names and pictures of Sealin Belbur and his staff at Ravens Claw; memorize them. I will leave them there for the rest of the day. When I leave, I suggest you go out of town and practice your combat spells in preparation for your meeting with Sealin Belbur.

Zealotte laughed out loud. Do you honestly think he could beat me? He had a nasty sneer on his face.

Yes, I do, replied Mibbs. You let your arrogance get the better of you before with Goodrick the Elder. Have you learned nothing?

Zealotte felt a rage swell up inside him but he knew better than to argue with Kanzil's messenger.

Mibbs stood up and said, Kanzil will keep you up to date with messages in your head, so stay alert, and then he left.

Zealotte lay down on the bed and closed his eyes. Nobody talked to him like Mibbs had and got away with it. But as Kanzil's messenger, he had to let it ride. *Right, Belbur,* he mused. *Come and show me what you've got. I will have you on your knees before me begging for mercy before I kill you. You are nothing but a pretender.*

Chapter 56

BELBUR RECEIVES A MESSAGE

The atmosphere at Ravens Claw Castle had the wizards choking with fear. Sealin Belbur had had no contact with the four wizards at Black Eagle and was almost spitting blood. All of his staff were afraid to even look him in the eye for fear of what he might do. He had called a meeting, and the wizards were arriving post haste. One by one they were taking their seats around Sealin's table, and as soon as the last seat was filled, Sealin began.

I am very disturbed by my loss of contact with four of our Death Riders I had planted inside of Black Eagle's grounds. They were working on a plan to kidnap Professor Gellit and bring him here, but we have had no contact with them for thirty-six hours.

May I speak? A tall, well-built wizard stood up. It was Thomas Clinck, a wizard who worked for Semach Siege in the miniature engineering department specializing in miniature information-gathering drones.

Welcome, Thomas, Sealin said. He was desperate for any information that might help. Please speak up, you have the floor.

As you know, I work in the police department, and my job is gathering information using the latest miniature drones. After our last meeting here, I took it upon myself to send two 'fly on the wall' spy drones into the observatory at Black Eagle to gather as much information on Professor Gellit as I could, and see what progress, if any, he was making with the meteor. I didn't bother you with what I was doing, Sealin, in case nothing became of it. But I received them back shortly before you called this meeting and I have here some extremely important information for you.

First, may I please start off with some bad and disturbing news, and that is, our four fellow wizards at Black Eagle are all dead. There was a loud gasp all around the table.

How did it happen? Sealin asked, looking quite shaken.

I'm not quite sure, but my drones were in place when Professor Gellit had a visit from the headmaster and two of his students. They told him four wizards had been discovered hiding out around the forbidden library and they had fought a losing battle and were killed. I'm sorry to bring you sad news, Sealin, but what I also found out makes that fade into insignificance. While Professor Gellit was monitoring the meteor that is pulling back Baldric Zealotte, it suddenly shot off on a tangent away from Earth. The professor has reasoned that because of Zealotte's links with Kanzil, Kanzil has used his power over gravity and pulled the time bubble down to Earth and sent the meteor back out into space, and Zealotte is indeed back on Earth and has gone into hiding.

It is all here in my report for your perusal, Sealin. He walked up to the top of the table and laid it down in front of Sealin Belbur and walked back to his seat. The silence was deafening.

It was suddenly broken by a wizard who asked, does anyone know what Baldric Zealotte looks like?

Sealin had gathered his thoughts together and was pondering that very question. *What indeed does he looks like,* he thought. There were no pictures or paintings or anything that would give them the smallest of clues. So, what now?

Sealin stood up and said, I know this is a lot to take on board, but if indeed Zealotte is back, he will be making contact with us very shortly. So be alert, and if anyone is contacted by him, let me know immediately. And remember, he doesn't know who we are, either.

That night Sealin lay in bed, desperately trying to think of his next move. He reasoned Zealotte could possibly seek refuge in Hobgoblin territory and it may be wise to go and pay Petrid a visit to see if he has any knowledge of Zealotte's whereabouts.

Suddenly, he sat bolt upright. A clear voice in his head said, *"Greetings, Sealin."*

Who are you? Sealin said in a startled voice.

"That is irrelevant," said the voice. *"Look over to your right and you will discover the whereabouts of Baldric Zealotte. Good-bye."* The voice disappeared as quickly as it had come.

Sealin looked over to his right and the wall had changed to a screen showing a map of Ozmil Town and a marker pointing to a house. At the bottom were the words: this is where you will find Baldric Zealotte. Sealin was amazed by what he was looking at but even so, he was memorizing the house's position. He lay back on the bed and fell asleep.

The next morning, Sealin was up early and ready to go, and over breakfast decided to take a visit to the bridge because now that he knew the whereabouts of Zealotte, he would take his time dealing with him and not go rushing in without a plan of action. His army training had taught him that.

When he arrived at the bridge, Ivor Craktit was waiting to welcome him and said, Greetings, Sealin, extending his hand. They shook hands and sat down in his cabin.

Are we making good progress? Sealin asked.

Craktit was beaming. We're way ahead of schedule, he gushed. The planners have really pulled out all the stops.

That's great news, Sealin said, because there's every chance we will be going early. Ivor, well done.

Chapter 57

A FIGHT TO THE DEATH

Two days after his visit to the bridge, Sealin had his plan completed and was ready to go and face Baldric Zealotte. He had picked three of his best and fastest Death Riders. There would be no margin for error; they would be in the background ready to back him up in case anything went wrong. He had invited Thomas Clink along as an onlooker as a reward for his help with the drones; it was just a last-minute thought that had come into his head. They all boarded the transport module and set off for Ozmil Town and within ten minutes they were stepping out onto the pavement two streets away from where Zealotte was staying.

Sealin began giving out his orders. At the top of this street make a right turn and then take another right turn two streets on and then split up and try to look as casual as possible and keep walking. About halfway down the street on your left you will see a blue door with the number thirty-three on it. Walk on past to a safe distance and ready yourselves for action. Is that clear? They all nodded in agreement. Thomas, you will walk with me, all right?

Yes, Thomas said, nodding his head. I understand. Once more, be one hundred percent ready; remember Zealotte's reputation. Now let's go.

They moved off at a casual pace, first the three Death Riders and then Sealin and Thomas. They were soon heading down the street where Zealotte was staying, and all of the Death Riders had passed number thirty-three.

Then, just as Sealin and Thomas approached number thirty-three, a voice came from behind. Welcome, Sealin, we meet at last. Sealin spun around at a lightning pace and there was a bright flash. Zealotte screamed and his wand arm was missing from the elbow down; it was lying on the ground still holding his wand and a look of panic was etched all over his face.

Sealin laughed out loud. The great Baldric Zealotte, he scoffed. The history books were right about you; you had a fatal flaw. The weakness of arrogance. You couldn't just kill me, could you? You had to announce yourself first. I took a gamble and it paid off, and now you are standing there defenseless, about to meet your journey's end. He raised his wand and there was a flash.

In a remarkable twist of fate, Sealin lay on the ground bleeding with his life ebbing away. He looked up and standing over him with his wand raised was Thomas Clink.

Why, Thomas? Sealin said.

Why? It's simple, Sealin, he said. You were never going to be our leader. The Black Watch have been operating underground from the day Baldric Zealotte was sent into space, and was kept alive in the hope that someday he would return. You have been but a tiny pawn in a much bigger game.

Helen, your wife, is and has been our leader ever since you joined the army and left her alone with two little children to fend for. She called on Kanzil for his help, sold her soul to him in exchange for great power, and because you are the father of her two sons, she spared your life by sending you to prison. You made it easy for her by brutally killing a whole wizard family and murdering their children without a second thought. Did it never even occur to you why the police captured you so easily? Helen drugged you and gave the police your location and got you out of the way so she could get on with running the Black Watch's plans for the bridge and the return of our leader, Baldric Zealotte. However, we did not anticipate your jail break, and it took us all by surprise. But we decided to go along with you while it suited our course.

When you engineered the death of six innocent students at Black Eagle . . . that was a step too far. Three of them were from Black

Watch families, so you had to be stopped. With the help of Kanzil, you have been brought here to be executed, and Helen has given us her blessing. So now you know the whole story. You are about to become a short sentence in the book of wizard history. Good-bye. There was a flash and the Black Watch were back to business.

Thomas turned to the three Death Riders and gave the order to summon the transport module. We need to get Baldric back to Ravens Claw and tend to his wound, he said. Luckily, Sealin used a Destro spell, so Baldric isn't bleeding.

Chapter 58

SEALIN BELBUR IS DEAD

The news of Sealin's death had spread around the wizard world like wildfire and was on the tip of everyone's tongue. All of the reports simply read that Sealin Belbur's dead body had been found lying in the street in Ozmil Town and his wife, Helen, had identified the body as that of her husband.

Well, what do you make of this? Savajic fired the question at Peggy and Owen.

To say I am surprised would be an understatement, Owen said, but he was unable to conceal his pleasure with the news.

Peggy looked more relieved than pleased and said, Do you know, I really thought someday in the near future I would have to face him down one on one and I wasn't looking forward to it, and now I won't have to. Thank you, wizard, or wizards unknown! She raised her mug of tea and said, cheers, and they all had a good laugh.

Seriously though, Peggy said, do you think this was the work of Baldric Zealotte?

I'm absolutely certain of it, Savajic said. There is no doubt in my mind. I'm not a great believer in coincidence, and I do not believe someone suddenly took it into their head to face Sealin Belbur and have the courage and skill to kill him. If we were not sure of Zealotte's return before, then I think this killing confirms he is definitely back with us.

Savajic had been down in his workshop most of the day, where he had been working on a strategy for Owen and Peggy to make them a team, to watch each other's back and think as one. He had reached the time to let go of the reins. Owen and Peggy had to go it alone. He knew his days in the field were over, and the attack on him at Ravens Claw had taken its toll on him physically. Now he would operate from home and they would do the field work. Zealotte was back, and he knew now the pace would heat up to fever pitch.

Savajic had thought long and hard about the news of Sealin Belbur's death, and just couldn't work out how Zealotte would have known where to find Belbur, let alone even know what he looked like. Given that, it would mean Belbur would have known where to look for Zealotte and seek him out for a showdown, but how? And then again, he couldn't believe with all Sealin Belbur's military training and planning ability he wouldn't have set a trap for Zealotte to fall into and afford him any chance to escape.

He had come to the conclusion that from now on, he would collude only with Peggy and Owen and Demodus, no one else. Not until the war with the Hobgoblins and the Gnomes was over and he was sure Zealotte would then go into deep cover.

Chapter 59
DEMODUS IS READY

Peggy and Owen appeared in front of Greco's massive gates. The guard knew who Peggy was, but demanded to know who Owen was. He is Owen Menglor, son of Savajic, Peggy said. The guard was satisfied with her answer and opened a small door in the gate. He called out to the guard inside and instructed him to take them to Demodus.

Once inside, they were given horses and asked to follow a mounted guard. They mounted their horses and began to follow, and rode for about twenty minutes, winding their way through cobbled streets until they came to the palace gates, and waiting there was Demodus.

Welcome, Peggy! It's good to see you again. And I believe this is Savajic's son, Owen. Welcome, he said, and extended his massive hand.

Owen shook it and said, Thank you, Demodus, for seeing me.

Demodus laughed out loud and said to Peggy, A charming young man, very much like his father. Come along to my rooms; I have much to show you.

They followed him to his rooms. They were lavish and beautiful. He led them to a large library, and in the center was chart table. This is where we do all our planning, he said. Now I want to show you the plans for the outside fortifications. We actually finished all the building work yesterday, and the wizard planners have returned home.

They have been monumental in the help they have given us and we are eternally grateful to them. We have started to arm the fortifications today, and should have everything in place in a few days. These are the plans. We'll go through them, and then you can visit them in situ. We also have maps given to us by Princess Sheiklin showing us all the strongholds and training camps the Hobgoblins have hidden away in the goblin nation. The positions marked with a red cross are targets for our drones to obliterate.

Demodus talked about the bridge and how they planned to destroy it. Princess Sheiklin wanted her nation back from the Hobgoblin tyrants, and he intended to give it to her.

Demodus said, Let's go outside the city gates and I'll show you what we have in store for the Hobgoblins when they come visiting.

They left the palace and mounted their horses and began winding their way through the cobbled streets and down to the city gates. When they got there, the guards took charge of their horses and let them through the door in the gate and they went outside.

Demodus pointed to his right. Over there are the bunkers with the gun placements, and over there, he said, pointing to his left, are the same, symmetrically opposite. Let's go and take a closer look.

They were about seventy-five meters from the center of the city gates and when they got up close, they were amazed at the huge size. The walls were a meter thick and six meters high and in the shape of five sides of an octagon. The Demodom soldiers were setting up the machine guns, pointing them through the slots built into the walls, and this allowed them to cover a large section of the forest. The opposite bunker would do the same. There were six machine guns in each bunker, and they were set out in three lots of two, pointing at three different angles. Next to each one, neatly stacked, were metal boxes of ammunition.

This will be our first line of defense, Demodus said, and then turning around he said, and this is our cavalry. Behind were two rows of cross-country motorcycles, twenty in each row. The mounted Demodom soldiers will have orders to leave each bunker and outflank the Hobgoblins from either side and directly behind, and as soon as the first Hobgoblin appears from out of the forest, they will have the signal to attack them. Inside the city gates are twelve marksmen snipers as a backup, just as a precaution.

Our drones are heavily armed and will hover above the battlefield to deal with any attack they may send by air. We will intercept them and shoot them down. As soon as the sky is clear, the drones will go and obliterate their designated targets and then they will self-destruct. Then when the Hobgoblins retreat and we have them on the run, the city gates will open and the drone army will pursue them until they are all running for their lives across the bridge. When they are all safely on the bridge, I believe your planners have a little surprise for them.

Peggy said, Yes, they have. They have built into the Levita foundation a collapse spell that will collapse the bridge on their command, and when they do, the Snack Worms will do the rest.

Now for the best part of the planners' building magic. He produced a shiny disc from his pocket. It had a red button in the center and he pressed it. A loud rumble noise filled the air and the whole defense buildings on each side began to sink into the ground and when it stopped, the ground looked undisturbed. Peggy looked at Demodus in disbelief.

It's wonderful! she said. Absolutely wonderful.

Demodus smiled and turned the disc over in his massive hand and on the other side was a blue circle in the center. He pressed it and the rumble began again and the buildings rose up from the ground. Demodus said, The planners gave me the disc to use so we can take down the façade and look perfectly normal. The idea is to wait until the Hobgoblins have committed themselves well out into the open ground, then rise up and let them have the full force of our defenses.

Peggy had been recording everything on her holograph video camera for Savajic so he could evaluate everything she had seen. Peggy turned to Demodus and said, I think Savajic will be amazed at the progress you've made in such a short time.

Thank you, Peggy, Demodus said. I can promise you this; once the Hobgoblins are three-quarters of the way across the killing zone and we open fire, they will think they have stepped into Kanzil's kingdom of fire and brimstone.

Owen shuddered when he thought of the consequences this war would have if everything went to plan. The whole race of Hobgoblins would be wiped from the face of the Earth. But then again, it wasn't his battle, nor that of the wizards, so he reasoned destiny would have the final decision.

Did Savajic tell you of Baldric Zealotte's return? he asked Demodus. Yes, he did, replied Demodus. He also told me of the history of the Sword of Destiny and Zealotte. I guess when all the fighting is over and done, he will be paying me a visit to try and reclaim the sword, and he might just have his wish granted. But not in the way he wants.

Demodus said, Well, Peggy, Owen, have you seen enough?

Yes, said Owen. I think we should get back and show Savajic the fighting machine Demodus has created.

You're right, said Peggy, and she turned to Demodus and thanked him for spending time with them and sharing his plans with them.

The pleasure was mine, he replied. Have a safe journey, and I hope to see you both soon. The coordinates were set and they disappeared.

Chapter 60

ZEALOTTE GOES TO RAVENS CLAW

The transport module soon had the four wizards back at Ravens Claw Castle, and Zealotte was quickly taken to a doctor who had been summoned and was waiting for him with his medical equipment. Thomas handed the doctor a cloth holding Zealotte's arm and told him there had been no blood loss.

That's good news, the doctor said, looking relieved.

They undressed Zealotte and lay him on a table and covered him with a white sheet. The doctor began setting up his graft tube and when he had it in place, he carefully fed the upper part of Zealotte's arm into it, and then in the other end of the tube he fed Zealotte's hand and lower arm. In the center of the tube was a crystal window, and the doctor began to manipulate the lower section of arm, lining it up precisely with the upper. When he was satisfied with the match, he lowered a metal box over the crystal window in the tube and flipped a switch. There was a loud buzzing noise and lights were flashing. Zealotte had been given an injection to make sure he wouldn't move, so he had no idea when he woke up he would have the use of his arm again. Wizard science had moved on since he was last on earth.

An hour later, Zealotte was awake and flexing the muscles in his arm and fingers, the look of relief on his face was there for all to see. He shook hands with the doctor and thanked him. I will not forget what you have done for me, he said.

Zealotte dressed and walked back into the main monitor room and as he entered, a loud cheer went up and a chant of: "Zealotte! Zealotte!" He held up his arms and the room fell silent. It's good to be back with my people, he announced. Please forgive me for my dramatic entrance but I had a little mishap on the way here. And now, if you will excuse me, I need to speak with Thomas Clink.

Thomas Clink stepped up and said, Baldric, if you will follow me, I will show you where your conference room is. They both moved, and Thomas led the way. They settled themselves down and Thomas called out for refreshments to be brought in.

Thomas, what's going on? Zealotte asked.

You may well ask, said Thomas in a stern voice. I speak for Kanzil. He warned you of your arrogance and you didn't listen; perhaps this time you will. If Kanzil had not foreseen what would happen when you met Sealin Belbur and told me what to do, you would have been dead and lying in the streets of Ozmil instead of him. You are a very powerful wizard, but wizard magic has moved on in the last two thousand years and there are more powerful wizards than you are. And Sealin Belbur was one of them.

Kanzil has told me to spell out this message to you once and for all. Cut out this all-conquering hero stance and get organized. With the help of Helen Belbur and the Black Watch movement, Kanzil has managed to get this far without the wizard world knowing about it, and we want it to stay that way until the Hobgoblins have conquered the Gnomes. Kanzil wants just one thing of you, and that is to get back the Sword of Destiny and return it to him. Then, after that, you will have Greco and the Black Watch movement and the freedom to do anything you wish. Do you understand what I am saying?

Yes, replied Zealotte. It was at last beginning to dawn on Zealotte that things had changed dramatically while he had been away, and now he also realized he had to change and adapt. He also realized that, had not the Black Watch been secretly formed by loyal followers of his and kept going for all of these years in an underground movement, his return to Earth would have been of little consequence to the now powerful wizard world. Sealin Belbur had proved that to him.

Thomas said, I'm glad you have accepted Kanzil's advice. Now take control of the Black Watch, and show them you can be a great leader. Helen Belbur is on her way to see you. Show her respect.

You owe her a great deal. She has worked tirelessly resurrecting your name and reputation and has been the mastermind behind the bridge and rousing the Hobgoblins to fever pitch for going to war with the Gnomes, and all in your name. She hated her husband, Sealin Belbur, but with the help of Kanzil she managed to make him believe all of this was his idea. She got him to approach the Hobgoblins and broker a deal with them to go to war with the Gnomes if he was prepared to build a bridge across the worm fields big enough to take his army across, and Petrid the Hobgoblin leader jumped at the opportunity. So, it all began.

Chapter 61
HELEN BELBUR

Helen Belbur arrived at Ravens Claw and was given a warm welcome by Zealotte. It's good to see you all in one piece, Baldric, she said, looking down while shaking hands with him.

Zealotte took it all in good spirit. He held up his hand and said, As good a new, thanks to our wonderful doctors. I'm afraid I didn't show your husband enough respect and paid the price.

Ex-husband, Helen said, correcting him.

Helen smiled at Zealotte and said, You have to realize that no one knows what you look like, so I have arranged for Thomas to take you to meet with the planners in charge of building the bridge. You will meet Ivor Craktit, who is in overall charge, and he will give you the grand tour and introduce you to everyone. Then you will go and meet with Petrid, the Hobgoblin leader.

When the war begins, we have no intentions of giving the Hobgoblins any help from the wizard world. Once the bridge is built, the wizards will all return home. If you decide to join them because you wish to regain possession of the Sword of Destiny, then that will be your choice, but you will do that on your own.

From the information we gathered from a spy we had planted in Greco City, well before we started to build the bridge, we know the Gnomes should give the Hobgoblins very little resistance because their army has grown weak and is a shadow of what it was. As for the Sword of Destiny, when you were sent into space, Goodrick the Elder hid it away from the world and his secret went with him to the grave. Only a few years ago was it discovered by a wizard, purely by accident, so fortunately for us, we know who has it. And would you believe it? The sword is in the possession of a Gnome, so there is a good chance it will be in Greco City. And if it isn't, you should be able to find out where it is when the Gnomes have surrendered. You have until the bridge is completed to make the decision as to go with them or not. I doubt if Petrid will care either way. From what I can gather, all he can do is smell the Gnomes' blood.

After the fighting is over, you will offer to do the same thing Sealin Belbur did, and that is to retrieve all the gold from the Gnome treasury and take it over the bridge to them, and we keep Greco City as our headquarters; that is our agreement with them. What will actually happen? Well, that will be a different scenario altogether. The Hobgoblins will return home in triumph after at last defeating their old enemy, the Gnomes. The sting in the tail will come when their army are all on the bridge. The planners have built into the bridge a collapse spell, which they will trigger on our signal and the bridge will collapse, scattering the Hobgoblin army onto the worm fields. The Snack Worms will do the rest. After that has been accomplished, we can move the contents of the Gnome treasury to our vaults in Ravens Claw Castle.

Baldric, your only problem will be to find the Sword of Destiny and return it to Kanzil, and then we can start to build our new empire together with all of your followers.

Chapter 62
SAVAJIC MEETS ZEALOTTE

Savajic was in his study, eagerly awaiting news from Peggy and Owen, when suddenly his wall screen appeared and a council member, Professor Stephen Blood, came into view. Savajic greeted him, Stephen, to what do I owe this honor?

I've been asked to contact you, Savajic, and ask you if you will meet with Enzebadier and the council at four o'clock this afternoon in the council chamber for an informal meeting. Would this be possible?

Of course, Savajic replied. Please tell Enzebadier I will be there.

Savajic was a little puzzled Enzebadier had not contacted him personally, as he usually did, but dismissed it, reasoning he was probably busy contacting the other members of the council.

When he had finished his lunch, he decided to wait for Peggy and Owen to return and see what news they had from their meeting with Demodus.

The time was three thirty and there was no sign of Peggy and Owen, so he decided to leave a message with Cooper, telling them where he had gone. He went to his room and changed his clothes and prepared himself for the meeting. It was a nice change to have a meeting without having to wear full ceremonial dress.

He set the coordinates on his pendant and disappeared. He reappeared outside the council chambers, and standing there alone was Stephen Blood.

Greetings, Savajic, he said. It looks like we are the first to arrive. Savajic didn't have a chance to answer because a Stun spell hit him between the shoulder blades and he fell to the floor unconscious. Two wizards emerged from behind a façade. They both had their wands drawn and as the façade disappeared, a travel capsule came into view. Quick, said Stephen Blood. Get him into the capsule. They will know what to do with him at Ravens Claw. Quickly now, we don't have much time before he wakes up!

At Ravens Claw Castle, preparations had been made to receive Savajic. They realized they were dealing with probably the most powerful and dangerous wizard in the wizard world, and had securely bound and gagged him. They had been unable to remove his wand because he'd put a powerful spell on it and only he alone could draw it. After he had been gassed and kidnapped by Demodus, he swore he would never again be parted from his wand, so he worked on the spell that now made him and his wand inseparable. And that being the case, the Black Watch wizards were taking no chances.

Savajic regained consciousness and as his eyes began to focus, he found himself in a room he recognized as the vault room in Ravens Claw Castle, where Peggy and he had been captured by Sealin Belbur.

But his captors had no idea it had been him and Peggy, as they had been hazing.

So, this is the great Savajic, is it? We meet at last. I am Helen Belbur. Her voice was high-pitched but it had a certain amount of gravel to it and a faint whiff of unpleasantness. For Savajic, it was dislike at first sight. Of course, it was impossible to answer her because he was gagged so he remained motionless, with his gaze fixed firmly ahead with the intention of showing her complete indifference; it worked.

Her voice turned into a growl. Remove his gag, she ordered, and one of the wizards stepped forward and removed his gag. But as he did, Savajic felt no immediate threat. He reasoned that, as they had taken all this trouble to capture him, there must be a good reason, and until they had gotten what they were after, he would be reasonably safe. But as soon as he felt a threat to his life he would use his Uncaptivus spell.

You seem to be a very well-prepared wizard, Helen said.

I try to be, replied Savajic. And by the way, how are you today? He was determined to wind her up and put her off balance if he could and it was working, but at a cost.

She slapped his face hard and screamed, "Cut the crap!" She was glaring at him now and growled, How do you release your wand?

It's very simple, Savajic said. I just draw it out. But I can't while I'm all bound up like this.

And that's how you are going to stay, Helen said. It works for me too.

You are probably wondering why you have been brought here and what we want of you, so let me explain. Several weeks ago, we had intruders who were captured by the late Sealin Belbur, but the fool let them escape without a trace—or so we thought. But one of our bright young wizards decided to dust for fingerprints, and lo and behold, he found some. Just two, but they were clear ones. With our connections, we put them up on the police databank but had no success; and then Stephen came up with the idea that Enzebadier kept a fingerprint database of past and present wizards on the council, so he gained access to it and lo and behold, he found a match. And that match was Savajic Menglor. Now that you are here and there is not the slightest chance of you leaving this place alive, I will introduce you to our leader.

A wizard stepped forward and dropped the hood on his robe to expose his face. This is Baldric Zealotte, announced Helen.

Savajic scanned every inch of his face, putting it firmly into his memory. He couldn't believe his luck; he not only now knew what Zealotte looked like, but he also knew where he was.

I'm sorry, Helen, Savajic said. But am I supposed to be impressed with yesterday's wizard?

Savajic had to endure another smack across the face from Helen. How dare you! she snarled.

Forgive him, Zealotte said. After all, they are the words of a dying man.

Savajic smiled at Zealotte and said, "The history books were right about you. There are no bounds to your arrogance. I sincerely thank you for your hospitality and sharing so much information with me. But enough really is enough; you are beginning to bore me. Uncaptivus!" There was a loud flash, and Zealotte was left staring at a pile of wood splinters and the rope that had been binding Savajic.

Savajic was safely back in his workshop and was delighted with what he had found out about Zealotte—and Stephen Blood, for that matter—and the part Helen Belbur was playing.

Suddenly Savajic cried out in pain and sat down heavily in his chair. Where he had been struck in the back by the Stun spell there was a burning pain. He leaned back in his chair and passed out.

Chapter 63
PEGGY ARRIVES BACK JUST IN TIME

Peggy and Owen appeared in the great hall and made their way to Savajic's study but it was empty. Father is probably down in his workshop, Owen said, so they went to look. Owen knocked on the door but there wasn't any answer. He must be somewhere else, Owen said, so they started to go back upstairs.

Suddenly Peggy stopped in her tracks. Did you hear that?

Hear what? Owen said, straining his ears.

Peggy was rushing towards the workshop and flung the door open and there, slumped in his chair, was Savajic. He was hardly conscious.

She rushed over to him and without saying a word scooped him up in her arms and began running to Savajic's room. As she went past Owen she said, Go and get Cooper, and get a doctor here right away!

Peggy laid Savajic on his bed and held his hands and then she closed her eyes. "Share, share," she said. Slowly the color began to come back to Savajic's cheeks. Five minutes later he was sitting up, and Peggy helped him off the bed and into a chair.

Cooper had arrived and was standing by Peggy. Is there anything I can do? he asked.

Yes, said Peggy. Will you make Savajic a nice hot mug of sweet tea? Cooper disappeared, and Peggy turned to Savajic and said, I must go outside and lie down for a few minutes. Promise me you will drink your tea and stay here until I come back and you have seen the doctor.

I will, Savajic said. And, Peggy, thank you for what you've just done. Peggy waved her hand and left the room.

Ten minutes later, Peggy was back in Savajic's room. The doctor had arrived and was giving him an examination and when he was finished, he gave him four capsules. Take one capsule a day and they will steady your nerves and stop them firing off. There is no lasting damage but you will have a sore back for a week or so, there is no need to worry. Savajic thanked the doctor. So did Peggy, and asked Cooper to show the doctor out to his transport.

Peggy was pacing up and down, unsure where to start, and Owen was sitting silently. Then Peggy started, You promised me faithfully you were finished with field work, and as soon as I am out of the way you do the opposite. Where is all the trust?

Savajic shook his head and said, if you calm down and stop jumping to conclusions, I'll tell you what happened.

I was contacted by Stephen Blood, a member of the wizard council. He told me Enzebadier had requested my presence at a meeting of the council and of course I said yes. When I arrived at the chamber, the only other member there was Stephen Blood. He said we were the first to arrive, and before I could answer I was struck in the back with a stun spell. The next thing I knew, I was bound and gagged in Ravens Claw Castle.

What would make them blow their cover like that? Peggy wondered aloud.

Well, Savajic said, you are not going to believe this, but not only did I find out that all this time Helen Belbur has been running the Black Watch movement, but she, and not Sealin, is the mastermind behind the building of the bridge, and she merely used him to front the movement. She used Sealin to rouse the Hobgoblins to fever pitch over going to war with the Gnomes and made him think the bridge was his idea. But even more unbelievable than that is she introduced me to a wizard by the name of Baldric Zealotte.

Peggy gasped. You've met Zealotte? I can't believe it!

Well it's true, Savajic said with a big smile on his face. Peggy, I think you owe me an apology.

I am so sorry, she said. But it's only because I worry about you. You've had such a bad run of luck, and I want you to be safe.

But why would they target you? They have no idea we know as much as we do about their operations.

It's entirely my fault, Savajic said. I put my hands up. When we went to Ravens Claw Castle and entered their headquarters, I snagged my latex glove and instead of changing it, I carried it in and I accidently touched a railing. Well, to cut a long story short, they found out it was me and lured me to the council chamber and stunned me and bound and gagged me and transported me to the castle.

Inside the castle, when I regained consciousness, they began to tell me things and made the mistake of taking my gag off. Only when they had given me all the information and started to question me did I use the Uncaptivus spell. I have no doubt they intended to kill me after I had answered their questions and was no longer any use to them. The problem now is, I am a marked man. So too is Owen; they will try to get to me through Owen. While we are at home we are safe, but the moment we leave, believe me, we will be under attack.

I'm not afraid, Owen said. They can't frighten me. I'll go after them and make them pay.

That is exactly what they want you to do. They will goad you out into the open; they know you are a speed champion and will set a trap for you to step into where you will be hopelessly outnumbered. I hate to tell you this, Owen, but you have to stay at home; Peggy, the pressure is all on you.

Chapter 64
PEGGY GOES IT ALONE

Peggy looked at Savajic and said, if that's the way it's got to be, then that's the way it's got to be. So, Savajic, where do we go from here?

Well, first of all, I have to ask whom we can trust. It certainly isn't the Council of Wizards. But we have to trust someone. I think we have to put our faith in Enzebadier but no one else, and he, too, will have to choose whom he can trust. I will contact him and tell him what I know about Stephen Blood and leave it to him as to how to deal with it.

Peggy, it's your turn to tell me how Demodus is progressing.

She began by telling him the wizard planners had completed all of the building work and he was putting the finishing touches to the placement of his soldiers. The wizard planners have all gone home and from what Owen and myself saw, Demodus is more than ready.

That is good news indeed, Savajic said. I think we should take a step back and let history take its course. And now, Savajic said, I want to show you some magic I am particularly proud of. He waved his wand at the wall and the screen began to show the work going on at the bridge. This will give us the exact time the Hobgoblins will begin their march on Greco. It was all completely new to Owen, and he was amazed at how much Savajic and Peggy had found out about the Black Watch's plans.

Peggy spent the next hour going into minute detail of the defenses and battle strategy Demodus had laid out, and Savajic was very impressed with his plans. Savajic said, I honestly think fortune has turned strongly in our direction. It seems that every time the Black Watch tries to get ahead, they shoot themselves in the foot.

Before I passed out, I used my brain scan camera on myself and we now have a perfect picture of Zealotte from my memory. I will give a picture of him to Enzebadier when I contact him so he can circulate it to everyone he feels he can trust. And when I discuss Stephen Blood with him, I will suggest that before he takes any action against him, we use him to pass on a bit of misinformation to Zealotte. I want him to find out that Demodus has the Sword of Destiny and he has no idea of its power and he leaves it lying around and very rarely wears it. I want him to find out that Demodus drinks heavily and spends most of his time asleep in a drunken stupor in one of the many inns in Greco. Hopefully this will tempt Zealotte to come across the bridge with the Hobgoblins, in the hope that he can locate Demodus and regain possession of the sword, with a good chance of meeting little resistance. But we know what kind of reception he will receive when he crosses the bridge, don't we?

Peggy, I want you to do one more trip for me, Savajic said. And that is to go and see Princess Sheiklin and find out for certain who the Hobgoblins have managed to get to help them, and how many of them there are. It will be invaluable for Demodus to know exactly what he is up against.

When would you like me to go? Peggy asked.

Tomorrow would be fine, Savajic said. We have no need to rush. But if we can get as much information as possible to Demodus, he can adjust his tactics to suit. In the meantime, we can relax and monitor the progress on the bridge. Now on a more serious matter, because Zealotte knows I have breached the security at Ravens Claw, he will make me the number one target on the Death Riders' hit list. But it's not just me; he will target anyone close to me. So I have decided that, although while we are indoors we are safe, to go out into the grounds would be far too dangerous and a risk not worth taking. Fortunately for us, Zealotte has no idea how powerful our magic is and how far we have advanced since he was last on Earth. With our transference magic, we can come and go as we please, and no one will know where we are; only we and whoever we are visiting at the time. Now, do you agree?

They both nodded their heads. Sounds good to me, Owen said. How about you, Peggy?

It sounds good to me as well, she answered.

Good, said Savajic. Then that's a done deal.

Chapter 65

PRINCESS SHEIKLIN

Peggy was ready to go. She had set the coordinates on her bracelet. Savajic was standing next to her and said, Please give the princess my best wishes and my apologies for not attending with you. Oh! And, Peggy, please, I want you to be very careful when you come out of haze and take a good look around first. Peggy gave him a knowing look. I know, he said, but I can't help worrying, can I?

Peggy said, I'll be OK, and disappeared.

She arrived in haze next to a pile of rocks that was scattered next to the mountain. Staying in haze, she took the time to look around and after she was happy she was alone, she came out of haze. Almost immediately the rocks began to move and formed an archway she recognized from her first visit, and again Princess Sheiklin appeared with her two guards.

Greetings, Peggy, she said. It is so good to see you again. Please follow me.

As they walked through the tunnel cut through the mountain, a loud rumble began behind them, but this time Peggy knew it was the entrance turning itself back into a pile of rocks. They entered the lantern-type room she recognized from her first visit and the princess snapped her fingers, and they appeared in the royal palace.

After they had settled down in the princess's private room, Peggy was offered refreshments but politely declined the offer. She was eager to get on with the business at hand.

The princess smiled and said, What brings you here, Peggy? I hope there aren't any problems with our plans.

No, our plans and preparations are in really good shape, Peggy said, and gave her a general synopsis of Demodus's work.

Savajic asked me to apologize for his absence and come here and bring you up to date with our plans; and I have something for you. She handed the princess a photograph of a wizard.

The princess looked puzzled. Who is this? she asked.

Who indeed, said Peggy. It's a long story so I'll be brief. It is the one and only Baldric Zealotte. Savajic managed to get it, so now we know exactly what he looks like. And because he is almost certain to come to meet with Petrid, he wanted you to know what he looked like so you would be aware, should your intelligence network come in contact with him.

Thank you, the princess said, but she still looked puzzled. I thought Zealotte was still on his way to Earth. When did he return?

A few weeks ago, Peggy said. We believe Kanzil used his power over gravity to pull him down to Earth quicker than we had anticipated, and tried to keep it a secret until he could lure Sealin Belbur into a trap and have him killed. And to this end he achieved his goal; Sealin Belbur is indeed dead.

Baldric Zealotte is now leader of the Black Watch and the Death Riders, and we believe he will lead the Hobgoblins into war. And now, Princess, the reason for my visit. Savajic wants to know if you have any information on the status of the Hobgoblin army, and more important, if he has enlisted any help from any other nation.

The princess closed her eyes and put her middle finger to her forehead and there was a flash. Standing before them were three goblins. They bowed and asked the princess how they could help.

Thank you for coming so quickly, the princess said. I want you to meet Peggy Goody. She has been monitoring the building of the bridge and the movements of the wizards behind it. She has come to us with a request about the current status of the Hobgoblin army and any help they have managed to muster. Now, Peggy, may I introduce you to my intelligence leaders. From left to right this is Flit, this is

Seek, and this is Sting. They have between them contacts in every corner of our nation; nothing escapes them. Perhaps, Flit, you could start.

Thank you, Princess, Flit said. May I start by thanking Peggy for helping us in our cause, and may I say on behalf of all our nation how we respect the help of both you and Savajic for risking your lives on our behalf. I am certain your names will be forever in our history books.

The Hobgoblins have been very busy and have managed to enlist the services of Flying Bull Hounds. They are creatures with enormous power and can travel long distances at fast speeds. We have found out there are four hundred of them on their way. This is going to be a formidable force to face on its own. Over to you, Seek.

Seek took over. Six Trolls have been enlisted to man a massive battering ram that has been constructed in the form of a tube with a reinforced roof to withstand most missiles, and underneath is the ram. The Trolls' mission is to reach the city gates and smash it down and gain access to the city. And as far as we can gather, they are not enlisted to join in with the fighting. Sting, over to you.

OK, weapons. The Hobgoblins have developed arrows that will go around corners and seek out body heat. We also believe they will do U-turns left and right and up and down, and this will be a deadly weapon. Put into context, there are one thousand Hobgoblins and each will carry fifteen arrows. Fifteen thousand arrows all with heat-seeking ability, and to add to that, each Hobgoblin will be carrying an axe with magic powers that will slice through pretty much anything.

Flit produced a red folder and handed it to Peggy. You will find everything you need in there. It is all we know of, and I don't anticipate any additions.

Peggy took the folder and thanked Flit and then she turned to the princess. They have much more than we thought they would have and we will have to make adjustments. Thank goodness you had this information.

One more thing, Peggy said. Savajic has found a way to monitor the progress on the bridge from home, and he will know the exact time when it is completed. He will make sure you are informed immediately so you can move all your people to safety, well away from all the targets that will be destroyed. And after the Hobgoblins are well into their march across the bridge, the wizard planners will collapse your end of the bridge as soon as the army has crossed. There will be no way back for them so you will have no fear of any kind of reprisals from them and you will be in control of your nation once again.

The princess held out her hand and touched Peggy and said, The sequel of this battle will not only determine the destiny of the Gnome nation but the very nature of our own. The task that falls to Demodus is formidable. The ability to go to war is beyond us because of decree many millenniums ago. So is it written in our law. But as I have told you, we have magic far in excess of the Hobgoblins and there is nothing in our laws that says we cannot use our magic in other ways. So I can promise you they may well have a few unpleasant surprises when they take to the battlefield and to that end, we are working tirelessly.

Peggy admired how cool and calm the princess was, taking into account the serious situation she faced, but now Peggy was itching to get back to Savajic with the information the princess had given her. May I take my leave? she asked politely of the princess. I need to get back to Savajic so we can see how we go on from here.

Of course, Peggy. She snapped her fingers and they were back in the lantern-shaped room. My guards will show you out, she said. Until we meet again, good-bye. She snapped her fingers and she was gone. The guards showed Peggy to the entrance of the tunnel and she used her bracelet and disappeared.

Chapter 66

A Folder For Savajic

Peggy arrived back and Savajic was eager for news. How did you get on? he asked.

Everything went well, she said and handed him the folder. I think you're in for a few surprises, Savajic.

He took the folder from Peggy and said, Let's go to the study where I can digest the contents.

As Savajic read through the Goblins' report, it dawned on him that with the help of the Flying Bull Hounds, they possessed a serious aerial threat to Demodus's drones, as they would be greatly outnumbered and furthermore, heat-seeking arrows that could change direction could easily knock out Demodus's gun emplacements, rendering the city defenseless.

Savajic re-read the report, committing every detail to memory while Peggy went over the day's events in her mind. Savajic dropped the report on his desk and said to Peggy, I take it you know what's in this report?

Pretty much, she replied.

OK then, let's take things one at a time. He turned to the screen showing the activity going on at the bridge and said, Flying Bull Hounds. The screen changed to a picture of a Flying Bull Hound. It looked a formidable beast, with a powerful body and large wings, and next to it was a column of information and physical limits.

That's interesting, Savajic said, pointing to a section stating the maximum height they fly at was twenty meters. This means they cannot fly over the city walls, and Greco is safe from invasion from the air.

What about grappling hooks? Peggy asked.

Savajic looked at her and said, I knew you wouldn't make this easy for me, and they both laughed. But seriously, he said, you have a good point. It would be quite possible to climb the extra ten meters of the city walls and cause a big enough diversion to let them get their battering ram to the city gates. OK, one solution is to get some of Demodus's guns up onto the top of the walls, but that alone is not enough, because the Hobgoblins have heat-seeking arrows and they are deadly accurate when throwing their axes.

Have they got any apparent weaknesses? Peggy asked. Savajic scanned the column and said, the only thing that will stop them is a clean shot between the eyes.

Then machine guns are no good, Peggy said. You will need snipers up on the wall so they can take the shot while the Hobgoblins are still out of distance.

I'm impressed, said Savajic. You're getting quite good at this, aren't you?

That's a bit patronizing, said Peggy.

I'm sorry, I certainly didn't mean it to be, I'm genuinely impressed. Peggy rolled her eyes. OK, she said. Let's move on.

Right, let's take a look at the arrows; now they could be a real problem. Come on, Peggy, let's put our thinking caps on. Got it! exclaimed Savajic. How stupid of me. The arrows aren't a threat at all. Remember when Sealin Belbur captured us by using infrared heat-seeking goggles? Well, when we escaped and got back home I was too weak to think straight. But when the fog cleared, I remembered that some years ago, the military was conducting tests on a new cloth claimed to be impervious to infrared heat-seeking rays and they were in the process of making a suit for the field operators. Let's do a bit of digging.

He turned to the wall screen. Enzebadier, he commanded. Within seconds, Enzebadier was with them.

Greetings, Savajic. Do you have some news for me?

Yes, said Savajic, and read out carefully the contents of the Goblins' folder.

Enzebadier stroked his beard and said, I imagine you and Peggy have gone through the contents of the folder in fine detail. Have you come to any conclusions?

Yes, we have, Savajic replied, and we have pretty much resolved most of the problems; all but one, and this is where I think you may be able to help us. Do you recall a few years ago when the military were carrying out tests on a material that was impervious to infrared heat-seeking rays?

I do, Enzebadier replied, and they were very successful and have gone on to make special suits for the field operatives. Ah! I can see why you have asked; a solution to the arrows, of course. How many will you need? he asked.

I'll have to come back to you on the figures, said Savajic, because they have machine gunners and snipers and cavalry. Now because of Thomas Clink, we have no idea whom we can or cannot trust, so we have to tread lightly.

I am aware of that, Enzebadier said, so I intend to give Commander Churmill the task. Agreed?

Agreed, Savajic echoed.

Then come back to me with the numbers and I will arrange for the suits to be ready for Demodus, and I will have them delivered to Greco.

I have some news for you, Savajic. Commander Churmill has a plan to surround Ravens Claw Castle as soon as the Hobgoblins begin their march over the bridge, and on his command, they will attack. And his order is to take no prisoners. They will then remove the gold from the vault and destroy all traces of their headquarters. They are not expecting Zealotte or Helen Belbur to be there because they have fallen for the story we planted through Thomas Clink, and we are certain they will be at the bridge, because Zealotte is desperate to regain possession of the Sword of Destiny.

Now one other thing; Commander Churmill has positioned field operatives at the homes of the planners and all of the crews, and on his signal, they have orders to kill all the members of the Black Watch keeping guard over their families. Please keep me informed of any developments. He disappeared, and the screen returned to the bridge.

Look at that! Peggy jumped up from her chair and pointed at the screen. Standing on the bridge were Baldric Zealotte and Helen Belbur.

She hasn't wasted much time, Savajic said. She is really pushing on.

Look, that's Petrid standing next to him and Helen. What do you think this means? asked Peggy. It's a pity that we can't hear what they are saying.

I'm working on that, Savajic said. But in answer to your question, I would imagine they are there to apply maximum pressure on the completion of the bridge. I now believe that by capturing me, and my subsequent escape, they will know Ravens Claw is no longer a secret, and everything they are planning will be speeded up.

I'm going to spend some time making out a detailed report for Demodus, giving him all our conclusions and what we would do. I will also tell him of the suits for his soldiers and ask him to have a number ready for you when you go to see him tomorrow. I should have it done by dinner tonight, so, Peggy, if you would like to take the time to relax, I'll see you at dinner.

Chapter 67
PLANS FOR DEMODUS

At breakfast the next morning, Savajic presented Peggy with the folder and said, Inside, Demodus will have a documented account of all the forces that are about to be pitched against Greco and what our suggestions to combat them are. I have asked him to give you the number of suits he will require. I have also put that he has no need to worry about the sizes of the suits, as wizard suits will fit whoever puts them on. Now let's enjoy our breakfast, shall we?

I'll drink to that, said Peggy, holding up a cup of tea.

Once again Peggy was standing outside the massive gates of Greco City and a familiar voice greeted her. Demodus came striding over to her. Welcome, Peggy, he said. Let's saddle up and go to my rooms, where we'll be more comfortable.

As they rode along the cobbled streets, Peggy couldn't help noticing how much Demodus's face had changed since she had first seen him. The almost fish-like face had all but disappeared and in a strange, rugged way he looked like a king's champion.

As they reached the palace and dismounted, two guards came forward and took charge of their horses, and they headed for Demodus's rooms.

This is a full and final update on the Hobgoblins' army and the help they have managed to get from outside.

Demodus took the folder and sat down and began to study it, going through it in minute detail. Finally, he sat up straight and put the folder down.

I have to say, you and Savajic don't leave much to chance. And this is a massive advantage to me to have you on my side. Now Savajic has asked me for a figure for the number of suits I will need. I have six machine gunners with six ammunition feeders so that's twelve; there are forty cavalries on each side so that's another eighty, and I will put twelve snipers on the walls; that's a total of one hundred and four.

But your army is much bigger than that, isn't it? Peggy said.

Yes, it is, replied Demodus, but they will be behind the city gates and waiting to charge out in front of the Gnome army once the Hobgoblins are in retreat, and they will chase them onto the bridge and follow them. Remember, my soldiers are clones, and they have no fear of death; it means nothing to them. They only know how to follow orders and kill. Should any of the clones survive the battle they will only have a very short life span. Peggy shuddered. It was like the living dead.

Peggy stayed with Demodus and had lunch with him and was amazed at some of the stories he told her of his travels with his father, Valyew Sellum. She could tell he had loved his father very much.

It's time for me to go, I'm afraid, Peggy said, standing up and stretching.

It's been a real pleasure to have you here, Demodus said. We must do it again when this is all over.

I'll look forward to that, she said, but all good things must come to an end. She set her bracelet for home, said good-bye to Demodus, and disappeared.

Chapter 68
COMPLETION

When Peggy returned, she found Savajic carefully studying the bridge. Has something happened? she asked.

Shush! Savajic motioned for her to be quiet. I've almost got it, he said. Peggy could hear voices quite plainly. I can hear, she said. It's Helen, Baldric, and Ivor Craktit. They are discussing the bridge's completion. Suddenly the voices come through loud and clear.

Got it! Savajic shouted.

Are there no bounds to this man's talent? Peggy asked in a mocking voice. Their eyes met and they both burst out laughing. They both sat and listened to their conversation. They spoke freely, totally unaware that they were being listened to.

How good is this? said Savajic. Straight from the horse's mouth. They had obviously cracked the whip with great success.

Seven days, Ivor said, without fail. It's a promise I will keep.

Zealotte was delighted. You have done well, Ivor. I will not forget it, and that is my promise to you.

Helen, we need to move quickly, Zealotte said. Can you organize four Death Riders to join you at the bridge to help you tidy up as soon as we are on the bridge and out of sight? Remember, there must be no traces of the planners or the quarry crews.

We shouldn't have too much trouble, Helen said. The quarry crew's wands have been collected and locked away, and I will take the planners' wands the day before you march so their power will also be diminished.

Zealotte said, I propose we go back to Ravens Claw and take care of the business at hand. We have several loose ends to clear up over the next six days. I don't want any last-minute hitches.

There won't be, Helen said. In fact, I'm quite looking forward to tidying up.

Helen Belbur is a cold-blooded murderer, Peggy said. They never had any intention of letting the planners or the quarry crews go home and they wouldn't spare their families, either. Well, I have had an update from Commander Churmill and his plans. He has placed two commanders at the bridge behind a façade who will give the signal the minute the Hobgoblins are on their way across the bridge. And on that signal, the Death Riders guarding the families of the planners and the quarry crews will be eliminated. What will the commanders at the bridge do to help the planners? Will they try to stop the massacre or leave them all to their fate?

That I don't know, Savajic said.

Why can't we do something? Owen said. Couldn't Peggy and I go to the bridge in haze and take them by surprise? They wouldn't know what had hit them.

I was thinking on that line, Savajic said. But it's a big ask of you both.

Owen laughed. Considering what they did to us at Black Eagle, I would think Peggy, like me, would be more than up for it.

Peggy looked at him and she could see the burning hatred that was in his eyes. It would be a pleasure, she said.

We need to warn Demodus that the Hobgoblins will be coming across the bridge in seven days' time, Savajic said. So he can be on the alert.

There's no need, Peggy said, because when I spoke to him he told me he had already positioned soldiers high in the trees on the far edge of the forest, and from there they can see across to the worm fields. As soon as the Hobgoblins emerge from under the façade, they have enough time to get back to Greco and give the alarm.

Then there is just one more thing to do, Peggy. I would like you to visit the planners and tell them their families will be safe and of the plan to deal with the Death Riders and Helen Belbur.

When do you want me to go? Peggy asked.

Savajic said, The day before the Hobgoblins march. The less anyone knows about our plans, the better. I would suggest you and Owen relax, and maybe do some practice on the range.

Chapter 69
A Dark Day

It's time to visit the planners, Peggy, Savajic said. He looked strangely tired.

Are you feeling all right? Peggy asked.

Yes, he replied. I've still got a bit of pain in my back but it's nothing to worry about.

Peggy went down to the pool where Owen was swimming. When he saw her, he swam to the side and got out. I'm going to meet with the planners now. It won't be until this evening when their work finishes, so when I get back we can start to prepare for tomorrow.

Okay, Owen said. Just be careful.

Peggy set the coordinates for the spot where she had been with Savajic, and as soon as she got there she put up a façade and came out of haze. She hadn't taken anything with her except for her board because she was just delivering a message and wanted to travel light.

It was just after lunch when she located George. He was down by the bridge and was working his way back toward the quarry and counting the number of slate plates. She waited until he was well away from the bridge and glided down behind him.

Don't look around, George, it's Peggy. I've come to see you and the planners, she whispered.

What are you doing down here? The bridge is to be finished the early part of tomorrow morning so I have to make sure there are enough slate plates to complete it before we close everything down in the quarry.

When do you expect to go back to the cabin?

I'm not sure, George said, but it will be earlier than normal, so you will have to keep in touch with me somehow. I'll be at least another three hours if that helps you, Peggy.

It's a great help, Peggy said. I can go and build up my energy level to maximum and haze for longer so I can keep close to you and follow you when you leave.

When Peggy got back to her camp, she lay down on the ground behind her façade and said to herself, three hours, and tapped her forehead three times. It was a method of setting a time in her head to wake up. Savajic had taught her how to do it when she had trained for her field work. Soon she was asleep.

Hello, Savajic. We meet again. It was the high-pitched, gravelly voice of Helen Belbur. Savajic spun around. He instinctively went to go for his wand but he was in agony and could hardly move his arm. What's the matter, Savajic? Has something slowed you down? Helen's voice was almost a hiss. I must admit, she said, I thought you would have expired by now because we hit you with a powerful Degeneration Spell and your body should have shut down by now. However, let me use the time you have left to tell you a story. Once upon a time there was a young wizard bachelor whose father was high up in the Council of Wizards and well connected, but wizard women were not good enough for him, were they? So, he chose to marry a human woman and have a half-breed son. Well, let me tell you, we were not prepared to have our race contaminated by you, and you were never going to get away with it. It took us quite some time but we managed to dispose of your beloved Megan. It was simple enough to give her an untraceable poison and good-bye, Megan.

Savajic tried to move but he couldn't. You monster! he said. He was sitting on the stairs in the great hall looking up at the painting of Megan holding their son. Forgive me, my love, he said.

"Forgive me, my love!" shouted Helen, mocking him. She raised her wand and blasted the painting into a thousand pieces. Now then, she cried. Let us put an end to this story. Bring the boy here!

Two Death Riders dragged Owen in. He was unconscious. He had been in the pool and didn't have a chance to reach for his wand.

And now, Savajic, the last thing you will see in this life is the half-breed son of yours die. She turned to the two Death Riders holding Owen. Kill him, she commanded. There was a flash, and Owen laid dead on the hall floor.

No! screamed Savajic. Not Owen! He is only the same age as your own sons! But his plea fell on deaf ears, and he began to sob.

In your arrogance, Savajic, you forgot that your Proti spell protecting you was only as strong as you are, so you just let us in through the front door; how considerate of you. I'm bored now, Helen hissed, finish him off. There was a flash and Savajic lay dead, slumped across the stairs. Spare the human, she said, pointing at Cooper. He poses no threat, and they all disappeared.

Peggy awoke with a start. For a split-second she thought she heard Owen's voice and she felt a stabbing feeling in her stomach, but it disappeared as quickly as it came so she dismissed it and got herself ready to see how near George was to the quarry.

She started at the beginning of the bridge and followed the line of slate slabs back to the quarry. The last Hobgoblin had already left, and George and his crew and the other crew were tidying up and stowing away their equipment. Peggy landed behind George and let him know she was there. He put his hand to his mouth to hide his lip movement and said, We'll be away in the next ten minutes. The Hobgoblins are desperate to get ready for battle; it's all they can think of.

George got the all clear from the Black Watch wizards guarding them and gave the crews the signal to go back to their cabins, and then he climbed onto his board and took off, with Peggy right behind him. As soon as George opened the cabin door Peggy slipped through and moved to the back, out of the way and staying in haze. It wasn't long before they were joined by Brixun and Shovel. As soon as they had put up their Exclusion spells, Peggy came out of haze.

You are such a welcome sight, Peggy! Brixun said. We were getting really worried. We have no faith in the words of Helen Belbur.

You're right to have no faith because they plan to kill you when the Hobgoblins are on the bridge and out of sight. But I'm here to tell you not to worry. We have a plan for Owen and me to be here under haze, and ready and waiting for them to make a move, and then we will deal with them. Now as for your families, they will be quite safe. Commander Churmill has his special forces stationed at all of your homes ready to strike the Black Watch guards as soon as the signal comes from two members of special forces who are stationed by the start of the bridge behind a façade. So Savajic has asked me to tell you, you have no need to worry. He has one request to make of you, and that is, after we have disposed of Helen Belbur and her Death Riders, you stay for one hour and collapse the bridge and then go home to your families.

The pleasure will be all ours, the three wizards said as one, and began to shake hands and embrace each other.

At last, said Brixun, and gave Peggy a hug. Thank you from all of us, he said.

I'm not going to hang around, Peggy said. We have much to do. She touched her bracelet and disappeared.

Chapter 70

PEGGY'S BLOOD RUNS COLD

When Peggy appeared back in the great hall she was met by Cooper. Oh, Miss Peggy there has been a most terrible time while you've been away.

Peggy looked up at the black mark on the wall where Megan's portrait had hung. What's going on? What's happened? She looked at Cooper. He was a big, strong man but tears were streaming down his face.

It's the master and Owen, Miss Peggy. They have both been murdered. I've laid them out upstairs. I couldn't let you see what they had done to them.

Peggy was running upstairs. She burst into Savajic's room and lying side by side were Savajic and Owen. No! she screamed. No!

She felt Cooper's strong arm go across her shoulders. I was present when it all happened, he said. Please come downstairs and I'll make you a drink and tell you exactly what happened.

Peggy looked down at the two twisted and burned bodies; they were almost unrecognizable. She turned and followed Cooper downstairs.

She sat in one of the big leather chairs with her legs curled up, just like she did when she was a little girl listening to one of her mother's stories, and cupping a hot drink in both hands.

Cooper, what happened?

When you left this morning, Master Savajic became very ill. He could hardly stand up, and the pain in his back was making him cry out. I wanted to get Owen from the pool but he told me to leave him there so I did. He got me to carry him to the staircase and set him down under the painting of Megan and Owen and he began talking to it, and that's when the door burst open and several wizards and a woman wizard called Helen Belbur came in. Two of them went down to the pool and took Owen by surprise. They stunned him and dragged him up to the hall and sat him in front of his father.

She said when they had stunned the master outside the council chambers they had hit him with a Degeneration spell and she said she was surprised he had lasted so long. And then she went into a story of how the master had married a human and produced a half-breed son, and how they were about to put it right. She told the wizards to kill Owen. The master pleaded with them to spare him as he was only the same age as her own sons. She just laughed and screamed, kill him! There was a flash and Owen lay on the floor, dead. Then she turned to the wizards and said, I'm bored now, finish him off, and again there was a flash and the master was gone.

Cooper could hardly get his words out, his emotions were running so raw, and then he said, Helen had told the wizards to spare the Human as I wasn't a threat.

Peggy had gone white, every last drop of blood draining from her face. A rage was rising up inside her and her blood was running cold. She turned to Cooper and said, please leave me now. I have to get things sorted out. Cooper got up and left the room.

Chapter 71
VENDETTA

Peggy knew she was about to become a killer. She had been handed a vendetta, and it was one she couldn't refuse. And after it had been carried out, there would be no turning back. Every time she had used her wand it had been in self-defense, using a Flecta spell, but this time she would kill in cold blood. She had to clear her mind because tomorrow there could be no slip-ups; she had the lives of the planners and the quarry crews in her hands.

First things first, she told herself. She turned to the wall. Screen, she commanded. The screen appeared and she said, Enzebadier. He appeared immediately.

Greetings, Peggy. How can I help you?

It's bad news, I'm afraid, Peggy said. Her voice was a voice of controlled rage.

While I was away visiting the planners at the bridge, Helen Belbur and some of her Death Riders somehow managed to break through Savajic's Exclusion spell and they took Savajic and Owen by surprise. And then they murdered both Savajic and Owen.

Enzebadier stared at Peggy in disbelief. He was shocked at the news and his mind was racing. Stay where you are, he said. I'll be with you in ten minutes. Enzebadier arrived and he had a medical team with him. Where are they? he asked.

Peggy showed them up to Savajic's room and stood aside as they went inside and checked the bodies. When they were finished, Enzebadier said to Peggy, We will look after Savajic and Owen. Do you intend to stay here tonight?

Yes, said Peggy. I have a lot of things to do before tomorrow morning, so I will leave you to it.

Peggy went upstairs to her room, entered, and closed the door behind her. She lay on her bed and closed her eyes. A vision appeared. Standing in line were Savajic, Owen, Charlie, and Lilly. The alliance was broken and gone. He was her mentor and her adopted father, too.

She was in no doubt as to who was to blame: Helen Belbur. But killing her alone would not be good enough justice for what she had done. According to Cooper's version of what had happened, Helen Belbur had said to Savajic she intended to wipe the Menglor dynasty from the face of the world. Well, she hadn't quite managed to do it while she was alive, because she had Savajic's blood coursing through her body, and Helen Belbur had made a big mistake.

Her eyes opened and she sat up. She knew exactly what she was going to do. She quickly changed and set coordinates in her bracelet for the White Eagle School for Wizards and went into haze. Her luck was in; just as she arrived, the gate was being opened for two teachers who had come back from an outside visit and she slipped inside in between them.

Most of the students were getting ready to retire for the night and she was searching for signs of the Belbur twins. She heard loud laughing and shouting coming from the dining hall and immediately recognized the voices of the Belburs, and sure enough it was them in their normal showing-off pose.

And now it was a waiting game. As soon as they were alone, she would strike. An hour later, the twins were unconscious and on the way to the bridge. When they arrived, Peggy laid the twins down and put up a façade. She had brought a roll of tape with her and began binding the twins' hands and feet together. *Should keep them in check until tomorrow,* she thought. She looked at her watch and estimated she could sleep for six hours, and that would give her plenty of time to get the twins and herself down to the bridge, ready and in position for tomorrow's showdown. And now it was time to sleep. She lay on her back and went through her alarm call routine, and then she could feel Mother Earth feeding energy back into her body and she was soon asleep.

The dawn broke, and Peggy was ready for the day ahead. She looked down at the twins and poked them with the toe of her trainers. Wake up, boys, she said. You have a busy morning ahead of you.

Where are we? they both said together, their eyes squinting in the early morning sunlight.

Where indeed, Peggy said. Before I tell you where you are and why you're here, let me tell you something about your mother and what she is responsible for. While your father was in prison for multiple murders, your mother—who, incidentally, had your father arrested in the first place by leading the police to him—was taking over the leadership of the Black Watch and the Death Riders. She arranged the deaths of the students in the Dragon Island Swimming Championships, and that is why both of you were pulled out of the race. As soon as Baldric Zealotte was back on Earth, she arranged for your father to be murdered. Last night, she broke into the home of Savajic Menglor and murdered him and his son, Owen.

And today, your mother and both of you are going to pay the price for murdering my friends and family; it's as simple as that. And before you begin to protest, don't waste your breath; I'm not interested. All you can hope for now is that your mother is as good as she thinks she is. And now it's time for your gags, boys Peggy said as she began to tape up their mouths. She took their wands from her belt and broke them into tiny pieces and mixed them up and scattered them all around. You won't be needing them again, not where you're going to, she said. The twins looked at each other, terror etched on their faces.

Peggy picked up the twins by their coat collars and mounted her board, then went into haze and they all floated down to the bridge. As soon as she landed, she set up a façade and dropped the twins down on the ground behind it.

There was a loud rumbling sound in the distance, and over the hill Peggy could see the Hobgoblin army marching down the wide road towards the bridge. As they drew closer, she could see that in the front of the column were Petrid and Zealotte, marching side by side.

As they reached the bridge, Petrid gave the order to halt, and Zealotte moved off just as Helen Belbur arrived. Zealotte came straight to the point. Have the Death Riders arrived?

Yes, they have, she answered. They are ready and waiting.

Zealotte said, That's good. I trust they know what is expected of them?

Yes, I've been over every detail with them and they are ready to obey your orders.

Make sure we are well out of sight before you act. I will march with the army until the fighting starts, and then I will throw a Proti spell over myself and wait until the gate to the city is breached. Then I will enter the city and find Demodus and regain possession of the Sword of Destiny. When you have finished here and tidied up, send the Death Riders home and follow me across the bridge. I want you by my side when we take control of Greco City.

Helen Belbur had an evil smile on her face and punched the air with a clenched fist and screamed, Success to the Hobgoblins!

Zealotte rejoined the column, and Petrid gave the order to march.

Peggy watched as they marched past her. It was a frightening thing to see. Two hundred Bull Hounds, each one mounted by a Hobgoblin soldier, then four massive Trolls pulling a covered battering ram, and then the Hobgoblin army stretching out of sight; a whole nation at war.

As they passed by and began to disappear over the bridge, Peggy could see Helen Belbur and four Death Riders herding the planners and the quarry crews together into a group.

Listen up! Helen screamed. I'm going to give you a chance to defend yourselves. In front of you are your wands. They're a bit mixed up but that's part of the fun! Now, if you can get to them before we can kill you, you will go free. I'm going to count to five and on five, go for your wands!

She began to count. One! Suddenly, the Death Riders fell to the ground one by one, screaming in agony with their arms grotesquely twisted.

What's going on? Helen hissed.

I'm going on! Peggy said as she came out of haze. Helen went for her wand but Peggy was far too quick for her. There was a flash, and Helen's hand grasping her wand was lying on the ground.

Let me introduce myself, Peggy said. I am the adopted daughter of Savajic Menglor and sister of Owen Menglor and trust me, I'm your worst nightmare. And now let me introduce you to someone you do know. She pointed her wand at the façade and made it disappear, bringing into view her two sons, bound and gagged.

What are they doing here? Helen hissed.

They are going to die with you, Helen, Peggy replied. They are going to take you over the bridge to the Hobgoblin war.

That was good news to Helen because she knew Zealotte would be waiting for her on the other side of the bridge. But why my sons? she asked.

It's simple enough, Peggy said. I want you to watch them die just as you made Savajic watch when you murdered his son. And now you will need them to carry you. There were two flashes and Helen lay on the floor, screaming in agony, with both her feet missing.

Time for you to move on, Helen, Peggy said, looking down at her. Then she went over to the twins and cut them loose. Let's see how far you can get carrying your mother, big boys.

The twins picked their mother up and she hung limply in between them. Let's get out of here! Jed said to Guy, and they started to cross the bridge.

Don't go without your friends! Peggy said, pointing at the four Death Riders. They got to their feet and followed Helen onto the bridge. They all watched in stunned silence as the twins began walking. The only sound that could be heard was of Helen's painful crying.

The wizards were all trying to sort out their wands from the tangled pile they were in and by the time they had all found them, the Belburs were some three hundred yards across the bridge.

Peggy turned to Brixun and Showvel and said, My family have paid a terrible price to save you and your families from being murdered, and now I ask you for just one small favor in return.

Anything, Peggy, just name it, they both said together.

Peggy looked out over at the Belburs fading into the distance and said, Collapse this end of the bridge. The wizards raised their wands and there was a loud rumble as section after section of the bridge collapsed into the worm fields, and the Belburs and the Death Riders became just another meal for the Snack Worms.

Thank you, Peggy said. Now please all go home to your families, who I'm sure will be missing you and will be worrying about your safety.

One by one they all thanked Peggy and flew away off home.

Peggy turned and looked to where the bridge had stood and with her powerful hearing skills she heard the terrified screams of the Belburs and the Death Riders as they realized what was about to happen to them. She felt no sympathy for them; in fact, right at that moment in time, she had no feelings for anything. Her vendetta had been executed, and now she had to go home and regroup and decide on her next move.

Chapter 72
THE BATTLE LOOMS

High up in the trees on the fringe of the forest, the Gnome lookouts suddenly spotted the bridge as the façade lifted and the Hobgoblins came into sight, marching in columns of ten. It would take them an hour to reach the forest, and the lookouts were already on their way down the trees and mounting their horses and would soon be back at Greco and raising the alarm.

As soon as Demodus had word of the advancing Hobgoblins, he began giving out orders to his clones. He made absolutely sure they were all in place and knew precisely what was expected of them. He had already programmed the drones with the coordinates of their targets, and once they took to the sky they would be on a one-way mission. The last drone to take to the sky would destroy the bridge and then carry on to its target.

His cavalry was mounted, ready and waiting for the signal to perform their pincer movement and attack from the rear. The snipers were ready and waiting for the sight of the first Flying Bull Hounds. Now it was a waiting game.

When Peggy arrived back she was met in the great hall by Cooper. He still looked very upset. You have a visitor, Miss Peggy. I've taken the liberty of putting her in the study and serving a light refreshment. Is there anything I can get for you?

No, I'm all right for the moment, she replied, and walked towards the study.

As she entered the study, she was surprised to see Princess Sheiklin sitting there. What a nice surprise! she said. But what are you doing here at a time like this?

The princess stood up and walked over to Peggy with outstretched hands. I came as soon as I was informed about the death of Savajic and his son, Owen. Peggy, I am so sorry for your loss. Peggy, we Goblins are on the verge of regaining our country back and living once more as a free nation, and none of this would have been possible without the hard work and clever planning of Savajic and yourself. We owe you a great debt of gratitude.

I am truly happy for you, Peggy said, and you have no debt to us whatsoever. The deaths of Savajic and Owen have been avenged, and the Belbur clan have been wiped from the face of the Earth. And yet I have an empty feeling, and have never felt such loneliness before. I know there is still much more to do if we are to defeat the Hobgoblins and banish them to the history books. Now this part of the battle is down to Demodus and his powers, and the sequel of the next few days will determine all of our futures.

Chapter 73
PETRID'S PLAN

The Hobgoblins were crashing through the forest at a relentless pace, spurred on by Petrid. In another five hours' time they would be at the edge of the forest and next to no man's land. From there on there would be no cover.

Petrid was taking nothing for granted, for he knew the Gnomes would know by now of their presence and would probably be panicking and putting their army on alert to defend themselves. He laughed out loud. They don't have a chance, he told himself.

His first move would be to position the Bull Hounds and get them airborne and give cover to the Trolls pulling the battering ram towards the city gates. The Bull Hounds would fly as fast as possible and deliver two hundred Hobgoblin soldiers to the city walls. Then the main army would charge in after them. Their only orders were to take no prisoners, and now the clock was ticking. He had two hundred of his best bows all carrying six heat-seeking arrows each. His plan was to fire all of the arrows over the city walls, killing as many Gnomes as possible and creating panic in the streets. When the soldiers on the Bull Hounds got to the city walls they would try and gain entry over the walls and attempt to open the great gates.

When they reached the far edge of the forest, he intended to camp for the night and rest his army after their march, and then when the dawn rose, he would attack.

Demodus had asked the king to order his army to make sure the entire population were barricaded in their homes, with all windows and doors securely closed. He knew the heat-seeking arrows would soon be on their way, but with no targets to seek out, they would land harmlessly. His clone army were to be put under cover. He was taking no chances, and had put them all under a massive wooden dome that the Gnome army used as a training venue. As soon as the all clear was given they would mass behind the city gates, ready to charge when the gates were opened.

Dusk was falling, and Demodus stood in front of the city walls. As he looked out over the vast plain of barren land that stretched all the way to the forest. He could smell the stench of death all around him. It was a smell that was familiar to him from his countless battles in the past. The sky had a deep purple hue and looked foreboding. Tomorrow it would be a sky overlooking a fierce, bloody battle, a killing field, with no mercy shown by either of the opposing sides. He gave a deep sigh, turned around, and walked back through the door in the city gate.

Chapter 74
CHARGE

As soon as dawn broke, Petrid was organizing the Bull Hounds and their Hobgoblin riders into columns ready for the first wave of the attack. The Hobgoblins had checked that they had all got a full quiver of arrows each and were raring to get started. Petrid checked and double checked that everything was in place, and when he was satisfied, he stood and looked towards Greco City and screamed: "CHARGE!"

The Bull Hounds spread their powerful wings and took to the sky, wave after wave followed, and as the last wave took off, the Trolls began pulling the mighty ram towards Greco's massive gates. And then the Hobgoblins began their advance.

The mould was set. There would be no turning back, and now it was kill or be killed. Petrid turned to Zealotte and said, tonight, my friend you will have your sword back in your possession and the keys to Greco City, and I will be counting my gold. They both screamed with laughter. Petrid said to Zealotte, until later, my friend, and took off to be in front of his army, he had the smell of victory in his nostrils, and all he could think of was glory.

Demodus was watching and waiting. He didn't want to show his hand too soon. The façade was due to disappear when the Hobgoblins were two hundred meters from the gates of the city. This would give him eight hundred meters of the Hobgoblin army in the sights of his guns. They would be cut down before they realized what had hit them. Trip wires had been laid so the first Hobgoblins would set off flares, and that was the signal for the guns to let loose. Then, as soon as the guns began to fire, the cavalry would take off and begin their pincer movement and attack from the rear. The snipers had been instructed to fire as soon as they had a clear target of the Bull Hounds. They were expected to come fast and furious. Two drones were in the air circling and ready to back up the snipers.

The flares suddenly erupted. The façade disappeared and the machine guns sprang into action; the noise was deafening. There was a look of complete amazement on Petrid's face as he fell to the ground, dying, but his army kept on advancing, not realizing what they were walking into, and now the cavalry were on their way and would soon be attacking from the rear.

The Hobgoblins riding on the Bull Hounds, however, were having far more success. Their sheer weight of numbers were too much for the snipers, and several of them had been killed. The Hobgoblins were swarming over the city walls and picking off the snipers, and as soon as the Hobgoblins were on the city walls, the Bull Hounds peeled off and flew away, their part of the battle complete.

The drones were blasting the Bull Hounds out of the sky and they were taking too much punishment. The last few suddenly turned and began to fly away. It was too late; the drones had been programed to destroy them and that is exactly what they did. As soon as the last of the Bull Hounds fell from the sky, their instructions were to return to base.

Demodus had re-entered the city and was doing what he was good at; killing the enemy. He cut his way through the Hobgoblins, showing no mercy. His sword was deflecting both arrows and axes and keeping him safe from harm.

It was late afternoon when the Hobgoblins had had enough and were in full retreat. They had managed to overcome and kill the drone cavalry, now it was all about getting back to the bridge and getting home. Demodus had opened the city gates and sent the rest of his clone army off in pursuit of the Hobgoblins, and as soon as he had word, the clones had followed the Hobgoblins onto the bridge and trapped them. He gave his final orders to his drones. One by one they took to the sky, all programmed for their own targets, their mission to destroy. The last one to go was the one programmed to destroy the bridge, all of them on a one-way mission.

The Hobgoblins were on the bridge, fighting for their lives, not knowing they were about to face their worst nightmare, the Snack Worms. As the drone moved along the bridge it released its missiles one by one, collapsing it section by section and then finally it smashed into the bridge and exploded. It was then that the Hobgoblins realized they were destined for the Snack Worms and the screams began, but it was all over for them. To the clones it meant nothing; there was no feeling and no fear.

At the same time the Goblins were all taking cover from the drones, the destruction of the Hobgoblin bolt holes had begun. Soon they would be a free nation once again, able to mold a new future for themselves.

Chapter 75
ENTER ZEALOTTE

All through the battle, Zealotte had been hiding safely under a Proti spell. Why take unnecessary risks? he asked himself. And he had been right. The battle had gone badly wrong and they had walked directly into an ambush. He was trapped, out in the open, right in the middle of the battlefield, surrounded by dead Hobgoblins. He knew that the instant he removed the Proti spell he would be vulnerable to attack.

However, his mind was made up for him.

Who are you? The question was fired at him and took him by surprise.

Baldric Zealotte, he said without thinking.

And you are the great Baldric Zealotte then, are you? asked a mocking voice.

Zealotte looked up at the mighty figure in front of him; it was Demodus. Your plan is in tatters, Zealotte. So what do you intend to do now?

Before he could answer, the ground suddenly began to rumble and shake and a great hole appeared in the ground and began to draw the bodies of the dead Hobgoblins into it. Demodus lifted up his sword to protect himself. The ground shook again, and a giant figure of flame appeared. There is no need for you to protect yourself,

Demodus! roared a voice. I have not come for you but for the souls of the Hobgoblins!

Kanzil! exclaimed Demodus. We meet again. Was this all your idea?

Not mine, Kanzil answered, but I intend to help myself to a healthy harvest of evil souls.

Please be my guest, said Demodus. Suddenly a swarm of Fire Imps came pouring out of the hole and began pulling the dead Hobgoblins down into the hole and dispatching them into the magma, and when they were done the dead Bull Hounds followed them and the hole closed in over them.

Kanzil looked down on Zealotte, who was now cowering in terror and roared at him, Despite all the help I gave to you, you have failed me miserably! And now you must pay the price of failing me. Demodus, you have the power of the sword. Use it!

Demodus levelled his sword and thrust it at Zealotte. It went through the Proti bubble and deep into Zealotte's heart. Blood poured from his mouth and he fell to his knees and died. Demodus looked up at the towering figure of fire and said, Kanzil, he is all yours.

We still have unfinished business between us! Kanzil roared. A little matter of my sword. Give it back to me now and let us both wipe the slate clean once and for all time. I will return it to the magma and destroy it, and it will disappear from your world forever. On this you have my word!

Demodus looked at the sword in his hand. It had been both his destiny and his loyal friend for so many years; how could he give it back? A voice came into his head; it was the sword speaking to him. *"Demodus, you released me from the stone that had held me captive for so many years, and when you took it and wielded it you became the master of your own destiny. It took a strange path, and now you have arrived. I now ask you to return me to my true master, Kanzil, so you and your nation can live in peace."*

Demodus held the hilt of the sword in a vise-like grip and he realized the sword was right. Good-bye, my loyal friend, he said, and threw the sword to Kanzil. It flashed in the evening sun like a comet in the sky. Kanzil caught it and the ground rumbled and opened and Kanzil disappeared, and Zealotte was also gone.

A Gnome soldier approached on horseback with a horse for Demodus. The king and our people are waiting for you, Demodus.

He mounted his horse and they rode towards the city gates. The gates had been opened, and the Gnomes were lining the streets stretching all the way to the palace and the king. They were chanting his name and calling him champion; Demodus the giant Gnome had finally come home. The king greeted him on the palace steps and pronounced to the nation that he had once more become the king and the nation's true champion.

After going through two hours of congratulations and compliments, Demodus asked to be excused. He requested he be allowed to go to his villa and rest. The king of course said yes.

Over the past few weeks, the Gnomes had been working on the villa in preparation for his return, and when he arrived it was warm and welcoming. Your bath has been prepared, Demodus, and the women have prepared warm oils for your body, said his guard.

Thank you, said Demodus. He was beginning to feel at home already, and it felt good.

After he had bathed and eaten, he retired. He had things to do before he slept. He asked for a pen and paper and sealing wax, then settled down and began to write out his will. That night he intended to take the Tiger Tooth pendant off for good. It had been a wonderful gift from his father, a gift that had enabled him to live through many perils and survive long enough to save his race from annihilation by the Hobgoblins. But now it was time to give it up. All through his long life of fighting and killing, only one creature had resisted all his attempts to kill. A young Human girl named Peggy Goody, a brave girl who had now grown into a woman and a true friend. He could not think of anyone who would put it to good use more than her. It would be her choice whether or not to wear it. He would leave her a letter about what it was and how to use it. His villa was to be left to the nation and turned into a museum.

When he had finished writing, he took the pendant from around his neck and put it into a box and locked it. He then wrapped the key in the letter for Peggy and sealed it, then he used the hot wax to stick the letter to the box so they could not get separated from each other. And now he was ready for sleep.

He lay down on his bed and closed his eyes. He had not felt such peace of mind for so long, not since before the death of his father, Valyew Sellum.

His mind was drifting to another time and place. He could smell the sweet and fresh air. He was back in Nectar Valley, walking through the grape vines. It was warm and sunny, and he was feeling happy. In the distance he could see two figures walking towards him and as they got closer, he recognized his father with a young girl. He began running towards them. "Father!" he shouted, and his father waved and shouted "Demodus!" He looked at his father; tears were flooding down his face.

I've missed you so much, he said. Valyew was crying too, so was the young girl.

Demodus, this is your mother, Mobo, Valyew said. She passed on shortly after you were born, but she lived long enough to hold you and give you your name.

Demodus looked down at his mother; she was so tiny, and he felt an instant love for her. And my father? he asked. Valyew said, alas, he is not of this world, Demodus.

Demodus held out his hand to touch his mother but he had no feeling of her and he pulled back his hand in surprise. Is this just a dream? he asked.

Valyew said, At this moment in time, Demodus, your body is asleep, but your spirit has entered an astral plane where all of our spirits go when eventually we leave our Earthly bodies. You have put your house in order, and will now decide whether or not you are ready to pass over. The choice is yours.

I want to join you, Father, and I want to hold my mother close to me. Then go back to your body and as soon as your heart stops and your brain closes down, your spirit will rise and we will all be reunited again.

Demodus was back in his body once more. His face was relaxed and peaceful, and his massive chest heaved a great sigh and his heart stopped beating. At long last he was at peace and going home.

Chapter 76
Peggy Goes To Greco

The Hobgoblin war was over, but the Gnome nation was in a state of shock as the news of the death of Demodus spread among them. It didn't seem possible, but it was true. Demodus, their great champion, was dead.

Peggy had received a message from the king informing her of his death and requesting her to visit him at the palace as soon as possible. She didn't waste any time; within thirty minutes she was dressed and waiting to see the king. She noticed the stunned silence all around and realized she was witnessing a nation in mourning. The king's guard showed her into the throne room where the king was waiting to greet her.

Peggy bowed her head, and said, Your Majesty.

Welcome, Peggy, said the king. I'm afraid this isn't the welcome I had intended for you, after all you have sacrificed for my nation.

I have something for you that was in Demodus's last wishes. He produced the box with the letter attached and said, You are to take it home and open it in private.

Peggy took hold of the box and thanked the king. I will obey his wishes, she said. The king held out his hands to Peggy and she held him in a firm grip. Their gaze met and Peggy looked into the king's eyes. She could see the pain in them.

His bottom lip was trembling as her said to her, Thank you for all you have done for me and my kingdom. We will never forget what you have sacrificed for us, and I will carry you forever in my heart.

Peggy said, Your Majesty, may I see Demodus before I return home?

Yes, said the king. He is lying in state at the Hall of Worship. He gave orders to his guard to escort Peggy to the Hall of Worship and clear a path through the thousands of Gnomes wishing to pay their last respects to Demodus.

The outpouring of sorrow and love, sobbing and wailing all mixed together was a testimony of their love for him. She gazed down at Demodus and saw something in his face, something she hadn't seen before; a relaxed and gentle side to him, a warrior at peace with himself. It seemed as though all the centuries of fighting battle after battle that had hardened and changed him had gone. He had returned to being the Giant Gnome he had been when he was banished all those years ago. Something in her head told her it could be a gift from the Golden Fairy Queen as a sign of her forgiveness. Peggy leaned over and kissed him on the cheek. Thank you, Demodus, for being a friend. She turned and walked away.

Chapter 77
THE GIFT

Peggy laid the box with the letter attached to it down on Savajic's desk and looked at the empty chair behind it. How had all of this come about? Everyone and everything she loved and treasured in this dimension had gone forever, all lost in less than a year. How fickle and cruel fate could be! She pulled the letter from off the box and opened it. Demodus began the letter by apologizing for not handing her the box himself, but he didn't want anyone trying to talk him out of his decision to leave his war-torn body, and said after his long journey and his final redemption he was now at peace and with his loved ones. Then he went into detail about what the Tiger tooth was and how it had kept him alive for so many years. He explained that once she put it on, only she could remove it. Anyone who tried to remove it by force would be struck down by its power. He went on to say its powers had to be kept a closely guarded secret, and she now had three choices. One, to wear it. Two, to hide it. Or three, to smash it into a thousand pieces and scatter it in the wind. The Tiger tooth was now hers to do with what she wished.

He went on to say, Peggy, you are the only person on earth I would give this to because you are brave and honest, and I trust you to do the right thing. Last but not least, I have killed Zealotte and dispatched both him and the Sword of Destiny to Kanzil, who has said he will cast it into the magma where it will be destroyed, and in return he has promised to leave us all in peace. One last thing; Kanzil has said he will rid us of the worm fields and the Snack Worms. He intends to draw down the bridge, the tunnels, and the Snack Worms into the magma and leave behind a great canyon.

Good-bye, Peggy, my friend. Demodus.

Good-bye, Demodus, she said as she placed the letter down on Savajic's desk, then she sat down opposite the desk and fixed her eyes on the box. If only Savajic were here, he'd know what to do. But he wasn't, and he would never be again. It dawned on her for the first time she would have to reason things out and make all of her decisions by herself for the rest of her life.

She had been so lucky. She had had the very best of teachers, who had been so generous to her with their secrets and knowledge, and most of all she had had Savajic, the master, who had made it all possible for her. He had shared his home, his magic, and even his blood with her. She wasn't about to let him down. She had carried out her vendetta, and she didn't intend to stop there. He had taught her to be positive but careful at the same time. She stood up and walked over to the box, opened it, and picked up the Tiger tooth pendant and placed it over her head and tucked it in behind her tee shirt.

The wall screen sprang to life and Professor Enzebadier was standing there. Greetings, Peggy, he said in a very sober voice. Peggy acknowledged the professor and asked him how she could help. I need to meet with you as soon as possible, he said. Could I come to your home in the next hour?

Certainly, Professor. I intend to be here for the rest of the day.

Good, replied Enzebadier. I'll see you later. The screen faded and Enzebadier disappeared.

As Peggy sat and stared at the blank wall, her thoughts dwelt on something Demodus had put in his letter to her about Kanzil ridding the world of the bridge, the worm fields, and the Snack Worms. Screen, she said. And then, The bridge. Her timing was perfect because as soon as the bridge rubble came into view, a loud rumble began that got louder and louder, and a massive crack in the earth appeared and stretched out of sight in both directions.

It was the most frightening thing Peggy had ever seen. But the implications of this was far more frightening. It meant that at any time, anywhere in the world, Kanzil had the power to wipe out all of the great cities in the world; his powers had no limit. She stood up and said, Clear, and the terrible sight of destruction disappeared.

She had spent many hours discussing Kanzil with Savajic, and he had come to the conclusion that as long as Kanzil could enter people and corrupt them, then the Human race would be able to survive. His victories were our defeats, and we walked headlong into his plans time after time. He used religion, race, greed, mistrust, and military power to feed his never-ending appetite for evil. And he concluded there would always be evil in the world, and it was up to us all to put up a fight against it and be on constant guard.

Chapter 78
SAVAJIC'S WILL

There was a knock on the study door and Cooper appeared. Your guests have arrived, Miss Peggy. Shall I show them in?

Yes, please, Cooper, she said, and stood up, ready to greet Enzebadier. Peggy was surprised to see the professor had two other wizards with him.

Please let me introduce you to Professor Goldberg and Simon Demooz. They are responsible for looking after Savajic's assets and capital. They exchanged greetings and shook hands and all sat down. Both wizards were carrying briefcases, and Professor Goldberg began.

To begin with, this will was drawn up some three months ago. Savajic had received the decision from the Council of Wizards rejecting his request for permission to marry a second Human woman. He had already obtained the blessing of the Council to marry his first wife, and have a son of mixed blood, and then he was given permission to mix blood with you, Peggy. This was already more than any other wizard had done.

And because of this, Savajic had decided to abdicate the wizard world and surrender his wand for destruction. All of this was planned to take place as soon as the Hobgoblin war with the Gnomes had come to its final conclusion and Baldric Zealotte was captured or killed. Unfortunately, fate had other ideas, and what I am here for is to show you how this all unravels. The line of succession was next of kin, his son, Owen. Owen was supposed to share certain assets between you Peggy and your mother, Rose. But the death of Savajic and Owen both at the same time has changed everything. Before I go on, please let me hand over to Professor Enzebadier.

Peggy, before I start, I want you to put your wizard head on and look at what I say from a wizard's point of view.

Peggy, as you know, the wizard world lives in a different dimension to the human race. This was determined by wizards and put into law thousands of years ago, and it was decided because of our magical powers. We were attracting too much attention to ourselves, so we removed ourselves to a fourth dimension, where we have lived out of sight ever since. But our law makers did not stop us from visiting the third dimension, as long as we left our wands behind and dressed and acted as humans. Over the years, many wizards have abdicated from the wizard world and relinquished their magical power. Savajic was one of the very few who managed to get permission to marry a human and bring her into the wizard world. But he was banned from teaching her any kind of magic.

Savajic spent four of his younger years in the human world and amassed a massive fortune of assets and international currency, and every part of his wealth is in the human world, including the house we are in now.

Peggy, you are now the only beneficiary, and you have got to decide what your next move will be. If you decide to go back to your roots in the human world, you will have to surrender your wand and your magic. You will retain the mental powers your wizard blood affords you. Your vast wealth will remain intact because it belongs in the human world, and you will be guided through the details by Simon Demooz. But before I hand you over to him, there is one more important issue to be addressed.

Your mother, Rose, will have to have all parts of the wizard world, including all memories of Eastly Abbey and of Savajic, erased from her memory. She will never remember anything, not even you going to Black Eagle. Savajic told me in strict confidence of your dealings and of the mission you underwent for the British Secret Service. You, of course, had to leave your wand behind before you left, but it didn't seem to hamper your mission in any way. Cooper and Henry will also have their memories wiped clean and will revert back to a normal butler and driver. Members of staff would replace Savajic's magical spells and an estate manager would be appointed.

Enzebadier turned to Simon and said, If you will please take it from here, Simon.

Simon Demooz opened his briefcase and took out a single sheet of paper. Peggy, if you will allow me at this moment in time I would like to give you a brief statement of affairs.

He began with real estate. You have properties in seven countries, they are all taken care of by a real estate company in London. In the same seven countries, you have the equivalent of five million pounds, sterling, in the various countries' currency. You have gold reserves worth in excess of a billion pounds, sterling. You have shares in aviation, natural gas, water and hydro-power. In all worth nine billion pounds, sterling.

Peggy looked shocked. It's too much for one person to handle, she said, looking at Simon.

You don't have to, he said, trying to reassure her. You have an army of employees all in place handling all of your businesses. All you have to do is turn up to a few meetings a year. Now, I think I should leave you with this statement to study, and before I leave, perhaps we could set a future date when we can spend a full day together.

Enzebadier asked Simon and Professor Goldberg to leave the room while he spoke to Peggy in private, and as the door closed behind them, he turned to Peggy and asked what happened at the bridge.

Peggy replied in great detail, withholding nothing, and then she told him what was in the letter Demodus had left for her.

How the Hobgoblin race had been erased from the face of the earth along with Zealotte and the Sword of Destiney. And Kanzil had promised to rid the world of the worm fields and leave the Gnome nation in peace.

Peggy said, Professor, I would like you to see this. She commanded, screen, and then, bridge. The bridge had disappeared and a great canyon was forming. Kanzil is keeping his promise to Demodus and is drawing every trace of the bridge and all that was on it and the worm fields, down into the magma.

Peggy looked at Enzebadier and said, Everyone I ever held dear to my heart in the wizard world has been cruelly taken away from me, but I will always regard myself very lucky to have had the chance to live in the wizard world and the gifts so generously bestowed on me. Now I feel my time here has come to an end and I ask of you just one thing, and that is, when all the events of this bloody war are written down in wizard history, Savajic and his son were responsible for the survival of the wizard world, and Peggy Goody is excluded from the events. After all, other than my teachers at Black Eagle and the War Council, no one knows who I am, so it shouldn't be difficult to wipe me from wizard history.

Enzebadier said, Peggy, we owe you so much, the least we can do is grant you your wish. Your mother will awaken tomorrow with no knowledge of the wizard world or anything associated with it; nothing will be done to harm her.

Peggy stood up. Professor, will you ask Simon to meet me here at 9:00 a.m. tomorrow and go over everything with me? I need to tidy it all up as quickly as possible.

Chapter 79
PEGGY GOES HOME

Simon Demooz was on time and ready for a busy day ahead. He had his briefcase and a laptop with him. Good morning, Peggy, he said as Cooper opened the study door for him to enter.

Good morning, Simon, Peggy said. She was quite excited and looking forward to the financial journey Simon Demooz was about to take her on. When she had woken up that morning, she realized she was probably one of the richest women in the world and it was not only a great responsibility, but keeping it a secret was going to be a very difficult task.

She had cleared her mind, exactly the way Savajic had taught her to, and was ready to memorize the massive amount of detail involved. Simon was very precise and had prepared presentations on his laptop, and apart from a small lunch break, it was non-stop for seven hours. As Simon came to a close, he gave the name and address of two humans. These are your business consultants. Each one was completely trusted by Savajic. Each one has complete control over the workings of your assets and capital and gold reserves, approximately fifty-fifty each. The names are never spoken, so I would ask you to memorize them and destroy the paper I have given you.

There are two final things for you to do, Peggy. First, to access your bank accounts around the world you will need a password. At the moment it is Zigbo, a word chosen by Savajic. But if you wish to change it you may do so.

Zigbo sounds good to me, Peggy said. I'd like to keep it.

Good, Simon continued. Now last of all I need to register an image of your right iris, then you are ready to use all of your banking accounts. From his briefcase Simon produced a disc, which he held up to Peggy's right eye. Look straight ahead, he said, and a light flashed and it was done.

Simon was packed up and ready to leave. Before I go, Peggy, may I suggest you go and see your financial advisers and introduce yourself to them at the first opportunity you get? They will be a very important part of your life when you return to the human world. I myself will have informed them that you are now the sole beneficiary of his estate and his fortune. I would like to take this opportunity, Peggy, of wishing you success in all your endeavors in the future.

After Simon Demooz had left, Peggy paced around Savajic's study, pondering on what lay ahead, and then it hit her. It wasn't Savajic's study anymore, it was hers. Eastly Abbey and the whole estate was hers.

She sat down behind the desk and sank into the soft leather chair. She had the strange feeling Savajic was looking down on her and nodding his head in approval. I won't let you down, she whispered, and lay her head on the desk. It was time to let go of all the pent-up emotions she had been denying herself. She wept uncontrollably until she fell asleep.

There was a knock on the study door and Peggy awoke with a start. Cooper entered and asked if he should lay out in the dining room for dinner. Not tonight, Peggy said, but I would like a plate of sandwiches and a pot of tea here in the study please.

Fifteen minutes later, Peggy was tucking into a plate of sandwiches. She was so hungry! She had hardly eaten anything all day apart from a few biscuits at lunchtime.

Tomorrow was decision day on whether or not to leave the wizard world for good. If that was her final decision, then she would have to surrender her wand to Enzebadier for destruction, there would be no going back. She decided to sleep on it and make her final decision in the morning after a good night's sleep.

Peggy was up early. She had eaten breakfast and was ready to go to the council meeting. Her mind was made up; she was going home, for good. She had written a short speech, thanking the wizard world for all she had received from them, and of her decision to go home, never to return. She set the coordinates on her bracelet, but suddenly she had an uneasy feeling of danger. Go there in haze, she told herself. Remember what happened to Savajic. Tread carefully, and be prepared.

Peggy arrived at the council chamber in haze. There were three wizards waiting outside. Why hadn't they gone in? The chamber was open. She stayed in haze and decided to look around, and as she approached the three wizards she saw that they had their wands drawn and were ready for action. It was a trap waiting to be sprung on her. But where were the others? She was sure they would want backup; it was the way these cowards worked. She skirted the area and sure enough, four wizards were hiding behind a façade. She was ten meters behind them and tempted to just blast them, but that would alert the others so she put them out of action and splintered their wands. Then she walked through the façade.

Good morning, gentlemen, she said to the three wizards. Are you waiting for me? All their wands shot up and pointed at her but they were far too late; the three wizards were dead before they hit the ground. She looked down at them with a cold stare. They were all strangers to her. She shrugged her shoulders and turned her attention to the other four wizards.

The façade had disappeared and the wizards were cowering in fear of their lives. Give me one good reason why I shouldn't just kill you, she said.

Information! one of the wizards blurted out.

OK, Peggy said. Let's see if it will be good enough to keep you alive, let's have it.

They are waiting in the chamber for you. They have taken Enzebadier and some of the council members prisoners and if you enter the chamber you will be killed on sight. Their leader is Silas Slift, a cousin of Helen Belbur. They were very close, almost like brother and sister, and he has sworn to avenge her death by killing you.

Are they all Death Riders in there?

Yes, said the wizard. They are the last seven; all the others are dead. We were ordered here by them and told to stun you if they missed you.

And would you have? Peggy said.

The wizard looked at her and said, They told us if we didn't do as they asked, our families would be killed.

Peggy knew he was probably telling the truth, thinking back to the planners and the threats they had worked under.

Listen carefully to what I say, Peggy said, looking down at the wizards sitting on the ground. Mount your boards and go home to your families. Do not stop on the way for even one moment, is that clear?

Yes, the four wizards said as one, all looking very relieved. Before you go, I promise you the Death Riders inside the chamber will never kill again. Now, get going.

Peggy stood quite still for a while, pondering which way to tackle the problem. She intended to kill the seven Death Riders but at the same time, she couldn't risk hurting Enzebadier and the other council members. She decided she would not use her wand, it was far too dangerous in such a confined area. She had all the skills she needed.

She took a deep breath and went into haze and walked through the open door into the chamber. Her senses were on full alert. She moved away from the door and scanned the chamber looking for likely hiding places and listening for sounds of breathing and any slight movement. Enzebadier was sitting in the Elders chair at the end of the chamber and the other council members were seated in their usual seats. It all looked normal except for the silence, and that was not normal.

This was going to take time because they were not going to offer themselves up. She was going to have to find where they were and pick them off one by one and maintain silence at the same time. She already had two big advantages, because she knew there were seven of them inside the chamber, so until she had seven dead bodies, she would stay in haze. Once again Savajic had come to her rescue. He wasn't there in person but she had his anti-façade baton tucked into her wand belt and she was almost certain they would all be hiding behind one.

She was standing on the left side of the door and decided to circle the chamber, staying close to the wall. She took the anti-façade baton from out of her belt and switched it on. At first nothing showed up, but as she got close to the first council member she could see a wizard dressed in black robes standing directly behind him with his wand drawn and pointing towards the entrance of the chamber, ready to blast her the moment she walked through the door. She knew the other six would be doing exactly the same. The good thing was, because they were close up to the council members' seats, she would be able to get behind them with sufficient room for her to attack them.

Here goes, she told herself. She came up behind the first wizard, who had his eyes firmly fixed on the entrance, and in a split-second his head was facing the opposite way, his neck broken and stone dead. Peggy laid him down on the floor being careful not to make a sound and to make sure he was out of sight because when the wizard died, his façade died with him. It took Peggy twenty minutes to circle the chamber but she only had six bodies. Where was the seventh?

She stood in the doorway, took out her anti-façade baton, switched it on and walked directly towards Enzebadier. She had sensed a change in the pattern and she was right. Crouched in front of Enzebadier was the seventh wizard, his wand drawn and pointing at the entrance, waiting for her to appear. The look on his face was priceless when Peggy snatched the wand from his grip. He stood up and looked all around, and his façade disappeared.

I believe you are looking for me, said a voice. It was Peggy. She had come out of haze and stepped out from behind Enzebadier's seat.

You sniveling coward. Peggy looked at him with contempt. You want to kill me but you hide behind others. I should kill you where you stand, but that would be too good for you, and I'm sure Professor Enzebadier has other plans for you.

Enzebadier stood up and said, Indeed I do have plans for this one, Peggy. I'm so very relieved to see you have come through this episode unscathed. He raised his wand and pointed it at Silas Slift. Shackle! he commanded, and Silas Slift was immediately in heavy chains.

There was shouting coming from outside the chamber and Semach Siege came bursting in, followed by a dozen policemen. Enzebadier held up his hand and declared, Everything is back to normal, Semach, you can stand your men down.

Semach looked relieved to find Enzebadier safe and well. We found four dead Death Riders outside, are there any more?

Peggy spoke up. Yes, there are six more behind the councilors' seats, all dead, and then we have this one. She pointed at the shackled wizard.

Enzebadier said, Semach, will you take charge of the situation please? I need to speak with Peggy. He turned to Peggy and said, Please come with me.

Enzebadier showed Peggy into his private rooms where they both sat down and began to talk. Have you come to a decision on whether or not you wish to leave the wizard world, Peggy?

I have, Peggy answered. She withdrew her wand and handed it to Enzebadier. I've decided it's time to go home, she said. And I will never forget what you have done for me.

We owe you a great debt, Enzebadier said, and I will make sure your wishes are carried out to the letter. Wizard history will show no trace of your existence, and all credit for the outcome of the war with Zealotte and the Death Riders will go to Savajic and his son, Owen. Your ability to enter the wizard world will cease when you leave. You have wizard blood so your mental powers will remain the same; how much wizard magic you will retain is unknown to us, and is something you will find out for yourself. Your mother has been visited in her sleep and all memories of Savajic and the wizard world have been erased from her mind. We have planted a story in her mind that you have been away working for the government on a secret mission for the last twelve months and she must not ask you questions about it. Eastly Abbey has returned to normal, and a full staff and an estate manager have been put into place. Cooper is still the butler, and Henry is still your personal driver. Both of their minds have been cleared of any knowledge of Savajic and his family. The stable staff remain the same, and their minds have had any memories of Savajic and his family removed.

Your mother believes you have inherited Eastly Abbey from an American multi-millionaire, whose life you saved on a secret mission for the government. We have researched all of the clothing you and your mother have worn while staying at Eastly and have put in place a comprehensive wardrobe to provide you and your mother with everything from evening wear to sports and leisure wear.

Cooper and the staff will address you as Lady Jayne and your mother as Lady Rose. Today, Peggy, is the first day of your new life and your future lies ahead of you.

Peggy, the wizard world and I wish you good fortune and a full and successful life in the Human world.

Peggy set her bracelet and said good-bye to Enzebadier. Nothing happened. She gave Enzebadier a puzzled look. He smiled at her and said, I'm sorry, Peggy, but that was Savajic's magic. It is no longer yours to use. Please don't worry too much. You will soon adjust to your loss of wizard magic. But you will retain much of what you have learned.

And now I have arranged transport for your return to Eastly Abbey. Ten minutes later, she was back home in Eastly Abbey.

Chapter 80
ONE YEAR LATER

Henry came to a halt at the lodge where the gatekeeper, old Ben, lived, and the massive iron gates began to open. As the car moved onto the long drive that led up to Eastly Abbey, he tipped his hat in a respectful manner. Henry reciprocated and drove on.

When Henry pulled up in front of Eastly, Cooper was waiting at the bottom of the steps with Mrs. Fairchild, the housekeeper. Welcome home, Lady Jayne, he said. It's so good to have you back. I hope your time in London has been successful.

It has, Cooper, thank you, she replied, and began walking up the steps of her home.

Peggy stood in the great hall. A year had passed by since her departure from the wizard world and her life had taken a dramatic turn since she had become the mistress of the magnificent Eastly Abbey. Peggy had adopted her middle name and was known now as Jayne, Lady Jayne. Her mother had reverted back to her maiden name and was now Lady Rose Estelle Fenchurch, and she was now back in her world, the world in which she had lived before her mother had died and before her father had gambled everything away. And now after all the hardships she had endured, it felt almost as if it had all been some horrible dream and she had at last awoken from it.

Welcome home, Jayne, her mother said, walking towards her. They hugged and walked out onto the terrace. Cooper had organized a teatime spread for them, and they sat down and were soon deep in conversation.

Tell me everything, Rose said.

Well, most of my time has been taken up with training, she said. For instance, I now have a driving license and a pilot's license, and I can hack into most computers; and the list goes on. Well, that's me done, she said. So, what have you been up to, Mother?

Rose smiled and said, Would you believe I have quit the laundry business? I made the decision a month ago. I've transferred the cottage, the land, and the entire business over to Jim Smiley. He is now sole owner of it all. If ever someone deserved it, it's Jim. He has worked tirelessly ever since we took him on and he has grown the business to where it is today.

That's great news! said Jayne. At last you can relax and take it easy; that is, almost relax. We have a guest arriving for dinner and I have asked him to stay for a few days. He is my peer mentor and has taught me so much, I'm sure you'll like him. Well, I'm going to have a swim and relax before our guest arrives, Jayne said, so I'll see you later, Mother.

Rose was walking down the staircase that led down into the great hall when Jayne walked in with her guest. Rose looked at him and froze, and then in total shock, she said, Oh my God! It can't be! It's not possible! They told me you were dead. Is, is it really you, James? And then she swooned and he caught her up in his arms before she fell to the floor.

The end.